Graceland

Books by Deborah Grabien

The JP Kinkaid Chronicles

Rock and Roll Never Forgets
While My Guitar Gently Weeps
London Calling
Graceland
Book of Days *
Uncle John's Band *
Dead Flowers *
Comfortably Numb *
Gimme Shelter *

The Haunted Ballads

The Weaver and the Factory Maid
The Famous Flower of Serving Men
Matty Groves
Cruel Sister
New-Slain Knight
Geordie *

Other Novels

Woman of Fire
Fire Queen
Plainsong
And Then Put Out the Light
Still Life With Devils
Dark's Tale

forthcoming

Graceland

Book #4 of the JP Kinkaid Chronicles

Deborah Grabien

Plus One Press

San Francisco

This is a work of fiction. All of the characters, organizations and events por-
trayed in this novel are either the products of the author's imagination or are
used fictitiously.

Plus One Press

GRACELAND. Copyright © 2011 by Deborah Grabien. All rights reserved.
Printed in the United States of America. For information, address Plus One
Press, 2885 Golden Gate Avenue, San Francisco, California, 94118.

www.plusonepress.com

Book Design by Plus One Press

Publisher's Cataloging-in-Publication Data

Grabien, Deborah.
   Graceland : book #4 of the JP Kinkaid chronicles / Deborah
Grabien.—1st. Plus One Press ed.
      p. cm.
   ISBN: 978-0-9844362-3-1
   1. Rock Musicians—Fiction. 2. Musical Fiction. 3. Murder—Fiction.
4. Rock and Roll Hall of Fame and Museum 5. Blues (Music)   I. Title.
II. Title: Graceland
   PS3557.R1145 G73 2011
   813'.54—dc22
                                                     2010936489

First Edition: April, 2011

10 9 8 7 6 5 4 3 2

For all those early influences

Acknowledgements

All the usual WIP readers, of course. All the usual suspects.

Thanks beyond the usual are due to Stephanie Lang, for providing me with the current information about heart conditions and the drugs to treat them; and to Caridad Ferrer, for showing me the Ohio River Valley, enabling me to create the town of Ofagoula.

A special thanks to Jesse Craine and Line By Line Productions, for the tech minutiae and timing of the induction ceremony.

Jay Thomson, Gene Rider, Craig Juan, and Tom Morgan, for the soundtrack. They'll know what I mean. You guys rock.

Daymond John, for letting me use FUBU as the sponsor of the Hall of Fame party, despite there being no rappers on the inductee list.

And especially Nic. The man had too much fun, coming up with the background for Farris "Bulldog" Moody, not to mention JP's childhood. *Way* too much fun.

Graceland

Prologue

"Ladies and gentlemen, I'd like to welcome you to the Rock and Roll Hall of Fame and Museum."

Oh, bloody hell.

I shifted from one foot to the other, listening to nerve endings that were threatening to make my life miserable, at least for the rest of the evening. This was going to be a tricky few hours to get through, if I didn't get to sit down soon.

The band had just finished up a photo session that seemed to go on forever. The woman behind the pricey set-up had wanted about eighty shots, and that was just of the band. Right around the time we thought we were done, she'd announced she wanted an entirely new batch, this time us with the Museum's dignitaries and local press people.

Of course we did it—extended photo shoots come with being

a member of Blacklight. But I seriously could have thumped her.

The heat of the lamps was bad enough. What really messed me up, though, was all that posing and leaning and bending, because the one thing it didn't do was let me sit down. I'd been standing in one place far too long, which is something no one with multiple sclerosis has got any business doing. Now things were letting me know about it: my right leg was tingling and twitchy, and I could feel both hands starting to shake.

"We'd like to thank everyone for coming tonight, to celebrate the opening of our new exhibit…"

Christ, he was going on and on. I gritted my teeth, and tried to shift the weight from one foot to the other. *Come on, mate. Just get on with it and let me sit…*

"Hang on." My wife Bree, standing at my right elbow, had noticed how dodgy my balance was getting. Of course she noticed—Bree always does. "I'm going to get you a chair."

She slipped off into the crowd. Now I thought about it, she couldn't have been very comfy herself; she was breaking in a new pair of high heels. Luckily, there were quite a lot of folding chairs lying about, since for some reason they'd opted to hold the press conference and official opening speeches in the Hall of Fame's cafe. Probably not a bad idea, that was—after all, the Hall's right at the side of the lake, and it was January. Not exactly the weather for holding it out of doors.

"…take this opportunity to express our deep gratitude to the members of Blacklight for their generosity in providing such an extraordinary wealth of memorabilia for the exhibit…"

"Here." Bree was back, opening a folding chair behind me. She sounded fierce, even though she was whispering. I noticed a pimply-faced guard, one of the event security staff, beet-red and glaring in her general direction. He didn't seem to have noticed who she was with. "Sit, John, please? Otherwise you're going to be wrecked later."

"Ta, love." I sat, flexing my knees and wincing. She and the guard seemed to be having a sort of non-verbal pissing contest, a major staredown. I raised an eyebrow at her. "What's wrong with the hired help, then? Lad looks narked."

"...*including the earliest days of Malcolm Sharpe and Luke Hedley's first band, Blackpool Southern, as well as rhythm aces Stu Corrigan and Calvin Wilson's original group, the Light Brigade...*"

"Yes, well, the little asshole tried telling me I wasn't allowed to touch any of the chairs. I told him to go fuck himself. Some people just shouldn't be allowed near a uniform." She gave the bloke one final glare, but it was wasted—he'd finally realised whom she'd demanded the chair for, and he was looking sick. "He probably thinks I'm a raging bitch. He's right."

"...*session guitarist and blues player extraordinaire JP Kinkaid, including a rare autographed copy of his hard to find solo album, Blues House...*"

"You're not a raging bitch. You're my very favourite raging bitch, is what you are."

I reached up and got one of her hands. She knelt down next to me; the bloke was still rabbiting on about all the gear we'd lent them for the new exhibit, and how generous we were. I kept my voice low. "High as those heels are, I'm surprised you didn't snag two chairs. One for yourself, you know? Gordon Bennett, isn't this bloke ever going to run out of breath?"

"...*and now, ladies and gentlemen...*"

"Oi. Just as I was getting comfy. Careful what you wish for, you might get it." I took a deep breath and stood back up. Bree had her hand under my elbow, a nice light touch, ready to pull it away if I shook my head at her. "So much for putting my boots up. Here we go."

"...*Blacklight!*"

Right. Showtime.

It actually turned out to be quite a nice party in the end, you know? We thanked everyone for coming; Mac and Luke, the band's founders and certainly the best speakers, each took a turn talking to the crowd, who were mostly press and Rock Museum people. The rest of us said a few words as well, about being gratified and all that. Carla Fanucci, the band's US operations manager and PR genius, had flown in from Los Angeles to keep an eye on things, and she was off to one side, looking approving. Mac's bodyguard, Domitra Calley, was never more than a few feet away from Mac. She can't seriously have thought there was likely to be any trouble, but with Dom, hope dies hard, yeah? You just never know when someone might do something stupid, and give her a crack at beating them up.

The crowd lapped it up. It was all business as usual; personally, I was just glad the people in charge had kept the intros brief and to the point, because I was starving. There was quite a lot of food set out, a nice catered spread, to go along with all the folding chairs. The place smelled good enough to remind me that I hadn't eaten since breakfast. The marathon photo session had seen to that.

Finally, Luke finished saying his bit, the official got back up to the mic, the exhibit was declared officially open, and we got to eat, circulate and relax.

I'll say one thing for the Hall of Fame, the Museum end of it, at least: they know how to feed musicians. The food was superb, and there was no shortage of it. Another nice thing was that, since we'd already met most of the people who kept coming up and wanting to rub shoulders, the party wasn't too stressful, even for Bree. Back in the old days, she'd avoided this sort of do as if it was the Black Death, but since we'd got married after twenty five years together, she'd begun coming along more often. It kept her from flipping out over my health, and besides, it gave her a good excuse to dress up. After all, what's the point of having a closet full of pricey high heels and vintage velvet dresses, if you don't get to show them off to anyone but your old man?

4

That made me realise that she wasn't with me anymore, and I looked around. When I spotted her, I found myself grinning; if she needed people to show off the shoes and cocoa brown satin dress from the 1930s for, she'd got them. Just that moment, she was nearly surrounded by a small crowd of blokes who looked like academics, halfway across the room. I was trying to catch her eye when I heard a woman's voice behind my right shoulder.

"Excuse me. Mr. Kinkaid?"

I turned and looked down. I'm not a tall bloke—bit over five foot seven—but she was tiny, maybe five foot tall, and she looked like someone's maiden aunty. She was about the same age as Miranda, Bree's mum, or at least, that was my best guess. She seemed harmless enough, and I lifted an eyebrow.

"Yeah, I'm JP Kinkaid. Have we met before? I'm sorry, I know it's rude of me, but I'm afraid I don't remember–"

"Sara Kildare." She smiled, and held out a hand. "And no, we haven't met. I'm very sorry to bother you, especially in the middle of a party, but I'm on the nominating committee for the Foundation, and I was wondering if I could have a word with you." Her face had gone pink. "Actually, I was hoping to ask a favour."

"Yeah, of course." I kept one eye on what was going on across the room—a much younger bloke had joined the group round Bree. My wife was drawing them in like flies. Of course, in that dress and those high heels, no big mystery, you know? The brown satin was as huggy as it gets, and at least two of her entourage looked as if hugging would have worked for them, just fine. It would have narked me if I'd thought she even noticed. "Ask away. What can I do for you, then?"

"Well…I was actually hoping that you might be willing to give me your choice for a nomination. Specifically, we're looking for a suggestion in the category of Early Influences."

All of a sudden, she had my full attention, at least enough of it to get my mind off that knot of blokes hanging round Bree.

"Right, sorry—I'm not usually quite this spaced, but it's been a long day. Did you say you wanted me to suggest someone to be inducted into the Hall? Early Influences?"

"Would you be willing?" Someone across the room must have waved at her, or something—she lifted her hand, and smiled and nodded over my left shoulder. "The committee decided to ask someone who specialised in blues this year, so I was hoping you might have a few ideas. There's no huge rush, you can take your time, although if you were willing and could see your way to letting me know between now and–"

"Moody."

"Excuse me?" She blinked up at me. "I'm sorry—I don't understand."

"Oh, right, sorry. That's the name, Moody. My suggestion. Farris Moody—he's known as Bulldog Moody." I'd interrupted her. Rude, yeah, I know, but I didn't need any time to think it over. "Delta bluesman, brilliant guitar player—sessions bloke, one of the great unsung guitar players. Chess Records, Sun, played with Sonny Boy Williamson and that lot."

"Oh, I see."

"Good." I smiled down at her. Quite a change, actually, talking to a woman shorter than me. "Sorry, I didn't mean to cut you off, but honestly, I don't need to think about this one, not for a minute. You want an early influence, he's my number one."

She opened her mouth to say something, but didn't get the chance, not just then. A small horde of people, mostly press, had just got done hitting Mac up for sound bytes and juicy interview photos. They'd apparently all smelled the buffet at the same time, because they came at us in a wave. I got out of their way in a hurry; I was just thankful I'd already loaded up a plate of my own.

Once they'd moved on, I found Sara Kildare watching me. She had a look on her face I couldn't quite sort out.

6

"Bulldog Moody, you said?" She seemed to be picking up the conversation up just where we'd left it. "And you say he played with Sonny Boy Williamson, back in—what? Would that have been the twenties?"

"More like the late thirties." There was a nice little mouthful of salmon on my plate, and something with potatoes and garlic. Oh, sod it; I'd done my duty to the Hall of Fame, I'd been doing it all day long, and I was hungry. I forked up a mouthful, chewed, and swallowed. Good stuff.

"Do you know Ches Kobel?" She was looking over my shoulder. "Ah, good, I thought he was here tonight."

"Afraid not." She was waving at someone, beckoning really. What sort of name was Ches, anyway? I turned around and saw who she was waving to.

It was the youngish bloke who'd joined the group of admiring males round my wife. At least, I figured this Ches Kobel had to be him, because he was waving back. He said something to Bree, or maybe it was to the rest of the group, and headed towards us. Bree shed her entourage and followed him over.

All right, I'll admit it: there was a part of me wanted to bristle. Ches Kobel was just the sort of bloke who might have been designed to push all my middle-aged buttons. He was twenty years my junior easy, he looked like he worked out—what's the word I want? Oh, yeah—he was personable. Charming, you know? Unfortunately, he was being charming all over my wife. Not a good foot to start off from.

And then Sara Kildare introduced us, and he got us right back on track. His eyes went wide, his mouth dropped open, and he turned bright pink; behind him, Bree caught my eye and winked, and I went pink myself. Of course, she'd caught my jealousy vibe. There's no putting that one past Bree. She thinks it's funny.

"Oh, wow." He shook my hand. "JP Kinkaid, for real! I only just realised, about two seconds before Sara waved me over, that

I was talking to your wife. This is so cool—hey, can I take a few minutes of your time? If not, no problem, I'll just be over here, being quietly overwhelmed."

"Yeah, sure, if we can sit." I felt myself grinning. It was some damned good flattery, that was, and it took some doing to remind myself that, right, so, he was a fan—that's not a guarantee of good behaviour. Some fans are nutters. But the nutters aren't usually introduced by a senior staffer at the Hall. Besides, his vibe was very straightforward. "Blacklight fan, are you?"

"Blues guitar. Well, blues generally—Delta, Chicago. I write a lot of reviews, articles and that kind of thing. Mostly, the Cleveland *Plain Dealer* runs my stuff." We headed for a corner and a couple of empty chairs. Bree stayed behind, chatting up Sara Kildare. "Damn, that didn't come out right, did it? What I mean to say was, yes, I do like Blacklight, a lot, but right now, I'm all about the blues. I'm writing a history of the movement of the blues in North America, the way it evolved in different areas. I'm planning a few chapters on Sonny Boy Williamson and some of the people he played with, back in the thirties. I read somewhere that he was a big influence on you. Is that right?"

"Who, Sonny Boy? No, not really—after all, he was a harp player. Mac's a huge fan of his. I liked some of the people Sonny Boy played with, though. And if we're talking about influences on me, it's really one of his protégés I listened to, pretty much nonstop, when I was first getting my chops, as a kid in London."

"Really?"

"Yeah." I eased myself down into the chair. Took me a second or two to sort out just how tired I was; I was going to be glad to get back to our suite at the Ritz-Carleton. "My main thing was for a bloke called Bulldog Moody—what?" He'd jumped, and made a noise.

"You're not going to believe this." He was grinning. "I had breakfast with him yesterday morning."

8

"You–" I was gobsmacked. "You had breakfast with Bulldog Moody? You're joking, right?"

"Nope. No joke. You didn't know he lived in Ohio? Other end of the state, down near the border of Kentucky."

"I didn't even know he was still alive. Sorry, mate, but that's fucking amazing. How old is he?"

"Eighty-six, and still does some of the most incredible rhythmic stuff I've ever heard, when his hands aren't bothering him." His head was tilted to one side. There was something familiar about Ches Kobel, visually at least, but I couldn't place it. "Want me to hook you up?"

"Bloody hell, yes! That would be brilliant." Patrick Ormand, that was it. Kobel had the same healthy look, the same close-cropped dark hair, the same way of moving around; concise, a bit elegant, definitely remote. Big difference in the eyes, though; Patrick's a cop and a predator and he looks it, light eyes that get cold and calculating. Ches Kobel had baby blues, a lot easier to read, and I was reading him loud and clear. "So, what I can do for you in return? Come on, I can see there's something. Might as well dish."

"Well…"

He told me. As I listened, I forgot about being tired, about not feeling well, about being put off by how young and healthy he was, and just got enthusiastic instead. I got so caught up that I didn't even notice Bree coming up, waiting for a break in the conversation to catch my eye. Ches actually noticed her first, and he got up and offered her his chair, same moment I did. Nice bloke, with good manners.

"No, that's okay. I'm good." She meant it, too, and I saw why; the nice new shoes were dangling from one hand, and she was barefoot. Heels that high, it takes time to get them comfy, Bree tells me. "Just wanted to see if John was ready to head out. We've got an early flight tomorrow, back to San Francisco."

"Well, actually love, I want to bump that a day or two, if that's all right with you." I slipped an arm round her waist, and pulled her close. "Unless there's something going on I've forgotten about, I mean. I know you've got that gig coming up, but you can head back without me, it'll be fine. Ches, here, is writing a book about the blues, and he's offered to take me to meet the bloke at the top of my list."

"John!" Her eyes were wide. "Is that Bulldog Moody? You mean, he's still alive?"

"Seems to be, yeah." I was grinning at her; Bree knows all about my particular icons, and she'd known right off who I'd meant. "Alive and still playing. Ches says he's down near Cincinnati, in the southern part of the state. Who knows, I may get to learn some new licks from the first guitar player I ever tried to steal from."

Chapter One

The next morning, with Ches Kobel at the wheel of a rental car and Bree in the back seat, we drove away from Cincinnati Airport, and headed southeast toward the town of Ofagoula.

It wasn't my first visit to southern Ohio. Blacklight's played here, many times—Cincinnati's always a stop on any major North American tour. Being on tour, though, that's very different from just being there. On tour, it's a flat routine with not much room for variation: airport, city, hotel, venue, soundcheck, dinner, gig, hotel again, and out. Mostly, a city is simply a place you play.

So I'd never got a good look at the countryside down here before, and it was a surprise to me. I don't know what I was expecting, but it had a nice familiar feel to it. Maybe it was how green it was, even with a scattering of leftover snow piled up in a few places along the highway. Or maybe it was the Ohio River. I grew up in South London, and of course London's got quite a nice river of its own. Whatever it was, I found myself relaxing into it.

We'd got a decently roomy car, which was lucky for poor Bree.

My old lady's got long legs and she does all the driving at home, since I've never been taught. She wasn't used to being crammed into the back of someone else's ride, and I wanted her as comfy as possible.

Besides, I knew damned well there were things she wanted to be doing, back in San Francisco. She had an enormous catering gig coming up, a silver wedding anniversary party or something, with over a hundred people on the guest list and additional staff to be rounded up. I'd told her I didn't mind doing this Hall of Fame Blacklight exhibit opening without her, but she'd insisted on coming along. And now, of course, with me having a shot at meeting Bulldog Moody, she'd told me flatly she was coming along for that, as well.

I knew why. My heart had been acting up, this arrhythmia I've got had been more noticeable recently, and she was damned if she was letting me out of her sight. It was nothing major, my own cardio bloke had told me not to worry, but she'd seen me get dizzy a couple of times. Standing there when I suddenly swayed on my feet and got unsteady on my pins, that was all it took. There was no use arguing about it, either, not when she got this stubborn.

So here we were, trip home put back a day, and she'd agreed to this little detour without a word of complaint—hell, she'd insisted on it. Right, I know, I'm a selfish, pampered git, but whatever her reasons were, I was glad she'd come along. Truth is, I'm always happier when Bree's with me; it makes me feel safe, for one thing. And it wasn't as if I hadn't taken a shot at being noble about it, but she'd stiffened up and used the phrase "little man." I hate that, and she only ever uses it when she's got her heels dug all the way in about something. No point arguing, once she's tossed "little man" on the table.

Just then, I was especially thankful for having her there, because I was a lot more nervous than I was letting on. I've been playing guitar since I was nine years old, thanks to a bloke called Denny Hensley, the older brother of my best mate, Davey. Denny'd been a sax player with a pickup band in South London—swing, really, played some local gigs down around Streatham, and Wandsworth. He used to pick us kids up in his van after school. Sometimes we'd listen to him practicing his horn, but other days, he'd take us to this record shop, Jimmy D's, that was owned by a mate of his.

So I'd got to hear quite a lot of stuff off American records. Thanks to those records, Farris "Bulldog" Moody was one of the first people I ever heard play guitar, and I'd never looked back.

Now here I was, about to meet the first influence I'd ever had as a musician, and I was nervous as a virgin. I must have done a piss-poor job of hiding it, because Ches glanced at me out the corner of his eye.

"Relax, JP." He turned the car off the highway. "Bulldog's one of the nicest people you'll ever meet. Get him talking about the old days and it'll be hard to get a word in edgewise—he's got some fascinating stories. You ought to hear him talk about handling Sonny Boy, back in the thirties. Ask him about that, he loves talking about it. It's really funny stuff. Besides, he's always delighted to meet another player."

"Is he married?" Bree'd reached over the top of my seat, and was rubbing my shoulders. "Is there a Mrs. Bulldog?"

"There was. Not anymore, though. He's a widower. He lives with his son, Sallie."

"Sallie?" Bree'd found a tight spot at the base of my neck; she was working it with her fingertips, trying to tease the knot out of the muscle. "As in, short for Sarah? Interesting thing to name a baby boy. In most schools, that poor kid would be getting his ass kicked and his lunch money stolen on a regular basis."

"It's short for Salas—the family were originally slaves in Cuba, brought over from Nigeria in the eighteen-forties. Sallie's named for his grandfather." He smiled at Bree in the mirror. "It's all in my notes for the book I'm doing."

"Oh, I see." She'd moved to my left shoulder, and found the tense spot there. I leaned back into it, letting her rub. "So, what about Bulldog's wife? What happened to her?"

"Lula? She died about twenty years ago. She had heart problems. So does Bulldog, as a matter of fact, so that gives us one more thing in common. His heart stuff's a lot more serious than mine is, of course. He's got angina, among other things. He hasn't played in public for, damn, must be twenty years or so now, even just locally, and that's why. When people want to jam, they come to him."

"You've got a dodgy heart?" Now, that was a surprise. Ches looked like your basic workout fiend, the sort who goes jogging in the rain because he doesn't want to miss his daily endorphin rush. He wasn't a big bloke at all, probably didn't weigh much more than I did, but he looked muscled, and very fit. "What's yours, mate? MVP and arrhythmia, here."

"Wow, you've got heart problems?" He got the car around a big-wheeler, and revved the engine. "I didn't know that—I knew about the multiple sclerosis, but not about that. Me, well, I have mild arrhythmia. Nothing serious, my heart guy says there's no reason I shouldn't live to be as old as Bulldog. Man, when did this messed-up heart stuff get so common? What do they give you for yours, when it acts up? Digoxin…?"

We'd passed a water tower, the kind I always think of as needing a target painted on it, with the words "Tornado: Hit Me" above it in huge letters. Of course, what it actually said was "Welcome to Ofagoula." I could see it in the rear-view mirror, fading off as Ches turned the car down and along a series of nice little streets, shady and clean.

There was something about the houses here that managed to be totally American on one hand, while reminding me of the

14

working class London neighbourhood I'd grown up in on the other. I may live in a Pacific Heights Victorian these days, but my dad was a sign maker at a local business near Brixton, and I went to Clapham Junior School. Our neighbourhood had a lot more grime on the buildings than Ofagoula did, but working class is working class, you know? No matter where you are.

"Here we are." Ches pulled the car into a space against the curb, halfway along a small side street; there was a sign at the end of the road that said *Manassas Road*. We'd stopped in front of a small house, painted blue. There was a small porch, a rocking chair, a battered swing suspended from the overhead beams. And there was someone standing in the doorway, a man in a red shirt. I could tell he was a big bloke, even from here. "And there's Sallie, out front."

I took a deep breath. *Right. Showtime.*

I hadn't realised I'd gone trembly until Bree got out of the car, and opened my door for me. She slid her hand into mine, and squeezed, very reassuring. I tugged her down and kissed her once, fast, and let her go again. Bless the girl, she'd caught how nervous I was. I haven't got much in the way of personal idols, and this was new territory for me.

Ches had gone up ahead. He was talking to Sallie Moody, gesturing back toward us. Sallie lifted his head and stared at us, and I had a sudden thought, completely paralysing: *oh crikey, Ches didn't ring to let them know he was bringing us. We're not expected.*

It wasn't possible to turn back, not at this point—we'd reached the end of the path and come to the three shallow steps that led up to the porch. Before I could completely flip my shit, Ches spoke up.

"Sallie, this is the friend I told you about on the phone—this is JP Kinkaid, and this is his wife, Bree. JP, Bree, this is Salas Moody. Where's your dad, Sallie?"

"He's inside." The impression I'd got from the car, about his size, had been spot on: Sallie was a big bloke, well over six foot. Once, he must have been built like a footballer, but he was old, certainly older than I was, and the flesh looked to be softening up on those enormous bones. He had a voice like a bell, a bell that someone had damped down, with padding round the clapper to stop it echoing too much. I'd have been willing to bet he'd been told so many times in his life to please lower his voice that now, in his fifties or maybe even his sixties, he wasn't capable of speaking any way but softly.

"It's a pleasure, Mr. Moody." Bree had no reason at all to be nervous, and she wasn't. She offered her right hand to Sallie— her left was still holding onto mine—and he took it. "Thank you so much for letting us come to see you and your father."

"Pleased," Sallie told her, and smiled back. Right then, I relaxed a tiny bit. What he'd said, that was the plain truth: he really *was* pleased. I found myself wondering if Sallie Moody wasn't simple. Uncomplicated, you know? "Dad likes company."

"Sallie! Company here?"

The voice, Sallie's bell but without a damper, came out from behind the screen door. Inside, the house looked to be not very well lit. My palms had gone sweaty, and my mouth was dry.

"They're here, Dad." Sallie nodded at us. "Would you please to come in? My father's wanting to meet you."

Looking back now, I'm not sure what I was expecting. I mean, it's not as if I'd ever seen Bulldog Moody playing live; he was a session player, not a touring act. So far as I knew, he'd never once gone out on the road as a headliner or a solo performer. And there was nothing in print for me to reference, either, nothing to index in my head, no record sleeves or anything else, that might have had his photo.

So I couldn't match up this bloke, sitting in a rocking chair that looked a lot like the one I've got at home in our house on

16

Clay Street, with what I'd imagined he'd look like. Took me a minute to realise that whatever I'd been imagining couldn't be real, because I'd never seen him before.

The way it turned out, it didn't matter. The first thing I saw when I walked into a cheerful little front room with pitched ceilings and framed pictures of people I've admired my whole life all over the walls wasn't Bulldog Moody, it was his guitar.

I walked in through the front door. Like I said, I was sweating and nervous, because meeting someone you've idolised can really break your heart. But I stopped halfway in, because there it was, sitting there on a handmade stand that looked to be as old as the guitar itself.

"Gordon *Bennett!*"

I stopped so suddenly, Bree ran straight into me, and nearly knocked me down. I didn't even notice. All the attention I had to spare was aimed straight at that guitar.

I'm a Gibson guitar fan. For a long time, it took a lot to get me to bother with any electric guitar that wasn't a Gibson—acoustics are a different thing, but with electrics, it's been Gibson, straight down the line. I've actually been a spokesman for the Les Paul line. One of the things on my dance card over the next month or so was a visit to Nashville; we were having discussions, not only about finally making me chambered touring copies of my two favourite Pauls, but about launching a signature JP Kinkaid model. Until Bree had paid a local Bay Area luthier a lot of money to build me a gorgeous lightweight electric guitar called Little Queenie as a wedding present, the nearest I'd come to anything that wasn't made by Gibson was a Zemaitis custom.

So, yeah, I'm susceptible to Gibsons. But there are guitars, and then there was this, because unless I was completely mistaken, this was the only one of its kind…

"Hey." The voice jerked me out of what was threatening to become a complete trance. I'd been right—same bell as Sallie's, but this one was old, cracked round the edges, and very friendly. It was also really amused, and that's what froze me. "You like that axe, son? Because you lookin' at her like you were wanting to buy her a drink."

Shit.

I pulled my stare off the instrument, and over toward the bloke who, presumably, owned it. Even in the iffy light, I could see he was grinning at me.

"I do, yeah." My ears were burning at the tips, and I felt myself wanting to turn bright red. Complete embarrassment, you know? Walking into Bulldog Moody's house and gawking like a damned groupie at his guitar, could I have been ruder? "Like it, I mean. I have a thing for Gibsons. I'm really sorry, that was beyond rude, wasn't it? But is that—can I just ask—that's not really a 1955 Byrdland, is it?"

"Nope." Bulldog Moody, eighty-six years old and rocking back and forth, grinned at me. It was a brilliant grin, lighting up his face, showing either good strong teeth or really good dentures. "It's *the* 1955 Byrdland. First one they ever made."

"Wow." Bree's voice, interested and amused, came from just behind me. Bless the girl, nothing ever fazes her. And bless her twice, giving me time to get my balance back, because I was speechless, and she'd sussed me. "Serial number one, sort of? That makes it a historic guitar, right?"

"Yes, child, it surely does. Bought it off Tom Lapworth at O.K. Houck Pianos, down in Memphis. He got it for someone else, Sid Manker if I remember rightly, but I got to take it home with me instead. That guitar cost me big money, five hundred dollars and then some. I had to pay it off in pieces, but that guitar, well, that Byrd sings my name. Last guitar I ever bought. That was all the way back in the nineteen-fifties, before you were even thought of."

He had his hands resting on the rocker's arms, and now that

18

I'd had my attention taken off the Byrdland, I kept looking at his hands. Musician's fingers, all right, solidly calloused, long and knuckled, gnarled at the top, but I'd have bet any money at all he could still play with the best of them. "Sallie! Get the lady a chair. You sit yourself, child. Aint no reason to be standing around, tiring out those pretty feet."

Child? Now, that startled me. I caught his eye, finally, gaze on gaze, just for a moment.

And out of nowhere, there we were, you know? He recognised me, in just the same way I recognised him: a couple of geezers who know another player when they see one. We can pick each other out of a rampaging mob at a hundred yards in the middle of a blizzard. It's one of nature's little mysteries, just something players can do. If I had to guess, I'd say it was probably something about the music we make, the smell of it maybe, lingering on the skin like pheromones. Whatever it is, whatever the cause, it's real. It's there, beyond argument.

"I'm John Kinkaid, and this is my wife, Bree."

I held out a hand, and he took it. Now he was using them, I could see that his hands were corded, the kind of weathering and veining you get with age. They were also huge. He had very long fingers; you'd have thought the bloke was a piano player, not a guitarist. I've got big hands for a bloke my size, but crikey, his were amazing. How in hell had he wrapped hands that size around that Byrdland's short-scale neck? "There's no words to tell you how excited I got when Ches told us you were willing to meet us. Because I'm so chuffed at getting a chance to meet you, you can't begin to imagine. But that Byrdland—right, I didn't mean to walk in and stand about staring, but I've wanted one of those since I first heard you and Walter Loudon on an old record, back when I was a kid in London. That's original, isn't it? Those are the old Alnico pickups?"

"Never changed a thing on the Byrd, son. Why would I, when

19

she's just right the way she is? Wait a minute, though—you telling me you were listening to the old Sundial Records session stuff in England? Me and 'Laughing' Loudon? You joking on me? Only record I ever played on with Loudon was one of the Sundial specials, song called 'Daisy Chain Blues.' That record came and went so fast, might as well have been a sunbeam." Bulldog looked over at Bree, who was settling herself into a straight-backed wooden chair, a few feet behind me. "Sallie, boy, let's have some daylight in this cave. Can't be asking company to sit around in the dark."

Sallie got a few of the curtains open. The room was full of sunlight, that pale sun you get in winter. I was surprised at just how light Bulldog's skin was. It reminded me of Mac's bodyguard, Dom; she's from Jamaica originally, and she's got a gorgeous tint to her skin that always makes me think of butter toffee, or caramel. Bulldog was nearly that light, and that surprised me, but I couldn't tell you why. "Missus Kinkaid, now, what can we get you? Chilly day out there—Sallie make you a cup of tea, maybe? And Chester, boy, I was so busy talking guitars with Mr. Kinkaid, here, my manners must have gone to Kentucky for the day. How you doing over there?"

"Me? I'm great." Ches had headed for the sofa, and parked himself there; he was so easy and comfortable in here, I knew it had to be someplace he'd spent enough time to feel at home in. "Bulldog, you know who JP is, right? You know about him being one of the two guitarists in Blacklight?"

Bulldog was looking at me. "Blacklight? That's rock and roll, right? English combo? See, now, I thought I knew your name from something else. Session stuff. Not meaning anything about your band, it's a fine band I'm sure, but someone with your name did a record I always liked, called *Blues House*. Lives high up on my favourites shelf, that record. But maybe that was another John Kinkaid?"

"No, that was me." There was a huge lump at the back of my throat. Talk about the best damned butter—one sentence, and the bloke I'd copied all my early riffs from had managed to move me, right to the points of tears. I swallowed, hard. "They were going on about it at the Hall of Fame last night, about how hard to find it is. Yeah, that's because it sold about eight copies, or something."

"Well, now." He sounded pleased as hell. "I surely am glad to hear that, because when Chester here told me he wanted to bring a London boy named Kinkaid to meet me, I did find myself hoping it would be the man who did *Blues House*. I'm hoping you won't mind autographing my copy for me...?"

After that, of course, it was all over. Any hope I had of being socially proper and well-behaved went straight out the damned window. I stuttered, said something that came out sounding like *you want me to sign are you having me on then first record I ever picked up a guitar and played to was one of yours bloody hell this is amazing you want me to sign it really* except less coherent, and that was it.

I've had a lot of interesting conversations about music in my day. Mostly, the best ones are with other players, people know what you mean, who you are, where you've been. They just *get* it. Sometimes, you get a really good interviewer, the sort who may not be a player but who loves it enough to have all the gen on what it is about the music that makes the people who can play, tick over. Ches struck me as one of those.

But this was the first time I'd ever sat at a legend's knee, basically, swapping some of my own stories as a kind of trade-off for as many of his as he wanted to tell. And I was doing it, in his eyes at least, as an equal. It was completely beyond my experience, this meeting. There was a feel to it, different from anything I'd ever had before.

It was as if I'd found the grandfather of my tribe, or something.

21

Every word he said stayed with me. I still remember everything he told me, every anecdote, every moment of personal history. And right, I know, people are always taking their memories, their icons, and polishing them, trying to make them brighter and warmer and shinier than the real thing ever was. But Bree was there, and she remembers it, as well. No polishing was needed, not for this.

He told me about his family, how his own great-grandfather, Maoudain Ferrer, had been something called a *bata* drummer, for religious rituals. I asked what sort of rituals, and Bulldog smiled at me, and sipped his drink, and said, Santeria—his grandfather had been a *balabao*, a high priest. He'd also been a slave in Cuba, kidnapped from a Nigerian village by slavers, apparently, but then there was a war or something, and the U.S. had got itself involved, and when all the dust settled, the slaves were all let go and the family went off to America.

I wondered, right about then, if maybe some of the rhythm chucks of Bulldog's, those unique little movements that were unlike any guitar I'd ever heard and had caught me and pulled me into wanting to play straight off, might not have started out as his great-granddad's *bata* drum riffs. They'd caught my ear when I was a kid, and they coloured every blues riff I played, and still do.

Before I could ask him, though, he'd moved on, telling me about his father, Salas Moody, about how he'd worked for the U.S. Army during the First World War, building bridges and things. Not that I'd ever thought too much about it, but I was beginning to get that all the hazy stereotypes I'd been carrying about in my head all these years, about how all the black blues players from the Delta were poor sharecroppers' kids, was bollocks. It was an eye-opener, listening to him.

We took a break from talking, not a long break, but I'm not likely to ever forget it. I'd been telling him about how I'd first started playing when I was nine, and that I'd first asked my dad

22

for a guitar after I'd heard some of the Sundial Records stuff at the local record shop, Jimmy D's. Bulldog listened, and then he nodded toward the Byrdland.

"You pick that up, Johnny boy. Sallie! You go get my Stella from my room." He caught my dropped jaw. "You can show me the slide thing you did on that Robert Johnson song, on *Blues House*. Been wanting to see how it was done, a good long time, now. You need a bottleneck for that run?"

So yeah, an hour of playing together, me starting out nervous as a bride on a honeymoon cruise, holding that Byrdland like it was made of platinum or crystal or something, watching Bulldog's fingers moving, just flying over the old Stella's frets, hearing those rhythms that just said to me, *Bulldog Moody and no one else*. And now I knew where he'd got them, from ancestors who were Santeria high priests and *bata* drummers, that made it even cooler, somehow.

Two hours later, we'd put the guitars back down. Bulldog was telling a story about how he'd once won ten dollars and a fried chicken dinner off a drummer called Rocky Dombier, from Gatlinburg, Tennessee by driving Sonny Boy Williamson into a frothing fit of rage in under one minute, when I thought I heard a tiny sigh from behind me.

I came back to earth—and the present day—with a huge, guilty thump. I'd forgot about Bree completely. She'd been sitting there in silence, just letting me do my thing, since Sallie first brought that chair in. So had Ches, but of course, the stuff me and Bulldog were talking about, that was meat and drink to Ches. I was willing to bet that anything Bulldog had talked about today would fetch up in Ches's book, somewhere.

My poor wife, though, that was a different story entirely. I caught Bulldog's eye, and he stopped talking. I twisted round in my chair.

"Bree, love, I'm so sorry—I'm a selfish sod. Get up and stretch

23

your legs, for heaven's sake. We'll get you some lunch in a minute, yeah? What time is it?" I wasn't nearly enough of a hypocrite to tell her she should have interrupted me, that she should have just got up out of the uncomfortable chair and stopped me talking to Bulldog. Her doing that was about as likely to happen as me getting asked to be one of Tina Turner's backup singers, and I knew it. "Bulldog, this has been amazing, but we ought to get moving—Bree took an extra day away from her own gig to come down here with me, and we've got a flight back to San Francisco from Cincy in a couple of hours."

"Pleasure, John. I surely do hope I'll be seeing you again." He must have seen something in my face. "You got something else on your mind?"

"Well..." I let it out suddenly, about Sara Kildare, and me suggesting him for the Hall of Fame. I don't know why I felt so shy, but somewhere inside, I was convinced he was going to not like it, tell me he wouldn't do it. Turned out I couldn't have been more wrong; he was quite chuffed at the idea.

"There's one thing, though..." I was really relieved, relieved enough to warn him ahead of time. "We do this, they're going to want to fly you to New York for the induction ceremony. And they'd probably want us to jam, for the television cameras. Would you be okay with that, Bulldog?"

He met my eyes. Odd thing—I'm a pale English white kid from South London, and he was the grandchild of a Nigerian high priest. But his eyes and mine were the same colour. One more moment of feeling connected.

I got another one of those moments when Sallie came back into the front room. He'd gone off to get his dad's raft of heart medicine. I saw bottles, at least two of them familiar; there were a few more than I have to take for mine, and of course, there would be. Ches had mentioned Bulldog having arrhythmia and angina, as well.

"You tell them I'll be there, if they want me."

He got out of his chair, finally, and I was gobsmacked. While he'd been sitting, I hadn't thought about his size, but Bulldog Moody, even stooped with age, was still at least six foot three, and probably weighed a good two hundred thirty pounds. Before time had brought him down, he must have been a giant. "But only if they let us play together. That's my condition. You tell them that for me, John, okay? And one other thing, too."

We'd reached the door, but I was still watching him. There was something in me that could have stayed right there, in that house, that room, for the rest of my natural life.

"Name it," I told him. I lifted one eyebrow at him, and damned if he didn't do the same thing, one eyebrow up, right back at me.

"You come back and see me again," he said, and waved us out into the chilly afternoon, towards Ches's car and Cincinnati Airport and our flight home.

Chapter Two

Anyone who thinks a major rock and roll tour is demanding ought to try living with a caterer with control issues.

We got home from Ohio safe and sound. I was in a good mood, about as mellow as I'd been in a decade or so. That interlude, playing and talking and listening and just being there in the house on Manassas Road, had put me into a perfect space, where it seemed like nothing could get through. There was something between me and Bulldog Moody; I didn't have the first clue what it was, but it left me relaxed and mellow. I found myself thinking *right, I spend too much time being stressy and ill, it's all just time passing anyway, no point in worrying.* Even the multiple sclerosis had stayed so quiet, I'd damned near forgot I had it.

Bree, on the other hand, wasn't what I'd call mellow, but then, she wasn't given any chance to be. I couldn't blame her for having a major meltdown, not after we walked into a shitstorm of messages and small crises about her upcoming gig.

It was really uncanny. You'd have thought the fates or whatever had been sitting there, rubbing their hands together, just waiting for the poor girl to walk in the door and saying *good, okay, here she comes, let's all pile on, yeah? Right, now, who's got the masses of miserable shit to unload?* It was even more of a drag, since she'd gone out of her way to make sure I got to meet Bulldog, even though she'd had to put herself into crunch mode to do it. Not fair at all.

We got back to Clay Street early evening, and found that our cat-sitter and occasional housekeeper, Sammy, had taken a few things out of the freezer, the way Bree'd asked him to. Sallie had offered to wrap us up some of what he called "fixings", to take with us for supper. Bree had declined the offer, not because she doubted he could cook—Bulldog let us know just how good a cook Sallie was—but because she'd already slipped out and rung up Sammy. That was standard operating procedure, when we had to be out of town for just a few days; Bree would ring up Sammy, give him our schedule, and tell him what to take out of the big Sub-Zero fridge. That way, there'd be something she'd already cooked, and all we'd have to do was to heat it up. Bree loves cooking, but not when she's knackered after a long plane ride.

Sammy'd taken some basic spaghetti sauce out to defrost for us. So far, so good, all we'd have to do was boil water and put noodles in. Unfortunately, that was about the last thing that went right for poor Bree until bedtime. She hadn't even finished scratching our Siamese, Farrowen, behind the ears before her cell phone started ringing. Once it began, it didn't stop.

Five minutes and four calls into it, her voice was getting ragged round the edges and she was scrabbling around frantically for one of the little notebooks she has all over the house. The snippets of conversation at her end were enough to explain what was happening to her voice: "*Hi this is Bree Kinkaid can I help you hey Lisa what's up what do you mean the client changed the number they've added HOW many people please tell me you told them the menu was fixed because there's no way we can do an extra thirty peo-*

ple on this short notice no there isn't any way and anyway the contract is specific about the headcount oh shit hang on my other line is going hello this is Bree Kinkaid can I help you hi Suzy what yes no the chocolate people told you what shit hang on my call waiting just clicked SHIT…"

Right around then, I decided the time had come to make myself useful. I picked up the pasta sauce, hunted out one of Bree's pricey saucepans, dumped the sauce in, and put it on the Viking's back burner to simmer. I know sod-all about cooking, but I've watched Bree a good long time, and I know which pan to use for the simple stuff. I rummaged around for one of her multi-pans to cook the noodles in, listening to her voice from out in the hall. It was getting shrill.

"Jay hi yes we just got back and my phone's going crazy what about the tablecloths oh goddamnit please tell me you're kidding no of course it's not okay the suppliers were told silver yes of course I'm sure it's a damned silver anniversary party for the love of what no battleship grey is NOT silver hang on my call waiting just clicked look I'll call you back Bree Kinkaid can I help you…"

I set the water on to boil, added a pinch of salt the way she always did, and put the kettle on. I was still feeling mellow, still in the Zen headspace. But Bree was going to need a cup of tea, or maybe a chainsaw, when she finally got all the messes sorted out. Okay—spare the girl as much to do as possible. Time to set the table…

She came into the kitchen a few minutes later, talking to herself, just sort of mumbling under her breath. That's never a good sign with her.

"Right. Sit, Bree, please. Good—here you go." I handed her a cup of Earl Grey. "Decaf, of course, and I put a dollop of honey in there. No arguing with me, all right? Water's just about ready for pasta, and the sauce is on as well. What the hell happened? Or shouldn't I ask?"

28

"Oh, nothing much. Just every possible goddamned thing that could go wrong, went wrong." She took a mouthful of tea, sounding bitter. "The bakery isn't sure about the cake, never mind that there's enough detail in the original order to make a Silicon Valley programmer happy. The warehouse providing the linens apparently can't tell the difference between silver and battleship grey—um, hello, silver is *metallic*—and they're all offended because my staff is cranky about it. The client wants to add thirty people—thirty!—to the guest list, despite the damned party being this weekend and the contract being signed and the cut-off date being ten days ago, and the chocolate supplier..."

"Bree, breathe, just—"

"...the *chocolate supplier* got the *order* wrong and got us about half what we needed so we need to find a supplier, by tomorrow morning, to get us enough sixty percent cocoa to make the *pots de chocolat* that we're using as place settings, and..."

"Right." Enough was enough; her voice was spiralling up toward the ceiling. "Here, you drink your tea. Where's the noodles? That water's on the boil."

That got her out of her seat, the way I knew it would; she wouldn't trust me with pasta. Hell, the only reason I'd been able to get the sauce bubbling and the water on was because she'd been distracted in the hall.

It's like I said: Bree's got some control issues. It's not that she's a perfectionist, at least not in the traditional sense. Doing everything perfect isn't in her world view, you know? But she gets really cranky and pissy when the rest of the world does anything that smells of incompetence, and it really shows when she's got her caterer's apron on. That and, oh yeah, when she's looking after me.

Her phone rang twice more during dinner, one problem fixed but, as it turned out, a whole new one rearing its head, and this one was major. Someone from the car rental place where Bree hires her trucks for really big catering events had completely spaced it, and somehow or other, they'd managed to lose track of the fact that she'd reserved a truck for tomorrow. They'd given their last one to someone for a week's rental. At that point, Bree hung up and started to shake.

" Hang on a minute," I told her. "I've got an idea. How big a truck was this?"

"SUV." There were tears on her face, pure frustration. "Great. Just great. I swear to God, there's a hex on this party. God damn it all to fucking hell! I've used these people for fifteen years, and they have to pick today to screw it up? Now I get to call all over the City, trying to–"

"Would your gear fit in a Range Rover?"

She blinked at me. "Probably. Why? We don't have a Range Rover, John. We have a Jaguar."

"No, we haven't got a Range Rover." I grinned at her, hoping for a smile. I didn't get it. "Tony does, though. Hang on, let me ring him up, all right?"

Tony Mancuso's my best mate here in San Francisco. He's a brilliant keyboard player, one of the founding members of the Bombardiers; he'd sat in with Blacklight a couple of times, when the band played locally on tour, and Mac and I had returned the favour after the Bombardiers' lead singer, Vinny Fabiano, had got his head bashed in with his own custom guitar. Mac covering the vocals had kept the record label off the Bombardiers' arses. I'd actually signed on weeks before the murder, partly because the Bombardiers are a fun band and old friends, but mostly because I love playing with Tony. He's got an old-school barrelhouse touch on a piano that just works with damned near everything I do, from slide to headbanger stuff.

Besides, as I say, Tony's my mate. And I wanted to tell him about getting to meet Bulldog. Bulldog had shared a couple of brilliant stories about the great piano players he'd known in Chicago and New York in the thirties and forties, and I wanted to share, as well. These blokes Bulldog talked about, they were Tony's idols: Meade "Lux" Lewis, Albert Ammons, Pete Johnson. Getting to hear about them by way of someone who'd actually played with them, he was going to hang on every word.

He picked up on the second ring. "JP? Hey, man, when did you guys get back? How was the Hall of Infamy, er, Fame?"

"About an hour ago, and it was—interesting. The trip was, anyway." I was grinning to myself. Blacklight, as a band, was inducted into the Hall as soon as we'd become eligible, and anytime the subject comes up with any of the Bombardiers, I got friendly grief over it, because they haven't made it in yet, and probably won't. "Listen, Tony, I need to beg a favour, yeah? It's for Bree, not for me."

I told him about the catering gig, about the extra days' layover in Ohio, and about the truck rental reservation going walkabout. I also told him what had made us late getting home by a day. Of course, he was right on it.

"Hell, yeah, no problem at all. Does she want to just borrow it? Or would it make more sense for us to be her minions while she catches up getting the actual work done? I mean, if she dumped a day's prep so you could trade bottleneck licks with Bulldog Moody...?"

"I hadn't even thought of that. Hang on, I'll ask her." Bree was at the sink, draining pasta. "Bree, Tony's had a brilliant idea. He says of course you can borrow the truck, but would it make sense for us to drop you at the kitchens? We could get supplies while you whip the troops into shape. Would that save you some time, us being your roadies?"

"Oh man, yes! But only if it won't get in the way of you doing stuff you want to do."

She flipped the pasta back into the pan, dumped the bubbling sauce into it, and with a couple of fast expert movements of her wrist, managed to blend the ingredients, without putting a fork or anything else near it. A cloud of steam billowed straight up. It smelled gorgeous, and I suddenly realised how hungry I was.

"Okay. Tony, we're on for tomorrow—Bree says she'd love for us to fetch things for her. Right now, there's pasta being served up, and I'm half-starved. Tell you what, why don't we ring you after dinner? I've got a few things I want to tell you about, anyway..."

Next day, with Tony driving, we dropped Bree off at the licensed kitchens she works out of when she's catering, and headed off with a list of things that needed getting.

The way it works in San Francisco is, most private licensed caterers don't own their own restaurants. And the problem is, the City's got a powerful restaurant union, and they've got a death grip on catering contracts. Also, they're not what you'd call welcoming of competition. The City doesn't let you cater out of your house, and that means people like my wife have to buy insurance and then wave proof of that insurance at one of the few licensed kitchens out there that aren't behind the doors of a restaurant. Industrial kitchens, those are; the one Bree uses is all the way out near the old shipyards.

Tony had seen Bree at her job before, but only once, and that had been twenty years ago. The party to celebrate the Bombardiers' acquisition of their own rehearsal space on Freelon Street had been her first professional gig as a caterer, and she'd been shy, nervous as a colt.

Yeah, well, like the saying goes, that was then, this is now. By the time we'd dropped her off and climbed back into the Range Rover with a detailed list and a command to ring her up if we had any questions about anything at all, Tony'd gone quiet and slightly pale, and his eyes were wide. This particular silver anniversary party she was heading up, she'd put together a staff of nine people, and she was in no mood to let anything else fuck up.

They'd already begun assembling a bunch of little moulded cups and brushing them with tempered chocolate before we arrived; one of the things on our list was about ten pounds of the stuff, the amount her usual supplier had shorted her. But Bree had her control thing all the way on, and she was cracking the whip. When we left, two of the helpers were assembling something she called ganache, to fill the chocolate cups with, and they were doing it fast, and without a lot of conversation.

While she was busy terrorising the catering staff, Tony and I were driving round the shops, getting her what she needed. We had a very nice time. I started off giving him the details about Bulldog and about Ches Kobel's book, and he called me a few rude names for getting to hang out with someone who'd actually known the great barrelhouse piano players, instead of him.

"Reminds me, I had a thought." We'd gone to the linens warehouse, over on the east slope of Potrero Hill. They'd been thoroughly snarled at by Bree over the phone, and by the time we got there, they'd put together a huge stack of tablecloths, all snowy white with bands of silver round the edges. The damned things weighed a ton, and they were going to take up most of the back of the truck; it was going to mean a run back to the kitchens to unload, before we got anything else in there. Lucky thing the kitchens weren't far...

"A thought?" Tony was panting a little—we're neither of us the lads we used to be. "Cool. Share."

"I'm planning to." I was panting, as well. Seemed to me there was a lot of tablecloths. How many tables did Bree have to cover, anyway? "I'm off to Nashville next week, the day after Bree does this party, in fact."

"I know that. And...?"

"I've got to talk to the people at Gibson, and I was thinking I might do a quick detour and see Bulldog, if he's up for it. Do you want to come along? You really should meet him and you'd love

33

the bloke, Tony, honestly. Besides, if you came along, I might be able to convince Bree to stay home. She worries about me, you know? But she never seems to get that I worry about her, as well. She's going to be a complete wreck when this party's over, and I want her to stay home and put her boots up for a couple of days. She might just do it, if she knows I'm not going off on my own."

"Shit, JP, are you kidding?" He heaved the last of the folded cloths into the truck, and latched the doors. "Man, wild horses couldn't keep me away—you said he knew Pete Johnson? Oh hell, is that your cell, or mine?"

"Mine. Damn, what in hell did I do with it?" I was patting my pockets and shaking a few jabs and jolts out of my legs. The MS had held back most of the day, but that wasn't going to last, of course, not with all the heavy lifting and running around I'd been doing, and that was without taking the inevitable jet lag into consideration.

I finally found the phone, and leaned against the back of the truck. "Hello? Damn, missed it."

"(beep) Hello, Mr. Kinkaid, this is Sara Kildare. We met earlier this week, in Ohio, at the opening of the Blacklight exhibit. You were kind enough to suggest Farris Moody for induction this year, and I'm calling to let you know he's been selected, in the category of Early Influences. If you're still willing to act as his inductor, please give me a call. We'll need to discuss the induction speech, and talk about assembling a band for a televised jam session at the ceremony itself."

I don't really know when the idea to invite Ches Kobel to come stay with us popped into my head, but whenever it was, I got lucky. Turned out Bree was as enthusiastic about the idea as I was.

I'd scheduled the trip back east to begin the day after Bree's big catering nightmare was done with. After all the grief she'd come up against planning it, of course the party went off without a single mess-up. Nice to know that, sometimes, Sod's Law works

34

backwards, yeah? I'd even thought ahead far enough so that, when she came home exhausted after ten hours on her feet, there was a steak dinner from our favourite place in the Marina, waiting for her in the range's warming drawer.

Here's a lesson for all you married blokes out there: that had a very nice effect, very nice indeed. After the day she'd put in, I'd expected she'd want to crawl into bed, pass out cold and sleep for ten hours. Instead, she got a look at the china on the table and a whiff of dinner in the air, and what I got were the big green eyes misting up and some gorgeous sex right after we'd locked the cats downstairs for the night. And it honestly hadn't even crossed my mind, that she'd react that way. Sod's Law can sod off.

We were both just the other side of drowsing off when she stirred, and sat up in bed.

"Shit." She swung her legs out from under the covers. "Just remembered—I need to pack for you. What time is your flight?"

"Eleven fifteen. Plenty of time to do that in the morning, Bree." I got one arm free from under the duvet, shivered—February gets chilly in San Francisco, especially in a house with fourteen-foot ceilings—and pulled her back in. "I set the alarm for half past seven, and Katia and Tony said they'd pick me up here, right around half past nine. It's all taken care of, so just get back here, lady."

"Oh, good." She sighed, relaxed, and curled up. "So what's the agenda? Nashville for the Gibson factory, and then what? Are you going to visit Bulldog, with Tony?"

She sounded wistful. Of course, since most of her face was muffled up against my left side, it was hard to tell.

"Yeah, we're stopping off in Ofagoula, to see Bulldog. I rang him up and got Sallie. Bulldog's expecting us. I may pick up one of the new chambered Pauls at the factory, and bring it back—that way, I won't have to feel so guilty about having to use that Byrdland, if we end up jamming."

"Good." She rubbed her cheek against me. "Are you going to talk to him about the ceremony?"

"Yeah, probably." I stroked the tumble of hair. "Tony's completely blissed at the idea of meeting Bulldog—no surprise, not considering some of the piano blokes Bulldog worked with. I may ask Ches Kobel if he wants to come down, as well. With any luck at all, he can give me some background stuff on Bulldog."

"Why would you—oh! The induction speech?" I could feel her breath, warm against me. Gorgeous feeling, that is, one of my favourite things about the follow-on to a good bit of slap and tickle. There's nothing quite as cool as having your old lady snuggled up against you, just right there, breath and skin and hair, and both of you relaxed and mellow. "It's not only about Bulldog's history, though, is it? Because I thought it would have some stuff about you in it, John. I mean, how he influenced you, that kind of thing."

"Yeah, that's got to be in there. But I've got a couple of weeks to write it. It should be okay."

"Mmmm." She was half asleep again. "Good. Don't let me oversleep. Need to pack…"

I didn't sleep as well as I thought I would that night, but it wasn't until I was halfway across the country, sitting next to Tony in first class, that I realised why: I'd never actually written a speech before, and I didn't have the first clue about where to begin.

I kept that to myself, just letting it simmer. When I'd rung Sara Kildare back to tell her that, yeah, of course I wanted to induct Bulldog, she'd given me a few details. I'd been so pleased at being asked to do it, I hadn't stopped to think very much about the fact that I was actually going to have to write the damned speech myself.

I ran it around in my head for the rest of the flight to Nashville. The speech would have to run a minimum of four minutes, maximum of six. That may not sound like much, but crikey, you try it, especially one that's got to not only contain details of two lives and get it all those details in, nice and pithy, but link the two lives together, as well.

Once we got to Gibson, I switched the focus entirely over to that. I checked out one of their new chambered Les Pauls, the Crates—the official name for the things is apparently "CR8". I quite liked it, but at over seven pounds, they came in heavier than I wanted; for the touring replicas of mine, I wanted them down to no more than six and a half pounds. It was going to be months before the new Blacklight CD was released, but when it did hit the stores, we were going to have to tour to support it, and it already looked to be a double disc.

Bottom line is, I wasn't getting any younger and the MS wasn't going to get any easier. Standing about for two hours with a guitar, I wanted it as light as possible, and that went for the signature JP Kinkaid model they wanted to issue, as well. And I was willing to dig in my heels over it.

Fortunately, I already had a weapon to get things done my way. The weapon's name is Little Queenie, and she's my custom Zemaitis knockoff, commissioned by Bree as a wedding present and built by a brilliant Bay Area luthier called Bruno Baines. And she weighs under six pounds. That guitar's become my favourite axe, and she was proof, right there, that the lighter weight could be done.

So we had a back and forth about that. It nearly got noisy, because, as I said, I dug my heels in. But they finally agreed to try to customise the chambered Pauls down to where the weight would be acceptable to me. I ended up ordering prototype copies of both my Pauls, and I also got to take one of the seven-plus pounders with me, for a trial. Good job, that visit was, nice and productive. I got a lot done.

We were only in Nashville for a day, and I rang up Ches in Cleveland, to ask him how he'd feel about meeting us at Bull-

37

dog's place. Of course, he was right on it, especially when I told him I had Tony with me.

"Tony Mancuso—the keyboard player from the Bombardiers?" Ches sounded really enthusiastic, and very winded. "Fantastic! Love to meet him. I'm not a piano guy, but I know he does a lot of Delta-influenced stuff."

"Right. Ches, you all right? You sound breathless."

"That's because I *am* breathless. I just got back from my jog, and man, it's cold outside. I think I inhaled icicles—it's really freezing, out there near the lake. I bet that damned groundhog stuck his nose out, said something nasty, and went back to bed until April. Look, JP, what time does your flight get into Cincy? Because I can reserve a car and meet you, and do the driving…"

So that was fixed up, nice and painless, and poor Tony didn't have to try and drive us round southern Ohio while I cocked things up trying to navigate. Just as well, since it was icy out there; not snow, just really cold. It looked to still be winter in the heartlands for awhile, yet.

This time, I'd had the sense to not rush it. The next actual commitment I had was the same one Tony had: we had a gig set up for our pickup band, the Fog City Geezers, Saturday night at the Great American Music Hall, back in San Francisco. But right now, it was only Tuesday and we had no planes to catch, and no reason to hurry.

And we didn't hurry. We sat in Bulldog's front room, the four of us, Sallie off somewhere else in the house, and we talked, just swapping stories, Bulldog making Tony as happy as I've ever seen him, telling brilliant moments of history. He had this amazing storehouse of memories and stories; we spent hours, talking about sessions he'd done at Sun, at Chess, at Sundial, some uncredited guitar parts while Elvis Presley was first rehearsing, sitting in with some of the great keyboard blokes out there, Jimmy Yancey out of Chicago, Pete Johnson. Tony's idols, every damned one.

The feeling I got—right. Same as it was the first time. There'd been this odd little section of my own life, where I'd listened to everything I could get that sounded at all like Bulldog Moody. I'd told Bulldog the truth, that first visit: the whole reason I'd first picked up a guitar when I was nine years old was because of "Daisy Chain Blues," Sundial Records, him playing those sessions. By the time I was fifteen, I'd learned every riff of Bulldog Moody's I could get my hands on.

So meeting him, that could have been a disaster, yeah? That's always the chance you take, when you meet someone you've idealised in your own head. I ought to know. I'm not stupid; I may see myself as a sideman, but I'm also a very distinctive guitar player and I've had people come up to me, wanting to meet me, telling me I'd had a hand in how they listened to music, or in how they played. It's like I said, meeting someone you idolise can break your heart.

But Bulldog, meeting him, coming back to Manassas Road again? That was perfect. It felt as if the part of me that was made to play, the part that was completely dedicated to the service of music, had come home somehow.

"...so I told Mr. Fineberg, yes sir, I'm happy to do a few sessions with Jimmy Yancey, but we got a problem, because the drummer, well, he's off on a three-day drunk..."

Tony laughed, leaned forward, interrupted, apologised. His face was bright, shining with interest, just loving it. He felt it, as well, that whole connection thing: another player, another one of us. We were family.

It came into my head, right then: *Here you go, Johnny, here's what your speech is about.*

"...but a piano player, he aint gonna think like me, no sir, because piano players are a whole different thing, they think end to end, and you got to watch the ones who get scared off playing up on the high end..."

39

Connections.

Of course, that was it. I was who I was, had become the guitar player I was, because I'd connected with a rhythm, a heartbeat, that had belonged to Bulldog Moody. His rhythms had become the basis for the style of play that said *JP Kinkaid* to audiences who listened to me.

Bulldog was the child of Santeria high priests, *bata* drummers. And their rhythms, from Nigeria to Cuba to the Mississippi Delta and up into studios in Chicago in the forties, in New York in the fifties, those rhythms were as much of me, had been inherited and carried forward by me, as if I'd been Sallie's blood brother. I hadn't needed the DNA, or even the upbringing. I had the music, and that connected us.

"...so there was the sax player, guy called Gil, out of New Jersey, he calls up Yancey the night before the session..."

My feet were tingling, waking up to a sharp little series of pains. It was an unpleasant reminder that no matter how much of an enchanted place the house on Manassas Road seemed to be, the MS wasn't going to be impressed by it, or kept at bay. I was a good two hours late for taking my afternoon meds, and anyway, it was time for a stretch.

I left Tony in a sort of trance, listening to Bulldog remembering playing cards in a Chicago recording studio with Champion Jack Dupree, and wandered out onto the front porch with my pills and some water. *Damn.* I'd meant to ring Bree, but my phone was inside, in my jacket pocket...

"How you doing, JP?"

I jumped half a mile; I hadn't heard Ches follow me out. "Not too bad. Just realising that I've got to write Bulldog's Hall of Fame induction speech. Should be okay—I got what it has to be about, the main thing, I don't know what to call it–"

"The theme?"

"Right, that's it. The theme. History and family." I told him

40

what I'd been thinking, my feeling that Maoudain Ferrer's *bata* drums were essentially being carried on like a kind of ancestral thing, and how I was privileged to be able to do it, to be a part of it.

"Family as a musical line, and not just a blood line?" He'd got it, straight off. He was nodding, focused. "Or maybe music, the music itself, as the connection, the substitute for actual DNA and blood, making up a family? Damn, JP, that's a kickass idea! You know, if you need any information about Bulldog's family, I've got all the notes I'm using for my book..."

That's probably when the idea first came into my head, and I didn't stop to think it over—the idea was just right, and I went with it. "Ches, question for you, mate. How's your immediate schedule? You up for spending some time in San Francisco next week?"

"Hell yeah." He zipped up his jacket. It really was cold out there; if I stayed outdoors much longer, I'd get back to San Francisco ill, and Bree would never trust me out on the road without her again. "What did you have in mind? Collaboration?"

"Actually, I was thinking more about one hand washing the other." I had one hand on the door. "You bring your notes, I'll fill you in on what it was like being a working-class blues guitar prodigy in South London in the early sixties. I can get the speech written, and you can get more stuff for your book. I'll need to ring home, and check with Bree, but if we haven't got anything on, I'm betting she'd love to have you come stay with us."

"Really?" His face was pink, whether because he was flattered or because he was half-frozen I didn't know.

"Really." We were back indoors now, out of the chill of the Ohio afternoon. From out in the kitchen, I heard a sizzle, and caught the smell of fish frying; Sallie must be making supper, catfish and red beans and dirty rice. "Music, connections—it's all in the family."

Chapter Three

"*Good evening, San Francisco!*"

The dressing room, backstage and downstairs at the Great American Music Hall on O'Farrell Street, is actually a decent size. Good thing, too, since we had a few more people than usual hanging out before the gig.

"Mom, can you grab some of that bottled water? Just a few bottles—Sandra's holding our tables, but we need to get out front." Bree was already at the dressing room door, one hand on the knob, straining to get up and out into the front of the house. "Lights are about to go down. Come on, mom, let's rock!"

I was tuning up the chambered Paul I'd been given back at Gibson, in Nashville, but I looked up at her, and grinned. Bree's a veteran of these local gigs, and she knows what the vocal cues are, from the house announcer. Her mum, Miranda, was a lot newer at it; she'd got a night off from having to practice medicine, had rung us up to see if she could talk Bree into cooking her a meal, and promptly got grabbed and dragged along to the show.

"I'm right behind you, dear." Miranda Godwin isn't what you'd usually expect to find in a dressing room. Okay, maybe in a green room at the symphony, or something, but not backstage at our kind of show. For one thing, she's in her sixties, and for another, she's so damned elegant and icy-looking, if you didn't know her, you couldn't imagine her unbending enough to enjoy any sort of rowdiness. Hell, I'd thought that myself until pretty recently, and I've known her nearly thirty years, now.

Truth is, I don't know whether she likes what I play or not. She's got such good manners, every note could be turning her nerve endings inside out and scraping them raw, and she'd never show it. What I do know is that she'll bend over backward to enjoy anything Bree enjoys.

"It's been awhile since we had the pleasure of having these guys on-stage at the Great American Music Hall, and we're always glad to have them back…"

"Man, this is so cool." Ches Kobel was looking as wide-eyed as a teenaged fanboy who'd somehow snuck in through a backstage window. It was really funny. I mean, crikey, he'd interviewed dozens of musicians in his day, blues legends, jazz players, even a few fusion types. There just seemed to be something about being in the dressing room with a bunch of rockers that had got him bouncy, and awestruck. "This is a lot more mellow than I thought it would be, though. And no drugs?"

"Ha! Were you looking for blotter acid and a hash pipe?" Billy Dumont was grinning. "Because we stopped doing that stuff when Reagan was president. And not because of Nancy and her *just say no* shtick, either."

Billy was moving a pair of drumsticks between his fingers, and actually, I think that was what Ches was staring at. I'd watched Billy doing it with the Bombardiers for donkey's years, and it still gets my attention, every time. He rolls the drumsticks in a very precise rhythm, over and around his knuckles, under two fingers,

43

and back out again. Thing is, you watch it for a few reps, and it suddenly hits you: he's doing it in an actual 4/4 beat. Completely unconscious, you know? The whole rhythmic thing is so ingrained, he doesn't even think about it. It was beyond cool, and the fact that he never screwed it up, just made it even cooler.

"So put your hands together and give it up..."

"Everyone ready?" Kris Corcoran was flexing his fingers. His old Fender P-bass was already tuned and set out onstage. This band wasn't the Bombardiers, it was a sort of amalgam, but we used the Bombardiers roadies. They'd been setting up for the band so many years, they could have tuned that P-bass in their sleep. I spared my usual moment for the usual thought, hoping the roadies had remembered the stool I need in case the MS flares up during the gig. "Sounds like a full house up there."

"...Tony Mancuso, Kris Corcoran, Billy DuMont, Jack Carter and JP Kinkaid..."

I headed for the door, and led the way up the stairs and into the artists' waiting area, just inside the backstage door. Bree and Miranda were already gone, out into the audience; their tables were reserved, just outside the backstage rope. The side of stage area's so small at the Great American, there's no room for tables, so the club management holds a couple for the band family near the backstage door. Katia and Sandra were out there right now, ordering food and drink for the break.

"Ladies and gentlemen..."

"Right, we're on." I opened the door, and led the way out. That was tradition; the band had been my idea in the first place, something to keep me playing in front of a crowd during the long stretches between Blacklight tours. I not only lead the band out onstage when the houselights go down, I also do all the speaking for the band from the stage. It's the only time I do any of that—with Blacklight, it's always been Mac front and centre, and it should be.

44

"...*San Francisco's own Fog City Geezers!*"

Showtime.

It was a good show, and a lot of fun. Geezer gigs generally are; there's no stress, no push to be perfect, no ego or heavy media or star power involved. A pickup band is there to have fun with, and when the band's enjoying itself, that vibe pings off the audience like sonar off a submarine, and pings right back at the band. It becomes a nice loop, the back and forth sharing and feeding of that energy with the crowd.

The Geezers play a two-set show, with a break at the halfway point; usually, we run about ninety minutes of music total, plus an encore. We play a lot of old standards, blues, rock and roll, everything from Fats Domino and Alan Toussaint tunes to old Delta and Chicago style boogie woogie to Chuck Berry numbers. If Tony's in the mood to play some honky-tonk, we've even got a couple of country tunes that make it into the set list as back-up: a brilliant Ray Price tune called *Crazy Arms*, Patsy Cline's *Walkin' After Midnight*.

Tonight, I'd weighted the set slightly heavier toward rock than it was toward blues, mostly because I wanted to really give the new chambered Les Paul a workout, see how it did. Turned out Jack Carter, the harp player who sits in with us whenever his schedule allows, had a few rock runs he'd been experimenting with, so that worked out well. In fact, we caught an edge and went off on a sensational unplanned jam, nailing Berry's *Roll Over, Beethoven* in a series of lead-tradeoffs between all the instruments up there. As a closer to the first set, it brought down the house.

When we finished, I stepped up to the mic, and got the crowd—they were cheering and hooting—to settle down. "Right," I told them. "We're going to take a short break, but don't worry, we'll be back in a few minutes."

With the houselights up, I was all set to head for the downstairs dressing room, but that wasn't on. Instead, the rest of the band turned left instead of right, and went straight out into the audience, to the cluster of band family tables.

I peered around Tony—he's taller than I am, and I was the last one offstage. The first thing I saw was Bree, at one of the tables. She had Miranda at one elbow, but she was deep in conversation with someone. Whoever he was, he had his back toward me.

For a moment, I thought it was Ches; same build, same close-cropped hair, same way of holding his shoulders. But that wasn't Ches, not unless he'd slipped out during the first set and changed clothes...

Bree saw me over his shoulder, smiled, beckoned. The bloke she'd been talking to turned his head, and lifted a hand, and waved at us.

It was Patrick Ormand.

I stood there a moment, just breathing in, breathing out, getting it nice and even, telling my heart to slow down. Right. No reason he shouldn't be there, not really. For one thing, Patrick's a music fan; he'd been backstage for Blacklight twice, at our invitation and with the band's blessing. And after all, cops get the night off, same way doctors do; Miranda was here, no reason Patrick shouldn't be.

But Miranda isn't a homicide detective, and none of the nice simple reasons I gave myself before I headed over there took away the little jolt that seeing Patrick Ormand on my turf always gives me. Knowing he was probably here for pleasure rather than business, just digging the band on a night off, didn't help.

"John, look who's here." Bree'd picked it up, of course. She knew damned well what my reactions to Patrick were; she had good reasons to remember some of those reactions.

The situation was tricky. The last time we'd actually spoken to each other to say anything more than hello or goodbye, Patrick had been picking himself up off the floor of my hired villa near

46

Cannes, apologising to us for getting us shot at, and for actually getting Mac injured. I wasn't about to say so to Bree—she probably knows, anyway—but I treasure that memory. Mac's bodyguard, Domitra Calley, had resented her boss nearly getting killed thanks to Patrick's wrong-headedness, and she'd shown her resentment by decking Patrick. Since she's trained in a few martial arts I can't spell or even pronounce, she'd really messed his face up. He'd had a shiner for the record books.

Tonight, though, it seemed he really did just have the night off SFPD, and had bought a ticket and stood in line, along with the rest of ticket-buying public. He got to his feet and offered me a hand.

"Hey, JP, nice to see you. That was a great first set. New guitar?"

"Yeah, fresh from the nice people at Gibson. One of the new lighter-weight chambered numbers—everything you wanted in a Les Paul, but less. How's it going, mate?" I shook his hand, and nodded at Bree. "Decided to hang out front, love? Got a seat for me, then?"

The entire band seemed to have decided to hang out front. Sandra, Kris Corcoran's wife, had ordered quite a lot of nosh, and the food had only just arrived. Dragging it all backstage seemed as pointless as abandoning it, and people were hungry. Now I thought about it, so was I. I reached out and grabbed a handful of chips. Bree'd had the sense to order me a burger, as well. It was a nice way to spend most of the break.

I sometimes forget what hanging out front of house is all about. I mean, you can't do that with a band like Blacklight. But it's really nice to be able to do it locally, at a smaller venue. People come up and want to take your picture, or ask you questions, or remind you that you've met at a show about thirty years ago. I quite like the interaction with the fans, but sometimes, you really just want to eat and not chat with strangers. If it gets to be too

47

much, I just slip backstage. Having both options available is nice.

There's one other drawback, though, and tonight, talking with my mother-in-law about the results of my latest round of heart tests, the drawback showed up. A pretty girl in her twenties came up to the table, wearing a faded Blacklight tour shirt, and asked me to autograph it.

I said yeah, sure, no problem. Problem was, she seemed to think the best place for me to sign my name was right across her chest.

Patrick opened his mouth and then shut it again; Ches, who'd been talking to Patrick but kept getting sidetracked by all the people coming over, made a noise and glanced at Bree. His eyes were wide. Meantime, the girl was standing there, holding the tee-shirt at the bottom, stretching it out tight. The idea seemed to be to give me a balcony to write my name on.

"Right." I caught Bree's eye—she was tapping her fingers on the table, trying not to glare. Not good. I probably shouldn't have been grinning, but I couldn't help myself. "Tell you what, I'm happy to sign it, but that particular location's a bit dodgy, you know? Makes me feel like a dirty old man. How about I sign the hem? Or maybe right across the back...?"

Like I said, a nice way to spend the break. A couple of minutes before we were ready to head back onstage, Ches leaned over toward Billy.

"Can I ask you something?"

"Sure." Billy's fingers had been doing their thing, tapping away on the table. He's a drummer all through, Billy is; no matter what he's doing, there's always a rhythm going on in there, somewhere. "What's up?"

"That thing you're doing, with your fingers." Ches nodded his head at Billy's hands, which gradually stopped tapping and went quiet. "That particular beat. I'm curious—sorry, it's the nosy writer in me. Just tell me to back off if I'm getting on your nerves.

But I really am curious—you must have listened to a lot of Cuban music, the old *son* stuff from Havana, a lot of *clave* from the fifties. Right?"

"Huh?" Billy blinked; the houselights had flickered twice, which meant we were just about due back onstage for the second set. "I know what *son* is, vaguely, but I have no idea what that other one is. What did you call it? Klah-vay? Because whatever it is, well, no. That rhythm I was just doing? That's basic Bo Diddley."

He ran it again, his fingers tapping it out on the table: *bomp ba bompa bomp, pause, babomp-BOMP.* On Bree's other side, Patrick was watching Billy's fingers. He looked absolutely fascinated. So did Miranda. "You mean this, right?" Billy told Ches. "Basic Bo, dude."

"Nope. Basic *clave.* Bo Diddley made it mainstream, but his stuff comes straight from the Havana beat, and that came straight from *son.* All from the original slave population in Cuba." Ches grinned at me. "Scary thought, isn't it, JP? The stuff all you rockers do, that three-beat thing? Sallie's great-grandfather was doing that back in Santiago de Cuba, a hundred years ago."

The houselights went all the way down right around then, the audience began the usual stomping and catcalling, and we headed back onstage for the second set. A nice evening, all the way around.

Halfway through the show closer, I looked up during one of those three-beat riffs Ches had been talking about—we were doing a cover of Bo Diddley's *Mona*, hot and sexy, and the place was rocking. I was looking for Bree, something that's become almost instinctive for me. It adds to my comfort level, knowing where she is, knowing she's there at all.

I found her right off; no surprise, since I know what to look for, her hair flying around her shoulders. She was near our table, dancing with Patrick Ormand. Miranda was sitting, talking with

Ches Kobel; I wondered for a moment if they were discussing music, or heart conditions, or something else entirely.

"Hey, Mona..."

I stepped up to the mic—Tony was singing lead, me and Kris were doing the back-up harmony together—and had to bite back a grin. First time I'd ever looked up from playing and seen Patrick Ormand dancing with my old lady, it had completely weirded me out. That had been at the end of the 2005 Blacklight tour, at Oakland, and just the sight of them together had put a knot at the pit of my stomach. This time, all it did was make me want to laugh.

...bomp ba bompa bomp, babomp-BOMP...

Definitely an improvement, you know? Maybe I was relaxing, after all these years. And maybe, someday, I'd be able to spend ten minutes in the bloke's company without getting all my defences up.

"Back in 1960, when I was nine, I went to school at Clapham Junior School, in South London. My best mate was a kid called Davey Hensley. Having Davey around, it was like having a brother—Davey was the reason I first picked up a guitar.

"See, it went down this way: Davey had an older brother called Denny, and Denny played saxophone for a local band, mostly swing, some jazz and blues stuff as well. So one day, when Denny'd picked us up after school, he took us along to his favourite record shop, this great place just off the High Street, called Jimmy D's..."

"Hang on a second, JP, please?" Ches had his recorder going. "That has a nice easy flow to it, but you have a lot of room to trim there, if you need to trim for time issues. Bree, what do you think?"

"About John's speech? I think it's starting out just fine. And I think you're probably right about time and trimming, but it's too early to start tweaking, is what I think."

She was unloading the dishwasher, putting things back where they belonged; we'd just had a party, the kind of thing she usually enjoys doing. This one had started out simple, planned as a thank-you for some of Bree's regular catering staff, for putting in a lot of hard work during that silver anniversary gig she'd done. Somehow, though, it had got out of hand, and we'd ended up with her mum, Tony and Kris and their wives, Billy DuMont, the two roadies who help out the Geezers, and four members of Bree's staff, with their plus-ones. Plus, there was Ches, who was staying with us.

Once it came clear that this was going to be a lot easier as a "wander straight on through, help yourself" buffet deal, rather than the polite sit-down meal Bree'd had in mind, we both said fuck it, and decided to throw an actual party. Bree's take was that this way was a lot easier than breaking out the good china and trying to keep it formal.

We'd ended up asking Patrick Ormand, as well. That had a sort of nice rounding-off feel to it, asking him to come round and eat Bree's cooking; as I say, last time he'd been a guest under our roof, he'd used my wife as bait to catch a sniper. I had mixed feelings about all that—yeah, he'd endangered her life, but he'd also flattened her and covered her, when the bullets started flying. He'd kept her alive.

So, right, this was sort of our way of saying okay, cheers mate, all is forgiven, and letting him know he was welcome under our roof again. Whether I'd actually ever forgive him for endangering Bree in the first place, well, that was something I honestly didn't know. Even if I did forgive him for it, I wasn't about to forget it.

I wasn't even sure he'd show up—he could always plead work pressure, and of course, considering his job, it might even have been the truth. But he showed up; he even brought Bree a bottle of decent champagne and some fresh berries. That was nice of him—I don't touch alcohol, I've been sober for over twenty years

51

now, and Bree's never had the faintest use for hard liquor. But she does love fresh berries in very dry bubbly stuff. It was nice of Patrick to remember.

If the party had been left up to me, there would have been a lot of people with nothing in common, standing about and not knowing what the hell to say to each other. I'm very bad at knowing how to get things started socially, and even worse at keeping them going.

So it was a good thing that keeping the party going was Bree's gig, not mine, because she's damned good at it. No one was there longer than ten minutes before they found themselves holding a plate of nosh, and deep in conversation with someone who had completely different interests. Bree swears it's all just because she knows how to provide exceptional food, that no ever whinges about being bored when there's great nosh, but I don't believe her. There's got to be more to it than that, you know? It's alchemy, or magic, or something.

I did my bit, of course, what with being the host. I got a word in with every guest, even if my thing was limited to waving people at the food, and asking if they were having a good time. I did manage to get some conversation in with Patrick; I need to take breaks at these things, sit, rest my legs. If I don't, if I forget and stay on my feet too long, the MS kicks my arse, good and hard, and that upsets the hell out of Bree.

So, once everything was going full swing, I queued up some vintage UK rock on the sound system, slipped off into the kitchen for a time-out, and found Patrick already in there. He seemed to be having a conversation with Wolfling, our elderly tabby, and I remembered, Patrick's a cat bloke. Surprising, that is—I'd expect someone with his kind of control issues to prefer dogs.

"Hey, JP." He had a glass of wine and an empty plate on the table. Wolfling was purring like a motorboat, his eyes half-closed, rubbing his head against Patrick's knuckles. "I came in to put my plate in the sink, but I got distracted. Which one is this, again? Wolfling or Simon? I know the Siamese is female."

"That's Wolfling. Furry old brown-noser." I tickled the cat under the chin, and the purr got even louder. "Oi, you been sucking up to the constabulary, mate?"

"Actually, I was sucking up to him. I always try to ingratiate myself with the housecats. You know the old saying, right? How dogs have owners, and cats have staff?" Patrick headed over to Bree's big double-wide sink, and rinsed his plate. "Did I tell you how much I enjoyed the show at the Great American the other night, by the way? I was really glad I had the chance to go. I don't get nights off that often, but this week, I get three. Unless someone decides to go on a killing spree—if that happens, all bets are off."

"Glad you made it out." I eased myself into Bree's computer chair; our kitchen's enormous, and it has an alcove that Bree uses for her office. The computer chair's an Aeron, cost a damned fortune, but it's worth every penny. I'd tried hers and I liked it so much, I ordered one for myself, for down in the basement studio.

I settled back in it, and stretched my legs; they hurt like hell, ominous little flickers along the nerves. I seemed to be getting tired out a lot more easily than I used to, just one more item to discuss with the neuro next time I saw her. "Bit surprising, you knowing I had a new guitar that night," I told Patrick. "After all, the new chambered Pauls, the one they gave me? Looks a lot like my Deluxe. Took a good sharp eye to spot the differences from the audience. I didn't realise you were a guitar bloke."

"I'm not." He grinned at me, a genuine grin. Patrick has a few too many teeth for my liking; when he's doing his cop thing, he goes into this predator mode, and the teeth look too sharp, all Red Riding Hood and the wolf in the fairy story. But this was just an honest smile, no threat in there anywhere. "Bree mentioned it, just before you came offstage. I understand you're getting ready to induct someone into the Rock and Roll Hall of Fame. Anyone with a name I might recognise?"

I told him about Bulldog. I wasn't planning on getting personal; I'm not close to Patrick and, besides, there's that whole trust thing. But he listened, and nodded, and then proceeded to floor me.

"Bulldog Moody." He'd sat down at the table, a few feet away in the main room of the kitchen, and was devoting himself to making Wolfling a very happy cat. "I know that name. Wasn't he a session guy, or something? Because for some reason, his name is familiar, and I'm mentally linking it up to my father's collection of blues records. Mostly stuff on Sundial Records, out of Memphis. Guitar player, very distinctive sound, heavy rhythm stuff? Am I thinking of the right guy, or am I talking out of my ass...?"

After that, of course, I ended up telling him the entire thing, including why Ches was here. I even told him about having to write the speech. And of course, he's a superb listener. He's got to be, what with his job, yeah? Also, he hears the stuff you aren't actually saying. That particular talent, that's got to be part of the whole cop thing.

"I wouldn't worry about the speech." Farrowen had joined Wolfling on the kitchen table, and every few seconds, I'd catch one dark blue cat's eye as the Siamese checked on me, making sure I wasn't going to do anything about her being where she didn't belong. One thing you can depend on a cat to do is not to miss out on a good thing. Both cats were blissed out, getting stroked and fondled—they knew damned well they weren't supposed to be on the table, but they weren't about to leave unless and until someone turfed them off.

Patrick looked to have found the spot high up on Wolfling's cheeks, a sort of nerve link that has this interesting effect on the cat: it turns him boneless. "After all," Patrick told me, "you've got your friend here, right? It sounds like you have the cooperative thing all set up. You guys are sharing each other's information. So what's the problem?"

"Yeah, the cooperation thing, that's all laid on. The problem is, I've never really written a speech before, not one that's got to follow time constraints and have a theme, and all that rubbish. I've got to get all my bits and all Bulldog's bits into it, and weave them together, somehow. It's about the connections, you know? Music, family, all that."

"Well—good luck with that." Patrick gave Farrowen a final rub behind the ears, and got up. The kitchen door was swinging open behind him. "I wouldn't worry. And if you need someone to practice on, someone who won't tell you it's a great speech even if it isn't, let me know. You can always come down to Seventh and Bryant and read it to me."

"Yeah, right. I'll just run right round to the cop shop and go through all the metal detectors to tell you and the other blokes at Homicide a bedtime story. Bree, love, need some help? Give me a moment—I just came in to give my legs a rest, but I'm coming back out. Here, let me get those–"

"No, stay put, John. I've got it." She had about two dozen dirty plates balanced on her forearms, but she got them into the sink without any trouble, before I could even get out of my chair— well, right, her chair. Once that was taken care of, she turned around and fixed Patrick with a long hard glare. Usually, I see that look, I'd expect the next words out of her mouth to be *little man*, a phrase I bloody well hate. She's got to be really narked to use it, but of course, it wasn't me she was glaring at, and thank God for it.

"I heard that comment." The look could have etched glass. "Just for the record, Patrick, I do not tell John I think something sounds great if I don't believe it. And what the hell are the cats doing on the table...?"

55

We actually managed to get everyone out reasonably early; by half past ten, there was just us and Ches. We'd loaded the dishwasher, put away things that had to be hand-washed, wrapped up leftovers, and put the kettle on. The tea hadn't even cooled down enough to sip comfortably before I'd got the first bits of my speech out, and was running them past Ches and Bree.

"...Jimmy D's was a fantastic record shop, complete magic cave for the local musicians. It had a downstairs, where Dominic kept his rare American stock—he'd got his cousin in Chicago to send him all these blues records: Chess Records, Sun, a lot more. The local musicians called the basement the Underground. Boogie, blues, jazz—it was all there.

"And one day, when Denny'd brought us kids over to the Underground after school, Dominic was playing a record from Sundial Records, and there was this amazing guitar being played, rhythms I'd never heard before. I listened to it, and I asked him to play it again, and then again.

"Turned out the song was called 'Daisy Chain Blues,' sung by a brilliant piano player called Walter 'Laughing' Loudon. But the guitar, that amazing guitar, that's what really got to me. My fingers were tingling, everything was tingling—I was humming it in my head, keeping on with the rhythm, and I wasn't making a sound. That guitar just talked to me—those rhythms went straight to all my nerves. So I asked Dominic who the guitarist was, and he looked at the small print on the back of the sleeve. He said the guitar was being played by a man called Farris 'Bulldog' Moody. And that night, I sat down at supper with my mum and dad, and told them I wanted a guitar."

Right. Maybe this wasn't going to be so tricky, after all.

Chapter Four

"*There's this image we white Europeans have, this idea about black American blues players, especially if they're from the Mississippi Delta, that they're all from poor backgrounds. And that's not wrong, not really—most of them were pretty poor. That's the rule. The thing is, every rule has exceptions, and in the case of–*" I got a look at Bree's face, stopped, and lifted an eyebrow. "What?"

"I'm not sure, but it just sounds—wrong. The whole sentence is, I don't know..." Her voice died off.

"Clumsy." If she was being tactful, Ches wasn't bothering about it. "Way too wordy. It's the sentence structure. You're using twenty words when eight will do just fine. You're getting a maximum of six minutes to do your thing. Tailor it, JP."

"Right." It was really odd. Musically, I have damned near no ego involved, you know? I just write and play. If someone says it doesn't work, I play it again, listen to it, feel it, and go from there. But having the speech criticised—damn. I had to make an effort not to bridle up and get defensive with every suggestion that the language was less than perfect. "Okay. How about something like this, then? *We Europeans tend to think all Delta blues musicians were sharecroppers or something. And many were, but there were exceptions, and Bulldog Moody was one of them.*" I looked at Ches. "That work?"

"It's a lot better, that's for sure. Do you want all my info about Salas Moody? When he joined the army, how he got so high up in the 809th battalion, how he met his wife, the stuff about him taking Bulldog along on the travelling tent shows? Because I've got all that handy, right here."

"Probably not for the speech, no. I do need what you've got on the roots of Bulldog's rhythm style, though—the *bata* drumming, all that." My neck was aching, and so were my eyes; everything was stiff. Comes from focusing too hard. More and more these days, I was becoming aware of little things. I had the feeling the next thing on my getting-old falling apart list might be reading glasses. It wasn't just the fine print on things that got blurry, these days.

I tossed my head, side to side, and got the vertebrae to pop. "That's better—my eyes were glazing over. Damned stiff neck. What you've got about Salas, I'd love to know about it, Ches. Just, not for the speech. The time limit's a bitch."

"I know. It sucks, having to write to a clock, especially since Bulldog deserves a couple of hours all to himself." He set his pen down. "Well, we've got the rest of the evening to work on this— my flight's not until noon. Anything of mine you need after that, I can always send overnight once I get back off the road, and home to Cleveland. Bree, I don't know what you're cooking, but it smells incredible."

"*Capellini con polpetti.* English translation, angel hair pasta and meatballs. I bake the meatballs in the oven, in the sauce itself, so you get a nice Bolognese, and the meatballs cook up so tender, they're perfect. That's why it smells so good. Pasta should be done in about five minutes, once the water boils—angel hair cooks nice and fast."

"Yum." Ches gave a long sigh. "Man, I'm going to miss this. I've never eaten so well for so long in my life. That's the suck part about being a bachelor who grew up eating fast food. I wish someone had taught me how to cook, but nobody in my family ever cooked. Hell, I probably wouldn't have time anyway. It's Chinese takeout or pizza, mostly."

"Poor Ches." Bree was filling one of those oversized multi-cooker pots of hers, the kind that come with inserts of different kinds, with water for noodles. "We're going to miss you too—it's been so cool, having you here. You said something about coming back off the road—does that mean you aren't heading straight back to Cleveland?"

"Nope, not right away." He got his notebooks and tape recorder off the table; I'd already got up and started setting the table for supper. Ches had been with us long enough to get Bree's timing patterns in the kitchen down. "I'm actually off to Memphis for a day, then on to Hattiesburg, over in Mississippi. This is a research trip—there are a few leads I need to check out down there, a few facts I want to check on for the book. I'll stop in Ofagoula Friday night, see if I can talk Bulldog and Sallie into having some dinner with me, and then home for the three-way phone deal we have set up. What are you going to be doing, JP? Besides writing the speech, I mean?"

"Making phone calls. I need to get a set list together, but I also need to start putting the band together for the induction jam. They've got some good house musicians, but I want to know who Bulldog wants. It's his party, he gets a vote, you know? My own thinking right now is getting Mac and Luke over, and asking Tony Mancuso from the Bombardiers to come along for the ride—Luke and Mac started out in a blues-based combo together. And, right, that phone thing Saturday morning—that's you, me, and Sara Kildare, ten in the morning, our time?"

"Right. I get home from Cincy Friday night, and I'm hoping to get a jog in, out at the lake, before the call."

"Good. I want to run something past Sara Kildare— I've got a song in me right now, an instrumental blues, and the damned thing wants out. If I get it done, I want to play it for Bulldog, and see if maybe we can cover it during the jam. A sort of tribute piece, you know?"

Ches nodded. The kitchen was warm, and quiet, and smelled brilliant; it was a nice relaxing moment, typical of the vibe Bree can produce at Clay Street. I watched her dropping pasta into the boiling water, stepping back as the steam billowed up from the pan, reaching for a long-handled wooden fork, stirring. She was singing under her breath, the way she often does when she's cooking, no matter who else happens to be around. It sounded like Paul Simon's song *Graceland*.

That surprised me. It was a change from her usual thing—she tends toward classic rock when she's crooning at her menus, Stones, Who, the odd bit of Bowie or even Motown, sixties vintage stuff, the four Tops, the Supremes, Carla Thomas. Once in a while, it's a Blacklight tune, but she always catches herself when that happens, and stops in mid-song. Damned if I know why—it's not like Mac is there to critique her vocals, and anyway, he wouldn't. For one thing, he's got very nice manners, especially with women, and for another, she actually sings quite nicely. Maybe what she was singing had come out of Ches's travel itinerary of choice, you know? Graceland, Memphis, Tennessee...

We had a really nice evening. Dinner, getting booted out of the kitchen while Bree cleaned up and got a dishwasher load started, sitting down in the living room, me in my rocking chair with my Martin and a metal slide, playing some old Delta stuff: Son House, Muddy Waters, but Robert Johnson mostly, because he always comes into it somewhere, you know? *Stop breakin' down, baby please stop breakin' down...*

We waved Ches into his taxi and off to the airport the next

morning, with a container of leftover pasta and meatballs, and I got down to business. First thing I did was, I rang up Bulldog, and told him what I was thinking about the jam band.

"Truth to tell, John, I don't know much about the younger players." It was amazing; if I hadn't known how old he was, I'd have thought he was fifty years younger, that's how vigorous his voice was. "But I do know about you. I tell you what, you think these boys can play, that's all I need to know. You got names, anyone you want to bring along, I'll be happy to sit and make a little music with them. Just so long as they're willing to make a little music with me, I'd be honoured."

So there was that taken care of, and I got busy. I got hold of Luke first—he needed a bit of convincing, since he was just back from taking his daughter to interview at yet another round of universities, but the convincing wasn't too hard, not once I told him what it was for. Once Luke had signed on, getting Mac on board was easy. Tony was thrilled half to death, of course. As for the rhythm section, I decided to go with the Hall's own drummer and bass player to back us up. For one thing, I didn't want to turn the show into Blacklight and Friends, and anyway, Blacklight's rhythm section aren't blues players at heart. Stu and Cal are rockers all the way, except when they're producing house and industrial techno for Euro bands, during Blacklight's downtime.

So that was the jam band all fixed up, one more thing to let Sara Kildare know about during the Saturday call. That being all done, I put together the set list. And I spent a day in the basement studio, just me and my 335, writing the tribute number for Bulldog that had been fermenting away in my head all week like a vat of John Barleycorn's finest.

Tell you the truth, I thought it was going to be tricky. I mean, yeah, I knew what I was hearing, and writing music is no big issue for me, not usually. But this was a piece that had to tell a story without a word being spoken, you know? It had to hold all the

61

stuff I was feeling and remembering, it had to let every single listener out there know where I was about family, about music, about connections and the sort of ties that history binds us up with. I had to do it right, not only for Bulldog, but for myself.

Because, see, there was a 9-year-old JP back there, the kid who didn't know he had any music in him, the kid who'd heard "Daisy Chain Blues" and gone straight home and asked his parents for something they couldn't really afford to give him: a guitar of his own to play.

They couldn't have known I'd turn out to be a prodigy. They couldn't have known that, by the time I was fifteen, my dad would be signing his approval for me to work on other peoples' sessions on school nights, that I'd be bringing home more money than he did. Maybe they sensed something I was too young to know myself, or maybe it was because I'd never really asked them for anything before. Whatever the reason was, they'd found the money somehow, and they'd got me an old Washburn. And that kid, the one with the music he only dimly guessed might be in there? He had to be in this song, as well.

Turned out the song was in there and ready. It was up-tempo, strong, talkative, but it was a blues, all right, with bits of the Delta and bits of Chicago in it. I rang Tony, and told him to come over—I had something to play for him, a new thing. When he asked me what it was called, the words just popped out: "Moody's Blues."

So by the Friday, I'd got a lot done, and everything was moving along quite nicely. The induction, from the Waldorf-Astoria hotel in New York, was in less than two weeks. Carla Fanucci rang up to discuss logistics, and Bree went shopping for a dress.

I woke up Saturday morning, not because the alarm I'd asked Bree to set had gone off, but because my cell phone was ringing.

"Shit!" I was up, fumbling for the phone; next to me, Bree was sitting up, bleary-eyed, her hair tousled. *Fuck.* How had she forgotten to set the alarm? And how in hell had we slept in so late? "Hello?"

"Mr. Kinkaid?" It was a woman's voice. The caller ID showed an Ohio area code. "JP Kinkaid?"

"Yeah." I was suddenly completely awake, every nerve on my body sending out little red alerts. It wasn't the MS, either, the usual morning dance of being woken suddenly, trying to cope with the needles and stabs of the damned disease; this was something else entirely. I was looking at the clock next to the bed. "This is JP Kinkaid."

The clock said twenty past seven. I hadn't slept in, and Bree hadn't forgot to set the alarm.

"This is Sara Kildare." Her voice was all over the place, trying to be calm, trying to hold steady, not doing any of it. "I'm sorry to be calling so early, but I'm afraid I have some very bad news."

Bulldog, it's Bulldog, oh Christ, oh Jesus, oh fuck, please don't let it be Bulldog. I wasn't saying it, because I wasn't saying anything. I was holding my breath. Next to me, Bree was taut, her shoulders hunched up against bad news. Because my face, my voice, the early hour, all that together? Bad news was what it added up to.

"I got a call from the Cleveland police a little while ago." Out of nowhere, Sara Kildare gave up trying to keep her voice even, and let the shock in. "Ches Kobel is dead. They found his body in the plaza, out in front of the Hall of Fame."

If there's any worse kind of wakeup call than what we had to deal with that morning, I can't imagine what it would be, and I don't particularly want to.

It took me a few seconds, trying to wrap my head around the news, trying to sort it out, trying to understand what Sara Kildare had just told me. Right, this isn't pretty, but I'll admit it: The first thing I really remember feeling was a sort of sick relief, at least I think it was relief. Because my first coherent thought was *thank*

63

God, it's not Bulldog, you know?

But of course, just about three seconds later, it hit and hit hard, that and feeling guilty about being relieved that we hadn't lost Bulldog so soon after I'd found him. I don't see myself losing the guilt trip over that one, not any time soon.

Meanwhile, on the other end of the line, Sara was trying to get her own voice and breathing under some sort of control, and she wasn't making a very good job of it. I swung my legs out of bed—the MS seemed pretty quiet this morning, and thank God for that, at least.

"Ches is dead? What in hell happened? Was it a car accident, or a mugging, or something?"

Sure sign that I wasn't completely awake yet: I'd asked the question before I remembered that Bree didn't know, couldn't read minds, couldn't hear Sara Kildare, hadn't got a clue what was happening.

So I said the first words, *Ches is dead,* and I heard a harsh, tiny noise from behind me, as all the breath went out of Bree. I'd been so concentrated trying to make sense of a situation I didn't want to believe, trying to get a handle on what the hell had happened, that I'd forgotten she was still next to me.

"Sara, wait, hang on a moment, can you? Just give me a moment, please." Sara Kildare was talking, and I interrupted her. Bree had started to shake, long shudders that rippled everywhere except her shoulders—those might as well have been granite. Her face had gone chalky. I dropped the phone on the bed between us, and got one arm round her.

"Damn, I'm an idiot. I'm so sorry. Let me find out what happened." I spoke into her ear, quiet, calm as I could make it. "We can't do anything about it, Bree, but let me find out, all right, love? And I'm right here. Not going anywhere. Okay?"

The shaking didn't stop, but she nodded. I picked up the phone again. "Sara? Right, I'm back again. Sorry about that—my wife's very upset. So am I. Ches was just with us, stayed here for a week. We'd got to know him, and like him." *One of the family*, I thought, but I wasn't saying that out loud in front of Bree just yet, at least not until she'd had time to take it in. A good, good bloke, Ches had been.

"All right."

There was a hard lump at the back of my own throat. Truth is, I was pretty gobsmacked and shaken off balance, myself. "Look, I know how difficult this is, but—what do the police think happened? Have they said?"

"It wasn't a crime." Sara had got a grip on herself; her voice was definitely calmer. "They called me about it because I was the first local number programmed into his cell phone, and he had that with him. He always took it along on his morning run. They didn't go into any details with me, but I gather they think it was natural causes. And he had no family they could notify, not locally—I think there's a sister or something, back on the East Coast."

Out of nowhere, her voice broke, just splintered. "I can't believe he's gone. He was only thirty years old, and healthy—it isn't right, it just can't be right. They called the paramedics, of course, and they tried to restart his heart, but it was no good. The officer who called me said it was probably a heart attack, or something. I know Ches had something not quite right with his heart, something he took pills for, but he wasn't sick or anything, not really. He jogged every day. He ran half-marathons, for heaven's sake!"

"Right." I'd nearly said it out loud, let it slip—*heart attack*—but I hadn't, and a damned good thing, too. That really would have had Bree melting down, what with me having a bad heart as well, same thing as Ches had only worse, and me being older. She'd have flipped her shit entirely, and no amount of pointing out that Bulldog had it worse than me and Ches put together, with a few other complications as well, would have glued her

65

back together again, even pointing out that Bulldog was not that far off ninety. When it comes to my health, she always sees the worst case, every damned time.

It was right about then, with Sara waiting for me to finish what I'd started off saying, that I suddenly realised something. Shit, shit, *shit*...

"Look, we're going to need to sort out what we want to do about the band for the induction, rehearsals, the set list, all that." I took a deep breath. "I know it sounds heartless, but the induction's in less than two weeks, and I've got some stuff to go over with you. But right now, I've got a question."

"What is it?"

"Has anyone rung up Bulldog, and let him know?" I was pretty sure I didn't want to hear the answer, especially since I probably already knew it. "Because he loved Ches, Sara. Hell, Ches said he was stopping off in Ofagoula on his way back to Cleveland. I don't know if did or not, but he told us he–"

"Yes, he did."

That stopped me for a moment. She sounded really certain, but of course, there was an obvious reason. Another moment of guilty relief; I didn't want to be the one to have to give Bulldog the bad news, and if she already had, I was off the hook. "So, you've spoken to Bulldog, then?"

"No. No, I haven't called him. I don't think he's heard about Ches yet. No, I meant, Ches called me this morning, about an hour before the police did. He said he'd got in really late last night, that he'd stopped off and spent yesterday afternoon down in the south state. He said Bulldog was really excited about the induction, about the chance to jam, especially with you, and about meeting some of the younger musicians."

I didn't say anything. The truth was, I didn't trust myself to say a damned thing. Her voice shook suddenly. "I keep seeing him, thinking of him, having his breakfast, lacing up his shoes, heading out for his morning run—oh, God. I hate to admit this—I'm a coward. I don't want to call Bulldog Moody. I don't want to have to tell him. It's going to be hard enough going over to Ches' place, getting his notes, trying to figure out what to do about his plants–"

"I'll do it."

The words were out before I even had time to think about it. And once they were out, I was stuck; there wasn't any taking them back.

Bulldog was going to be heartbroken, and shocked with it. From what I'd seen of them together, Ches was almost as much a member of that family unit as Sallie was. There was basically nothing in the world I wanted to do less than tell Bulldog about Ches dying.

But I'd offered, and that was that—no backing out of it. I did keep Sara on the phone, getting the details that wanted immediate attention sorted out: the length of Bulldog's segment, which of the musicians were likely to want to join the jam that would close the telecast, me hunting out everyone's phone numbers to give her, so that the Foundation and Museum people could extend the formal invitations and get names as to who they'd be bringing with them.

Halfway through this, my legs got shaky and I sat back down. A few moments later, Bree tapped my shoulder, and handed me a glass of water and my morning meds. I had a weird thought as I was taking them, unsettling, big black wings flapping over my own grave, as my mum used to say: these days, I take my morning anti-spasmodic drugs, my anti-inflammatories, my pain pills, and my heart meds. Not quite two years ago, there'd been blood pressure meds and blood thinners added into the morning mix. Ten years ago, it had been just the anti-spasmodics and the pain pills. And twelve years ago, right around the same age Bree was now, I hadn't had to take anything at all.

It was sobering, that was, but it wasn't the part that raised gooseflesh on my arms. What did that was realising that Ches, a good twenty-five years younger than I was, had probably taken the same damned heart medicine I was about to swallow, just before he laced up his running shoes and headed out into a cold morning in Ohio. And the medicine? It hadn't helped. It hadn't saved him. It had done sod-all...

"Hello?"

"Right. Sorry—I was taking my meds. Hang on a moment, yeah? Almost done."

Bree'd seen it, there in my face, in what I hadn't said. She waited just long enough for me to set the glass down, and then she curled up next to me on the bed, one hand rubbing the back of my shoulder, a light touch rather than a hard rub. It was meant to comfort and console, not to work out knots. I blew her a silent kiss, but I suspected she'd missed it—she'd ducked her face away, so that I couldn't see it.

I gave my attention back to Sara Kildare. There was something I still needed to ask her.

"Look, I've got a question—no, not a question, a request. Did you say you were going to deal with his plants? Because does that mean you've got a key?"

"Yes, I do. Why?"

"Well—it's his notes, the ones for his book. He told me he could overnight them to me when he got back, so that I could use them putting the speech together. There's a lot about Bulldog's history as a musician I know sod-all about, and Ches told me I was welcome to check out his notes. When he said he'd send them overnight, he probably meant he'd copy them, but, well, copy or original, I could really use those, and as fast as you can get them here."

"Of course. I'll be heading over there as soon as we're off the phone here; anything I find, I'll send them Fed Ex." She was quiet for a moment, and then I heard her sigh, a long exhale. It

68

was very mournful, somehow, mournful for waste and loss and regret. "Thanks for calling Bulldog for me, JP. I honestly don't think I could have coped with having to do that. I'll get those notes out to you—hopefully you'll get them Monday morning."

Chapter Five

"...Outsiders, especially Europeans, may think all Delta bluesmen were sharecroppers' kids. But Farris Moody—nicknamed Bulldog by an exasperated Son House because Farris was so strong-minded—was an exception. The son of a civil engineer under contract to the U.S. Army, Farris was born in Mississippi in 1921. The child of three generations of life-masters of the traditional bata drums, the rhythms of Afro-Cuban music were in his blood and in his world..."

One ring, two rings. Nothing yet. No answer.

I was sitting at the kitchen table with my cell phone in my hand. My second cup of coffee was on the table. I'd taken my meds, I'd eaten my breakfast, I'd showered, I'd got dressed. Basically, I'd run out of excuses for not making the phone call I didn't want to make. The best I could hope for, now, was that no one would answer.

Bree sat across the table, not saying anything, just being there. Three rings, four. Maybe...

"Hello?"

"Sallie?" I heard my own voice—it sounded completely normal, which was nuts. I didn't feel normal. "This is JP Kinkaid. Look, I've got something I have to tell you, and also tell your dad."

"Okay."

The big, deep, damped-down bell of a voice was impossible to take any cues from. I took a long breath, and reached out my free hand across the table, toward Bree. Right that moment, I wanted some contact, some comfort, touch. Moments like that, no one else will do me.

She covered my hand with her own, watching my face. I knew—hell, we both knew—that if I'd asked her to make the call for me, she'd have done it. She's always trying to get the universe as perfect as possible for me, or at least as easy as she can. This time, though, she couldn't fix what had happened. This particular grief, this chore, was mine to handle.

"It's about Ches Kobel, Sallie. It's—he–" I swallowed hard. "I'm afraid I've got some very bad news."

Nothing. Silence. But I thought I heard him take a breath, and hold it. I closed my eyes for a moment, listening to the voice in my head telling me, *just get on with it, Johnny, just get it over, yeah? Don't draw it out, don't pile it on, just fucking tell him and be done with it.*

"Ches had a heart attack this morning." Bree's fingers had started up a light, rhythmic rubbing, moving up and down the fingers of my left hand. Her own hands were warm. Made a nice change, that did. I needed warmth just then, and trust her to know that, and provide it.

"I surely am sorry to hear that." Sallie's voice went even deeper; I wouldn't have thought that was possible. "He going to be okay?"

"No. No, he isn't." Damn. He hadn't understood me; I'd forgot about him being simple. I was hating this, just fucking hating it. I'd known I would, but this…I took a long breath. "Sallie, he's

71

gone—Ches is gone. He was out jogging this morning, and he had a heart attack. He was alone—there wasn't anyone with him, no one to help him or get an ambulance."

Across the table, Bree made a soft noise at the back of her throat. I looked down and saw that I'd tightened my grip on her hand without noticing. I was squeezing so hard, her fingers were blue-white. I eased up, and waited for Sallie to say something.

When he finally did, I heard the change in his voice. He'd gone sombre, somehow.

"You saying Ches passed. That what you saying?"

"Yes." I lifted Bree's fingers to my lips, just for a moment, breath to living skin. "That's it. I'm sorry, Sallie."

"Do you want me to tell Dad? 'cause he won't be taking this well, Mr. Kinkaid. This thing bound to upset him." I heard him breathe, long and ragged. "Me too. Ches, he was like my little brother. He come and talk to my dad about music, like I couldn't do. I don't know about music, not a lot. Him talkin' with Dad, that made Dad happy. He loved Ches."

"You don't have to tell Bulldog, Sallie." There it was, the out I'd been hoping for, the offer that would get me off the hook, and of course I couldn't take it. The news, the details, all that? It needed to come from me. "I think it would be better for me to tell him. I'll try not to upset him any more than I have to."

"OK. I go see if dad's woke up from his nap, yet. You wait a couple, two-three minutes, Mr. Kinkaid?"

I'd waited to make this phone call until I'd heard back from Sara Kildare. She'd rung me from Ches's apartment, in tears, very shaken up. Not exactly a surprise, that reaction; she'd walked in and there was Ches's stuff, his place, his nest, where he hung his hat and kept the stuff he valued. It was bound to bring him straight up in Sara's mind, in her eyes, make the loss that much more real, more tragic, more pointless.

She'd found his notes with no trouble at all. Ches had been

very organised, and all the stuff about the new book was in his briefcase, along with his thumb drives. Rather than try to sort out what I needed and what I didn't, Sara'd let me know she was going to ship the lot out to me, papers, notebook, thumb drive and all, and let me decide what I wanted to use.

That worked for me. I'd already decided I was going to dedicate the live version of "Moody's Blues" to Ches's memory, acknowledge that the speech wouldn't have been possible without him. Let the millions of people who watched the induction telecast know that we, the musicians, the blues community especially, had lost a good one, and lost him too damned young.

While we were on the phone, something really creepy had happened; Ches's house phone had rung. That was completely chilling—ghostly, you know? A device that connects people, ringing and ringing in a room that's had the life go out of it, is all wrong. It's like something out of a nightmare. Ches had been there, lacing up his running shoes and maybe having a quick breakfast, just a few hours ago. And he never would be again, not here, not anywhere. He'd simply ceased to be.

We'd both gone quiet, me and Sara, listening to the answering machine kick in, Ches's voice doing the recorded message, coming out of the tinny little phone speakers: "(beep) Hi you've reached Chester Kobel, I'm not available to take your call, if you'd like to leave a message, please wait for the sound of the tone (beep)."

I heard Sara catch her breath. We waited a moment, and I heard a voice in the background, just a distant blur of third party sound, and then Sara asked me to hang on, it was Ches's only relative, his sister Paula, on the line, ringing from Baltimore or somewhere. Apparently, she'd got a garbled message from the Cleveland police, and didn't realise that they were ringing her up to find out about things like an autopsy and release for cremation.

So I'd waited, hearing Sara's voice at the other, speaking too quietly for me to be able to make out any words. Eventually Sara got back on the phone and let me know Paula Kobel had been deeply shocked, very upset, but she'd said I could use whatever I wanted of Ches's stuff for my speech...

"Johnny? Is that you?"

"Yeah. I'm here, Bulldog." It's weird; up until Bulldog, the only people in the world who didn't call me JP were Bree, Miranda and Mac. Even my first wife had called me JP. But Bulldog had started out calling me Johnny, just the way Mac had done.

"Sallie says you got some news you looking to share with me." He sounded sleepy, older than I liked; actually, he sounded drugged. "What's going on with you, son?"

"It's news, all right." Eighty-six, and a bad heart of his own. Christ. I wanted to ease him in; I had a moment of total panic, wondering, what if the news killed him? "Bulldog, look. I think you need to be sitting down for this."

"I'm in my bed. Can't be much more sitting than that." He was waking up; I could hear it. "You tell me what's going on, John. You prepared me plenty. What, now?"

"It's about Ches." Maybe it wouldn't hit him so hard, after all. In his late eighties, it might be harder to shock him than I'd thought. "He had a heart attack this morning, while he was out jogging."

I stopped. Somehow or other, the words just dried up on me. I couldn't make myself tell him. And of course, I didn't have to, because he's been around for the better part of a century, and he let me off the damned hook.

"You telling me Ches passed?" He'd gone quiet, so damned quiet. All the depth had gone out of his voice, and there was no sound from behind him, either. Bree was holding her breath, and the cats were off in different parts of the house. It was as if the entire world had gone silent at the news, Bulldog and Sallie, me and Bree, the air around us: a moment of silence for a good bloke, who had no business dying the way he'd died, or when.

74

"Yes. That's it. He's gone, Bulldog." I was beginning to shake, and there was a major sting going on at the back of my eyes and throat, the weight of tears wanting out. "I'm so sorry. It isn't fair, or right, you know? But it happened. He's gone."

This time, the silence seemed to go on for hours. I held the phone, waiting for him to say something. I could have kept talking, you know? But I'd have broken down crying if I'd tried just then, and since I was the one who was supposed to be offering some comfort along with the bad news, I didn't really want to go down that road.

"John." Still quiet, almost numb. "I got to ask you something, a favour, a thing you have to do. You still there? You still on the line?"

"I'm here." I swallowed. "Tell me what you need."

"I need you to come on out here, is what." All of a sudden, I couldn't read his voice at all. "You come out and spend a day with me. Bring a guitar with you. Bring that piano boy you know—Tony. Bring that pretty girl you're married to."

"Right." I shifted the phone. "Okay. I will."

"We'll give a day to Ches, is what we'll do. Make music, Sallie can cook us up a good dinner, figure out what we going to be doing at this induction thing we been talking about. We gonna get together and sing and play that boy straight up to God." He sounded stronger, more awake. "You up for doing that?"

"A day at your place, to celebrate Ches? You want me to bring Bree, and Tony?" I caught Bree's eye. She smiled suddenly, a beautiful, beautiful smile. It's not an expression she does often; after so many years of not having a lot to smile about, she seemed to have got out of the habit. But she was smiling at me now, and nodding, and I thought I'd never seen her smile quite that way before.

"John? You can make that happen?"

"Hell, yes." My eyes were damp. We'd give Ches so much music, Ofagoula would echo with it. "And while we're there, I want to play you an instrumental number I wrote, something I want us all to cover at the show."

In the end, our memorial to Ches Kobel turned into something a lot bigger than I suspect Bulldog had in mind when he asked me to do it. I not only brought Tony and Bree along, I ended up bringing Luke, Mac and Dom, as well.

The way it worked out was a stroke of amazing timing, the sort of thing that always leaves me wondering about stuff like invisible universal connections and whether or not anything is really a coincidence. I'd barely hung up talking to Bulldog when my cell rang in my hand.

"JP?"

"Hello, Carla." Good timing, right there—I was going to need roundtrip flights to Cincy, plus a rental car and a hotel as well, once I rang Tony. "Glad you called—I need to book a few flights."

"Well, that's what I'm calling about. I just got off the phone with Luke. He told me he and Mac are doing the Hall of Fame induction ceremony with you at the Waldorf. They wanted to know when you were heading to New York, so that I can book them flights and hotels and whatnot. I told them I'd check."

"Hang on a minute, yeah?" An idea had popped into my head. "Carla, look, can I ring you back? I'm heading to Cincy, probably Monday morning, me and Bree and hopefully Tony Mancuso as well. But I want to ring Tony, and also Mac and Luke."

"JP?" Something in my voice must have twigged her. "Is everything okay?"

"No, it's not. We just lost a friend." I explained about Ches, about Bulldog's request; I was sorting out what I wanted as I was running it past Carla. "What I'm thinking is, it would be amazing if we could get Luke and Mac out to Ofagoula. We're looking at Tuesday, assuming Tony hasn't got anything on that conflicts

76

with that. Do you think they'd be up for coming out to Ohio for a day, and then either back here until next week, or else to New York? I don't know their schedules, and I'm betting you do."

"You'd win your bet." She was obviously mental making notes and sorting it out in her head as she went along; when it comes to this sort of list, the whole organising thing, the girl's beyond capable, and well into scary. "They were actually planning on heading out of London tomorrow night or Monday. And tell me if I'm misunderstanding this, but wouldn't having them come out to Ohio actually take some time off the rehearsals? I mean, if the whole band for your guy is right there, at his house, you can get each others' stuff down, can't you?"

"It's not actually the entire band—we'll be using the Hall's own rhythm section on the night. This is about Bulldog Moody, Carla, not about me. I don't want to turn it into Blacklight and Friends, and I can't see Stu and Cal getting into the whole Delta blues jam headspace anyway. Not really the Bunker Brothers' thing, the blues."

"No, they're way more into funk and techno in their spare time." Carla was beginning to sound enthusiastic, which meant she was getting into it, the planning aspect, I mean. Carla's always happiest when she's got both hands on what she calls the big picture. "Look, why don't we try it this way? I'll call Mac and Luke and suggest they fly out to Cincinnati instead of New York. You talk to Tony Mancuso and see if he can make it, and that way, I can handle the entire booking deal and make sure you guys are all synched up. What else? A ticket for Tony's wife? Hotels in Cincy? Limos...?"

So that was all taken care of, and I could take my mind off it. If there's one thing I've sorted out over the years Carla's been handling American operations for Blacklight, it's that everything goes a lot more smoothly if the band just backs off and lets her get on with it.

77

I rang Tony, and told him what was going on. He went quiet and stayed quiet, too long for him.

"Tony?" It was unnerving. "You there, mate?"

"Yeah, I'm here." He sounded shocked, and badly spooked. "I was just thinking about Anton. That guy Ches—shit, JP, he was just a kid. This sucks. It's not right."

I knew what he meant. The Bombardiers had lost their founder and lead singer, Anton Hall, just about two years ago now. Anton had spent damned near forty years abusing the hell out of his liver, sucking down Southern Comfort the way I used to suck down Jack Daniels, before Bree stopped me drinking.

Anton, as fucked up as he'd been and as careless as he'd been about anything that didn't feel good while he was doing it, had hung on well into his fifties. But here was Ches, healthy except for one small thing, gone at just a few years older than I'd been when I'd nearly died from OD'ing on a little blend of coke and heroin. Life is really peculiar, some days.

Right. There wasn't a damned thing we could do change what had happened. Bree, across the room, had been overhearing my end of the conversation. She was looking sombre again; any more of this, and all three of us would break down and blubber like babies, and I wasn't having that. So I told Tony what Bulldog had said. I thought I heard his voice doing that tight thing that means someone is trying not to cry. That wasn't exactly what I was trying for, you know?

"Tony—look, right, I know. But here's the thing, mate. Carla's just rung me, and she's had a brilliant idea." I ran it past him: Mac and Luke, me and Tony, working out with Bulldog what we wanted to do at the induction. We'd probably get two songs during Bulldog's segment—normally, that might only be one, but what with the Hall's big exhibit at the moment being Blacklight, I was betting on two.

And, of course, there'd be the big jam that ended the ceremony; that would have to be rehearsed on the day, at the Waldorf. I remembered the basics of the procedure: getting in at least two days early, hooking up with the liaisons for both the Foundation and the production company, going over the tech set-up, getting comfortable with the wireless and the acoustics.

I could see the jam this time being fantastic, with a good solid blues theme to it. This year's big-name inductee was Traitors Gate, and they'd made their name back in 1980 by playing wicked melodic blues riffs, right around the time every other new act out there wanted to be either the Eurhythmics or Spandau Ballet.

"...so if Mac and Luke meet us at Bulldog's, we can rehearse what we're going to do." I had one eye on Bree, but her cell had rung, and she'd taken it out into the dining room. "Get a leg up, yeah? We haven't got a lot of time—the ceremony's in ten days. And if we can combine a day to celebrate Ches with a day of getting the Hall of Fame rehearsal in there, I'd lay money on Ches being out there somewhere, cheering us on. That would be right up his street, that kind of party. You up for it? And what about bringing Katia? I need to ring Carla back."

"Jesus, JP, what do you think? You have to ask? That's a big hell-yes." He'd eased up. Good. "I bet Ches would have loved the idea of Mac singing at his memorial. Shit, if Katia found out I'd gone and hung out in someone's living room with your lead singer, she'd be so pissed off, I'd never get laid again. This way, I can go over some of the stuff I sent Luke for your cover of 'Liplock.' Kill two birds with one stone."

I was so busy trying to wrap my head around the details and logistics of getting everyone together in Ofagoula, more than half the country away, that it took me a moment to sort out what Tony meant. Blacklight had spent a few weeks together, the entire band, early summer of last year, down at Luke's mobile studio at his farm in Draycote, in Kent. We'd gone in to get the founda-

79

tion of our next CD together, and instead, we'd ended up with a double CD that was as close to ready as it was going to get, barring some final tracks and a mixdown.

It was miraculous, that project. I've never seen anything like it. The damned thing had come together at light speed, every piece just falling into place as if the music itself had been sitting there, just waiting for us to get into the studio and get it down. Five of the song lyrics had been written by me, which is fucking amazing when you consider that, up until this lot, I'd never written a lyric in my life. There were eighteen original songs total.

This one had a different flavour to it, a different feel altogether, from anything else we'd ever done before. We'd all noticed it, felt that difference in the music. It was Mac who'd sussed out where the difference was, and when he'd done that, Luke had come up with the CD's title—or, rather, the title had declared itself. More magic.

"Crikey," Mac had said, and laughed. I remembered that day, taking a break after we'd finished up on a heartbreaking song Luke had written, called 'You Never Kissed Me Goodbye.' "You know, I've only just realised it, but this damned thing has eighteen songs, and only three of them are about sex. Seriously, have you looked at these lyric sheets? Johnny's tunes are about being married, and what a drag it would be to not be married, and how nuts he is about his wife—well, okay, 'Remember Me' is about politics, but even that one's got him being married in it. Luke's are all about loss, and getting your life back together. Good God, even my stuff's sounding wistful, when it's not political. Either I'm losing my touch, or else we're turning into adults, or something."

"Grand themes," Cal had agreed. He'd contributed two sets of lyrics, himself; both songs dealt with being middle-aged and the miracle of still being madly in love with the same woman he'd married thirty years ago. "It's like daytime telly—what are those things we always used to watch, first couple of times we toured the States? Soap opera or something?"

"Days of our lives, that's us." Luke was dead serious. "Mac's right, this one's different. All about where life's taken us, up until now, right? Sort of like Blacklight's personal book of days."

So there it was, the next Blacklight studio release, about six months ahead of schedule and ready to rock and roll. We were about to release *Good Evening, America!*, the live CD and DVD of the 2005 American tour. But this one, *Book of Days*—it just felt different. Besides that whole adult thing, there was another difference: we'd decided to cover a Bombardiers song, one that Mac had actually done the vocal for on their last CD, a hot sexy thing called "Liplock."

I've got a fondness for that song. We'd played it at our wedding reception at the Bellagio, in Las Vegas, and it was always going to have good things associated with it, so far as I was concerned. So when Mac said he wouldn't mind recording a cover version, I'd not only jumped at it, I'd suggested asking Tony to sit in on piano. The song really does need a hot, strong boogie-woogie piano to make it cook.

Besides, the guitar part on "Liplock" is brilliant, just huge fun to play. I'd actually laid some extra guitar tracks down in my own basement studio, using Big Mama Pearl, the pearl-top Zemaitis guitar I'd used when I'd recorded the song for the Bombardiers. The damned thing has incredible custom electronics and it just growls and scratches; if I'm playing it right, the whole effect is like a woman's nails dragging down her man's back. It's all about the bedroom.

"…Tuesday?"

"Sorry—my brain went walkabout there for a minute." Tony had been talking, and I'd missed it. "Tuesday for Ofagoula, yeah, that was the original plan, but it depends on Mac and Luke.

Monday might make more sense. Look, Bree's waving at me—I'll find out what's going on, and ring you back, yeah? Cheers."

Turned out Bree's phone call had been her mum, wanting to know if we could get together for dinner. Bree was looking tired and stressed—she'd told Miranda about Ches, and that hadn't been easy, or fun. So I was prepared to come the heavy husband over Bree and tell her, no cooking tonight. But it turned out Miranda was offering to take us out to dinner.

We ended up with Bree driving, us picking Miranda up and heading out to our favourite Italian restaurant, Angelino's. It's right on the water in Sausalito, just over the Golden Gate Bridge; the food's brilliant, the people who run it are very cool, and on clear nights, the view of the City can knock you back on your heels. Tonight, though, we weren't noticing the view, and the fog was rolling in anyway.

If Miranda had just wanted a nice evening out and some decent food, she was out of luck. Bree was quiet and withdrawn, I was thinking and talking mostly about the upcoming get-together in Ohio and the induction ceremony itself, and Miranda herself seemed uneasy. Between swallowing mouthfuls of food, I found out why.

"This news about Ches Kobel." She was done with her food, but she seemed to want something in her hands. She's a surgeon, and her hands are usually very quiet, very sure—restful. Not tonight, though. She didn't seem to know what to do with them, and that was a sure sign she was bothered. "I'm not comfortable about it."

Bree dropped her fork. She'd just swallowed the last bit of food on her plate, so nothing spattered, but it fell into her plate, clattered there, and finally stopped. A few heads turned toward us, and then turned away again. I looked at my wife, and nearly dropped my own fork. She'd gone white. What the hell...?

"He had a heart attack." I turned back to Miranda. "That's

what the Cleveland cops told Sara Kildare, anyway. Why aren't you comfortable with it, Miranda? Ches had a heart condition—he told me he did. Oi! Bree, what is it?"

"Nothing." She was shivering. "Just—no, it's nothing. Go on, Mom. Sorry."

"He had a mild arrhythmia." Miranda had her professional face on, now. This was a woman who knew what she was talking about. "Very mild, in fact. We had a nice long conversation about it. You may remember that we sat next to each other at your Great American show last weekend. Neither of us was about to get up and dance, so we talked. I know exactly what his health problem was, a simple intermittent condition that only reared its head very occasionally. I know what medicine he took for it—the same medicine I suspect you take for yours when you need it, John. And–"

She stopped, and met my eye. And out of nowhere, I suddenly got this sense of urgency, a complete *oh, shit!* moment, a huge, dark feeling that something, somehow, was very wrong.

"Right." I heard myself, sounding grim. I'd got hold of one of Bree's hands; it was cold, and I felt her trembling. Whatever was off, whatever her mum was thinking, Bree'd sussed it already. "And what, Miranda?"

"And I know who his doctor was." She was looking at me, and her eyes—they're a nice easy blue—were steady, chilly, just a pure laser beam focus. Something moved in my stomach, not pleasant; she reminded me of Patrick Ormand in full cop mode. "Ches told me that. He was a patient of Stan Minkus. And if Stan Minkus told Ches his condition was not going to kill him, then Ches shouldn't be dead, period."

"Who—why–" Bree was staring at her mother. She was still chalky. "Mom, who is Stan Minkus? Do you know him?"

"Of course I do. I've known Stan for years—he's one of the great names in cardiac medicine. We've done three symposium panels on preventive care together that I can remember, and there are a good dozen papers out there with his name on them. Stan Minkus is one of the greats. There is no way in this world that he'd tell a patient to expect no trouble at all and then have that patient flatline out of nowhere."

"Miranda..." I swallowed hard. She sounded fierce, and angry, and upset. That, by itself, was enough to get my full attention. This was the woman who'd stayed calm enough to drive her own nearly-flatline teenaged daughter to the ER and pump her stomach after a suicide attempt involving a bottle of my pain pills and a fifth of tequila. Miranda just doesn't flip her shit. "Look, I know this is your thing, but, well..."

"I know what you're going to say." She met my eye. "No, doctors aren't infallible. Yes, people die unexpectedly. Of course they do. Heart disease is one of the major killers in this country. I know that, and good heavens, I ought to know it; it's my job. But I also know Stan Minkus, and I talked to Ches. And I don't like this."

I took a good long breath. It was weird, playing role reversal with Miranda; I'd never seen her this upset, this emphatic. It's not her thing, at all. "Look. Ches went jogging. He was alone, all by himself, yeah? This isn't someone shooting him or bashing him or robbing him or anything else, is it? He went jogging, he had a heart attack, he died out there. I don't get it. Are you saying you think there's something dodgy about how he died? How could there be? I mean, you can't just wave your hands and give someone a heart attack, and this was the big cement plaza out in front of the Rock and Roll Hall of Fame. It's not as if someone jumped out and yelled boo, right? So, what do you mean? What do you think happened?"

"I can't tell you that, John. I don't know, not yet." She caught the waiter's eye, and signalled for the bill. "But I can tell you this. I've got a call in to Stan's office in Cleveland Heights—I left him a message, asking him to call me back. I want to know what he thinks happened. Because something isn't right. That boy simply shouldn't be dead."

Chapter Six

"...When Farris was nine, he went along with his dad, Salas Moody, on a construction job, working on the river levees, near a town called Lyon, Mississippi. They were eating lunch at a local park, and fortunately for the rest of us, Son House and Rube Lacy were there, playing with James McCoy, for tips.

"Farris listened. He watched. The whole time—he was nine, remember—he was tapping out the rhythms on the park bench. What he was doing got the players' attention. McCoy, especially, noticed. Those rhythms were complex, rooted in the family drum training. Bottom line was, Farris Moody was good enough to play with them. And that's just what he did..."

We flew out of San Francisco early Monday morning. Mac and Luke had decided that, between the Hall of Fame gig and playing with Bulldog, flying straight to Ohio and then back to San Francisco for a few days before we all hit New York made the most sense. Of course, they were right—I had the home studio, the guitars, and Bree, who'd be fussing over them and feeding them brilliantly. Besides, this way, they'd be able to work with Tony, and give the polish on the *Book of Days* cover of "Liplock" one more rub.

The plan was, we'd fly out Monday morning, get to Cincy late afternoon, and spend the night at the Cincinnatian Hotel. Nice comfortable hotel; I've stayed there before, touring with Black-light, and Carla'd booked rooms for everyone concerned. Mac and Luke were due to arrive before we were—they were flying out of London around ten in the morning, which got them there at just past two Monday afternoon.

We were actually at the airport, getting ready to board our flight, when my cell rang, and Carla's number came up on the caller ID.

"JP? Hi, listen, there's a slight change of plans." She sounded rushed. "This is going to sound a little pushy, but I just got off the phone with Bulldog Moody. I took a look at how many people were coming to this thing, and I couldn't help wondering if his house was going to be big enough for everyone. So I called him, and talked to his son, and then to him. I hope that's okay."

"Yeah, of course it is. That's not pushy, it's just common sense." People were beginning to queue up. "Carla, look, we're about get on the plane—they're calling first class boarding. What do I need to know? What's different?"

"It's about the venue. You have two limos booked, with local drivers, from Cincy to Ofagoula, and then back to Cincy tomorrow night for the flight back out to California. You're all booked on same flight back, first class."

"Okay."

"So: the limo service will call the hotel, and be there to pick you up when you're ready tomorrow morning. But Bulldog—God, he's a doll—he says that with seven people, half of them playing instruments and one of them playing a piano, you aren't going to all fit, not comfortably, anyway. He says his living room's too small to hold everyone, that you'd be bumping elbows. Plus, there's Bree, and Dom, and Tony's wife—there'd be no room. And anyway, there's no piano."

"Right." The airline representative was talking into her mic, and her voice crackled out over everything: *Ladies and gentlemen, if you are seated in the first class compartment...* "Look, we're boarding. What are we doing, and where, and when are we doing it?"

"You're picking him up at his house, in the limo. From there, you're all going to a place called the Backroom. Bulldog told me he used to play there a lot—the owners know him. He says he even still jams there, occasionally. It's a little blues club, owned by the local musicians. Bulldog can give the drivers directions; just call him when your car gets into Ofagoula, and he'll be ready to go. Oh, and the Backroom has a house PA system and their own piano, so we didn't have to rent one for Tony."

"Good." Bree had stowed her bag overhead, and settled into the window seat. I always take the aisle seat when I'm flying; with the pins and needles that come along with the MS, I never know when I'm going to have to get up and move my legs and feet. "Okay, they're going to tell us to turn off all small electronic devices any minute now. I wanted to ask you, are we all set at the Waldorf? Everyone booked for a couple of nights? Because the induction ceremony's next Wednesday."

"It's all taken care of." One of these days, Carla was going to prove she was actually human, and maybe slip up on something. As far as I was concerned, though, she could go on being super-human forever; it makes my life a lot easier. "I've been liaising with a woman called Sara Kildare in Cleveland, and with the production staff for the actual ceremony, in New York. They're very on top of this stuff. They ought to be, since they do it every year. I just made sure they knew your suite had to have a fridge, for your meds. Anyway, we'll go over your travel details for New York when you get home."

88

"Ladies and gentlemen, the captain has turned on the seatbelt sign. At this time, we ask that you turn off and safely stow all portable electronic devices..."

"Right. Look, I need to power down. Thanks—ring me if anything comes up, will you?"

"You bet. Have a great time in Ofagoula, and say hi to everyone for me."

It was a nice easy flight, comfortable, not even anything major in the way of bumps. I tend to forget that flying first class isn't standard for most people, including some of my mates, so I got a reality check and a nice moment, as well, watching Katia react to good food, decent champagne, flight attendants being respectful, all the perqs that come with flying first class. The Bombardiers haven't done any major touring in a while, and when they do, the tours are much lighter on the frills than Blacklight tours. The Bombardiers' record label doesn't run to first class travel.

Mac and Luke, with Dom in tow, had already checked in and had lunch by the time we got there; they'd even managed to get their hands on some amazing ice cream, with black raspberry chips in it, from a place called Graeter's. We had a nice evening, sending down for dinner from room service, talking about what we were going to be doing, going over suggestions about music in general, everything from tomorrow's memorial with Bulldog to the order of songs on both discs of *Book of Days*.

One we'd finished eating, I plugged in my 335 and Luke got his old Strat ready. Carla'd arranged with the hotel for a handful of rented amplifiers, nice little forty-watt Wild Cats, complete with reverb. They can give you quite a lot of volume when you crank them up, but of course you don't want to really push them, not in a hotel. The other guests tend to get shirty if you do that.

First thing I did was, I played them "Moody's Blues", the instrumental piece I'd written for Bulldog, keeping the volume reasonably low and level. Halfway through, Tony got his portable keyboard, a Korg Triton Extreme, plugged into another Wild Cat, and began adjusting the settings until he found one that worked with what I was doing. Ten seconds after that, he played a stone fucking gorgeous blues run, a fantastic cascade of boogie-woogie that was so perfect, I stopped playing, grinned at him, and started the song again, from the beginning.

Luke had already got his Strat plugged in and was playing easy, talkative little runs against my slide work. Mac was blowing along with a mouth harp, noodling with it, sorting out where the harp would work between the guitars and the keyboard, looking for the best places to ease it in and punch it up. This is what a working jam, a jam with a purpose at the end of it, is supposed to do: clarify the music, show it the road it needs to go down.

The women had all perched, watching and listening. We were in our suite, with its king-size bed; at one point, I came up from what I was doing long enough to look around for Bree, and she wasn't there—she was in the bathroom, opening the ice chest we'd travelled with, and I suddenly remembered, right, this was Monday, which meant my weekly interferon shot.

And out of nowhere, really, I got hit with a memory, of a conversation I'd had with Luke last summer, just before we went onstage at Frejus, in France. That had been the anti-racism awareness gig we'd played just after the Cannes Film Festival wrapped up. We'd stood there, and I'd said something about Bree keeping me alive. And Luke had stared straight at me, and told me, *she does more than that, mate; she gives you the space to be who you are.*

I'd remembered that, and I wasn't likely to forget it. Coming from Luke, who'd lost his own wife when their daughter Solange was barely out of nappies, those words had carried a lot of weight...

"Fucking fantastic." Mac was staring at me. "I'll tell you what, Johnny, that's a sensational bit of music."

"Ta." I was feeling a bit stoned, a sure sign the piece had worked; the entire room seemed to be echoing with it. "You think it'll fly for the ceremony, then? That Bulldog will like it?"

"Hell, yeah." Tony ran the piano line, truncated because the Korg is a mini; it only has sixty-one keys. "JP, are you thinking of recording this somewhere? I mean for release? Because, man, I'd kill to guest on that one."

"Don't know yet." I put the 335 aside, and got up to stretch. "But if I do, you've got it."

Tony'd actually heard the song before. He'd come over right after I'd finished writing it, and had actually run some nice acoustic piano riffs to it on the old Bechstein upright in my basement studio. But this was the first time either of us had done it with other musicians, and the song was finding new ways to surprise me.

Truth was, Mac was right: it was a killer piece. His harp added a good sharp edge of soul to it, kind of like a distant train whistle, wailing away. And Luke, well, there's a reason he's one of rock's legendary guitarists. Just give the man a rhythm line and something to bounce off musically, and he'll make magic for you, every time.

"I wonder if we shouldn't think about adding it to *Book of Days*." Luke was looking at Tony. So was Mac. "JP, would you be up for that? I know this is a very personal number for you."

"Can't see why not." Something was going on here, and I was missing it. They were looking at Tony, and Tony was very red and trying to look unconcerned. "Where else would I record it? Not as if I'm planning on a solo album anytime soon."

"You know, there's quite a few numbers on the new one that would be all the way better if we added some really world-class keyboards." Mac had put the harp away, and opened a bottle of spring water. "I mean, I'm decent on the keyboards, but really, I'm a singer."

I turned my head and looked at him. There was something in his tone, a bit too casual...

"'You Never Kissed Me Goodbye.' 'Moody's Blues.' That beautiful thing JP wrote, 'You Left The Light On'—I could hear something like the piano off the Stones' Angie, on that one." The Strat was back in its case, and Luke was ticking off song titles. "'Will You Miss Me When I Go.' That nasty pissy little monster of yours, Mac, 'Hammer It Home.' There's at least four more songs that would get booted straight over the top with piano added. That doesn't even include 'Liplock.' And not just on the disc, either. What about the tour?"

Tony was carefully not meeting anyone's eye. Right. You're probably thinking I'm completely dim, but I got it, finally.

"Tony, mate, would you be up for it? If things worked out? Because they're right, the piano would rock."

"Tour with Blacklight?" The penny had just dropped for Katia, as well—she was sitting up, staring at us. "You mean, Tony doing a full tour with you guys?"

"Why not?" Luke got up, and headed for the loo. Bree was in there rinsing out glasses; he grabbed a hand towel, and started in drying. He stood in the doorway, talking over his shoulder. "The new CD is going to be a double—we'll probably add extra dates to support it. Personally, I think adding a dedicated keyboard would be brilliant. It would also free Mac up to just do his thing. And there are quite a few songs where I think having both harp and piano would add all kinds of layers and possibilities. I almost forgot that hot little thing of JP's, the one about money—and damn, can you imagine what a good piano line would do to 'Remember Me?' The song's already a bloodbeast, probably going to be the sleeper hit off the CD, but shit, with a piano?"

"Wow." Something went down my back when Luke said that. I'd written the lyrics to that one in the weirdest way you could imagine: I'd been onstage at Frejus, playing someone else's stuff,

92

and the entire song, lyric, structure and all, had come into my head and just basically set up shop. "Yeah, I can. Tony, think about it, okay? We'd need to talk to Cal and Stu, make sure they're okay with it, but I can't think of a single reason they wouldn't be. And if they are, and you are, let's set something up to discuss it, all right? Ian would need to be in on it. He has all the numbers."

"Sounds good to me." Tony turned the Korg off. He wasn't pink anymore—he just looked really pleased. "Bree, you've got your 'very nice party, thanks so much for coming over, everyone please go the hell home now' look going on. Does that mean you're kicking us out?"

"Yep." She looked around. "It's Monday, and Monday is when John gets his weekly shot. Anyway, it's after ten and the cars will be here at eight in the morning. Good night, everyone."

I hadn't forgotten about that conversation with Miranda; I'd just pushed it to the back of my head until we could get home on Wednesday. There wasn't a damned thing I could do about it, not from here, not until she heard back from Ches Kobel's cardiologist. Anyway, until we got back to San Francisco, I was concentrating on celebrating Ches' life, not worrying about his death.

The two limousines, complete with local liveried drivers, were out front of the hotel at eight the next morning. That's earlier than I usually wake up, mornings not being the best time of day for my MS. Tuesday mornings are a dice-roll anyway, what with usually having my injection Monday night. There's just no way to know when the weekly shot is going hit me next day with what the manufacturer of the drug calls "flu-like symptoms." It's weird: I can go for months, sometimes years, with no problem at all. Then, for no particular reason, the stuff lays me out for two days, sweating and shivering. "Flu-like symptoms", yeah, right. They can call it whatever they like, but this is closer to what I imagine severe pneumonia would feel like, assuming you topped that off with being flogged with wet ropes for a couple of hours first.

Bottom line is, the meds are as unpredictable as the damned disease is. It makes scheduling a tour tricky—that was one reason Blacklight's 2005 tour had been so light on dates.

This time, there was no problem, and Bree was right there with my morning meds when the front desk rang with the seven a.m. wakeup call. We'd ordered breakfast before we'd gone to bed last night, so I got toast and eggs and coffee and juice, in bed no less, while Bree hit the shower. She doesn't like to eat before she washes her hair, I've never really known why.

We were actually the last ones downstairs—everyone else was waiting for us when we got there. I stood for a moment, just breathing in, wondering why it felt different, and then I sussed it. I'd been in Ohio twice in the past few weeks, and I'd got used to it being cold. The air this morning tasted warmer. The green seemed a bit greener, somehow, and even that early in the day, there seemed to be less frost on things.

"John?" Bree touched my shoulder. "Are you okay?"

"Yeah, I'm good." It was a lie, and she knew it. For a moment, I'd been remembering Ches on the phone, me telling him he sounded breathless, him saying he'd just got in from his morning run near the lake, how cold it was, he thought he'd inhaled icicles...

I shook it off, and smiled at her, a real smile, a private signal just between the two of us, letting her know it really was okay, now. "Everyone ready? Let's get the guitars into the back, then."

We took the first car, with Tony and Katia, and let Mac, Luke and Dom follow in the second. I'd been worried we might have to sit in traffic—that never agrees with me, and travelling right after the Monday night shot is always iffy—but the roads were pretty clear, and we hit Ofagoula in less than an hour.

94

I'm not sure what I'd been expecting from Bulldog, what sort of head space he was likely to be in. When I think about it now, there's a sort of wall up in my memory, blocking me out from remembering certain feelings properly, things that had started with Sara Kildare's call telling me Ches was gone.

I hadn't been able to read Sallie's reaction, but then, Sallie wasn't an easy read anyway. Bulldog was a different story. I felt so close to him that it was a shock to remember I'd met him just a couple of weeks ago. It gobsmacked me, realising that all our interaction amounted to two days in each others' company, and some conversation on the phone. I felt as if I'd known him forever; somehow, he was a part of me. We were cut from the same cloth. It was bizarre, having to admit to myself that I didn't know what was going on in his head, or in his heart.

That last conversation, when he'd told me to come, to bring whoever I wanted and that we'd play Ches straight up to God, he'd sounded—determined? Fierce? I don't know; I haven't got the words for it and finding words for it wasn't important anyway. Thing is, whatever had been firing that tone when he told me to come to Ofagoula was still there.

He wasn't smiling, when Sallie let us in, but he was awake, and aware. There was a kind of light in his face, in his eyes. Maybe I could read it because his eyes were so much like my own, but there was something going on, fire, a sort of passion. It sat very bright on that lined, elderly face. Whatever was up, he was ready for it.

"John, good morning to you, son. You're looking ready to play." He'd got one of my hands between his own, and he must have seen something in my face, because his voice dropped down, that big bell damping down like Sallie's. "I know, John. But we'll shake the rafters, don't you worry. No matter where he is, Ches gonna hear us. I plan on making so much happy noise, everyone be able to hear us. You with me?"

95

I just nodded at him. There wasn't anything to say to that, really, and besides, if I'd tried, I might have started bawling.

He looked around me, at the crowd of people jammed into his front room: Mac in black, holding out a hand to Sallie, Luke with his pale gold ponytail, and of course, the women, Bree with her eyes on me, Katia shy and charming, Dom, well, she's just Dom, you know? Not much change from place to place there, not when she's on the job, watching out for Mac.

Bulldog got very courtly with them, kissing Bree's cheek, making Katia welcome. He got to Dom and I saw him lift his brows at her bleached-white crop do. She lifted a brow right back at him, and he grinned at her, that huge encompassing smile of his, impossible to resist. She didn't resist it, either; hell, she actually allowed him to take her hand, and hold it for a moment—*old man's privilege, child,* he told her, and one corner of her mouth twitched up. She didn't relax, not completely; as I said, she rarely does. But her reaction, that not quite smile she'd given, that set the tone for the day.

As we were heading back out, Bulldog pulled me aside for a moment.

"Listen, John." He lowered his voice, and nodded his head, back toward the kitchen. "Need to ask you for something. Just a favour, but you tell me if you don't want to. Okay?"

"Sure." He sounded worried, just enough to worry me. "Anything you need, you've got it."

"I'm thinking to give poor Sallie a rest from the music." He kept his voice low. "Music, it's not what he understands—you probably already saw it, he don't understand too much, and what he does understand, that don't go too deep either. He didn't get my music, and he didn't get his mama's smarts, either—she was a sharp one, my Lula. There's plenty would say that he got a healthy body and a healthy heart, that's a fair trade. I don't know."

He stopped. I waited. He went on, finally.

"He loved Ches. He loved that boy like the baby brother my poor Lula never did give him. Times I'd be aching in my bones and Ches would be here, and all I'd want was a good sleep. They'd cover me up and the two of them, they'd be all over the place, down to the market, get some fish or some chicken, maybe. They'd let me sleep and they'd come back and I'd hear them in the kitchen, cooking, laughing, just letting me rest."

"Right." I had a hard lump at the back of my throat; I could see it, nice and clear, almost as if I was in Bulldog's body, looking out through his eyes, remembering with his long, long memory, instead of my own. "I get you, Bulldog."

"I'm thinking you do." He squeezed me hand. His were chilly, and it suddenly spooked me, reminding me of the hundreds of times I'd got Bree's hands between my own and how they were chilly, every damned time. "And this, everyone making music he can't join in with to show the love and respect to Ches, that would be a cruelty. You get what I'm saying?"

"Yeah, I do. Not why, though. Come on, Bulldog—tell me what you need."

"What I need—what I'd like is, for you to put the boy's mind at ease." He paused for a moment. "You go in there, you be willing, and tell Sallie he can stay home with a quiet mind today. You'll be with me all day long. You'll look out for me. You'll hold on to my medicine, make sure I take it. Let him know you won't let me talk you into being soft with me—you tell him you can make me take my meds and won't take me saying you no. What are you laughing about?"

"Nothing, really." I couldn't tell him he was asking me to play Bree to his John, but that's what it came down to. "But is that all? Of course I will. Hang on a minute."

I headed off into the kitchen, where Sallie was doing something to what looked like an entire fish, head, tail and all. The convincing took a while, but when he finally got that I'd be fierce with his dad if fierce was what was needed, he nodded, headed off into the back of the house, and came back out with a worn leather toiletry case.

"You take this." He put the case into my hands. "This got what my dad needs. This here is the medicine, for his heart—one kind of pill, one kind of capsule. Those, he take one, that's for when his chest hurts, the capsule, I mean. Come five o'clock, you got to make him take it. Don't be letting him make a face, and say it's too big. He got to swallow it just the way it is, with some wa-ter. Don't be letting him open them up and spill the stuff out. Has to take it whole. And don't be letting him have no grapefruit juice, either. Grapefruit, that's bad with his medicine. Them two together don't go."

"Right." I opened the case, and looked; it had aspirin, a comb, and two prescription bottles, both big. One of them was full, and I recognised the pills. Digoxin, the same stuff I take for my ar-rhythmia. The second one was almost full: the bottle said *Vera-pamil, one capsule daily, for angina. Do not double up on doses of this medication.* "Crikey, those capsules are huge, Sallie. Can he actu-ally swallow the damned things? I'd probably choke to death if I tried. Why can't he open them–"

"No! That's bad." He shook his head. "They have to get into Dad's blood slow. You got to promise me, okay, Mr. Kinkaid? Take them down whole, and no grapefruit."

"Okay. Not to worry, Sallie. I'll make sure he swallows it on time, and I won't give him any grapefruit juice, either." I zipped the bag; through the kitchen window, I saw one of the chauffeurs helping Bulldog into our car, next to Bree. Bulldog had to duck his head to avoiding smacking himself on the limo door; he really was a huge, huge bloke. The second driver was putting a battered guitar case into the back; Bulldog was bringing his Byrdland. "Does he need to take one of the pills, as well? They're Digoxin, right? I take mine at bedtime. When does he take his, Sallie?"

"Same time as his capsules." Sallie smiled at me, a vague smile, as if he wasn't sure what he was smiling about. A sweet bloke, but the more I dealt with him, the more I got that he was a bit wanting, somehow. "Might make him sleepy, but that's okay—he always wake up better than when he close his eyes, and he don't sleep long. You make him take his stuff, Mr. Kinkaid. I'll stay home today, and happy to do it. I got to finish cleaning up this fish, anyway. Not gonna cook itself."

The Backroom, ten minutes by car from Manassas Road, was the sort of place I'd always fantasised about playing. It had a look to it, the right look, and the right feel as well: hard old floors, the kind that had seen fifty years of people dancing. It had small tables, a beat-up bar with what looked like a tin counter, a stage with a piano at one end and four steps at each side, leading up to a place where you could pull up a stool and take your bottleneck or your harp or your percussion of choice, and just jam for hours.

Carla had told me it was owned by some local musicians. She hadn't said—probably because she hadn't known—that the local musicians in question were mostly contemporaries of Bulldog's, within a decade or so, and that every last one of them was a walking breathing blues legend.

When we pulled up in front of the club, a bloke I didn't recognise but thought I probably ought to came out, squinting through a pair of dark glasses. He was smallish, bent over; there was something about the curve of his back and shoulders that said *piano player*, and I wasn't wrong. Tony was sitting nearest the window, and he took one look and made a noise, something like *omigawd*, about three times, fast. So, yeah, obviously Someone with an upper-case S.

Before I could sort that out, the driver was opening the door for us. Bree and Katia climbed out, me right behind; I wanted the guitars out of the back. Bulldog got out, moving slowly. I wondered if he'd stiffened up during the ride over.

99

"Hey, Dance, my man." They shook hands. "How you doing, my friend?"

"Squeaky and creaky, that's how I'm doing. Damn winter been keeping on so long, this arthritis not looking to turn loose of me anytime soon. I need me a warm day, is what I need. How you been keepin,' Bulldog? Sallie not come with you today? This is some sad stuff, about Ches..."

Dance? I knew, now, why I'd thought he ought to look familiar. Behind me, Tony had got out of the limo, and I heard him make that noise again. I glanced over at him, and grinned; he was pop-eyed, and I didn't blame him. Now that I knew who this was, I was with Tony, right on the edge of making a noise myself. And I'm not even a piano player.

"Everybody, this is Dance Maxwell, old friend of mine. We must have played a dozen albums together, me on the guitar and Dance, here, tickling up the ivories. We got John Kinkaid and Luke Hedley—my boys for guitar. And this is Malcolm Sharpe—we're talking one damn fine singer. Plays a killer harp, too, or that's what I'm told." He looked over his shoulder, smiling, easy. "Tony! Come on over here, if you please. Dance, like you to meet Tony Mancuso. This boy knows his boogie-woogie near as good as you do. You get to hear him today."

"Hi." Tony barely managed to get the word out. He looked to be in a state somewhere between worship and terror, and I couldn't tell what was higher on the list. I didn't know whether to be glad or sorry Katia was behind me; she wasn't used to Tony worshipping anyone, and I wasn't sure how she'd deal with it. "Wow. This—wow. It's an honour."

"Honour, hell." Dance shook his hand. "Always pleased to find me another boogie player. Come on in, I'll show you around the place. What we got there—oh, electric guitars? Amps all set up. We gonna burn the walls down for poor Ches Kobel and we're not looking to power down until the stars come out."

Chapter Seven

"...At this point, you're probably thinking, hang on a minute—this kid was a drummer. When did the shift to guitar come about, and how? The answer to that is, just about three days later, and this is the stuff legends come from."

"Oh, perfect! Well, almost perfect. Mac, I think that bit toward the end of the bridge, where you dropped out on harp? I think that needs to be an inhale, then a sharp exhale. Almost a punch, yeah? Syncopated."

"You got it, Johnny." Mac lined up the harp to his lips, inhaled, exhaled. "Yeah, that's done it—you're right, it's much better. What do you think, Bulldog? Luke?"

"After a few days, Salas Moody realised he could leave young Farris safely with the players in the park, while he did his job, overseeing work on the levees. Toward the end of the third day, there was an incident. Rube Lacy's porkpie hat was full of tips. McCoy wanted to split it four ways, but Son House said no, that since all the boy was doing was banging on the bench he was sitting on, he wasn't a real player, and hadn't earned a share."

"What I think is, John wrote this thing, he bound to have some feeling for how it supposed to move." Bulldog was fiddling with one of the tuning pegs on the Byrdland. He tweaked it, and caught both Luke and me, watching him.

"This B-string, it wants to wander," he said, and grinned. "Damned if I mean to let it. You got to show your guitar who the boss is, some days."

"See, that's all the problem you guitar folk got." Dance was lounging against the side of the stage. He'd waved Tony over to the piano, saying that since he wasn't going on this New York trip of Bulldog's, no need for him be doing more than listen right now. "You got to be messing with your axe every time you move. Seems like someone sneeze out back behind a cheap motel somewhere in Kansas City, you all got to stop and tune up in Memphis. You played a piano, now, that a whole other story."

"So Rube Lacy handed Farris his guitar, and showed him a chord: E-seven, voice of the blues. The boy got the fingers of his left hand round it, and held it. McCoy asked him, can you strum what you were tapping, there, boy? Can you do that same rhythm on the strings, with your right hand, that you did on the bench over there?"

"You know, Bulldog, I love that cascade effect you get. Rhythmically, I mean. It's fantastic." Luke had pulled out a bag of very old tricks for "Moody's Blues;" he'd gone deep into the kind of finger-picking he hadn't done since he and Mac had first played as a folk and blues duo called Blackpool Southern. That was close to forty years ago. These days, any of the Blacklight stuff that wanted slide, bottleneck, Delta stuff, that was me doing it. Luke had been playing mostly good hard innovative rock for a long time, now. "Almost Bo Diddley, but more—what? Something. It just tastes like the Caribbean to me. Not Jamaica; Haiti, maybe? Anyway, it's perfect, using the rhythm that way. Did you say you learned it off a drummer?"

"You got a good ear, son—you hearing Cuba, is what that is."

102

Bulldog was looking at Luke, and I heard approval in his voice, maybe respect. "I learned it off two drummers. My grandaddy was a *bembè* drummer, and everything he had, he learned it from his own dad. Granddad was a priest—Yoruban, not Christian. My dad used to bring me with him around all them road shows, the tent shows, I mean. You know about the travelling shows? I'm talkin' about revival meetings—you got the spirit in you, music go on for hours. We used to call those revival meetings 'ring shouts.' A whole lot of drums there, black folk, white folk, didn't make no nevermind. All about the rhythms, all the folk looking for the spirit, going with the drums."

Bulldog put the Byrd back on its stand. He was taking it easy, but he had the song down, and what's more, he'd had it down the first time we played it through. Everyone else, they were close, but after all, we'd done it a couple of times back in Cincy, at the hotel. That magic, that synch, the lockup I'd had with Bulldog first time out? It was on, hot, clicking.

"Let's take a break, yeah? I want a sit-down." I caught a movement; Bree, at a table with Katia at the front of the stage, had heard me. I smiled down at her. "No, love, I'm fine. Just need to let things settle, yeah? I'll take my meds in a bit."

It was almost a cliché: the musicians onstage, all men, two generations celebrating the memory of a third, while the women stayed quiet, out of the way and nearly invisible. It's a damned good thing I knew Bree was okay with it, that there was a reason and we both understood it, that we both knew today was special. Otherwise, I might have got edgy about it. I've got reasons for not wanting her to slip back into the habit of thinking that being invisible around my professional life is okay.

We'd gone down that road for twenty-five years. People had died because of it, I'd nearly lost Bree because of it, and I wasn't about to let it happen again.

She smiled up at me, a small curve of the lips. I blew her a kiss, a tiny one, and watched her mouth twitch. I'd been playing my 335; even thought it's a hollow body, it still weighs enough to notice. I was suddenly glad to have a rest.

"Bulldog," I asked him, "how'd you make the jump from drums to guitar, anyway? Can you tell that story? And can I use it in my speech?"

"Uh-huh, here we go." Dance rolled his eyes, and I grinned to myself. "You had to ask, 'course you did."

"And Farris did. First try, he'd got the rhythm down, on an instrument he'd never touched in his life. There was the E-seventh, beginning of half the blues that had been written up to that point, but it was different, because what Farris was playing there was the rhythm he'd been drumming, the bembè beat from his great-grandfather Salas who'd been a Yoruban priest from Ife-Ile in Nigeria. There it was, that three-two beat."

"That was Son." Bulldog was rubbing his right arm, a light, even rub; I doubt he even knew he was doing it. His eyes were bright, mischievous, and he suddenly looked very young. "Son House, I mean, a great player, one of the best. I figured I could play, he said I couldn't. I was maybe eight, nine years old, we were playing for tips in the park, down in Lyon. You know Lyon? Over in Mississippi, not far from Clarksdale. Son just got out, off the farm when we met up with him. He killed a man, did some hard time. They let him out and told him, boy, get yourself the hell on out of Mississippi and don't be coming back. He was on his way north, just trying to make a few dollars to get him on his way…"

From across the stage, I heard a snort; Dance was rolling his eyes again. Bulldog, looking over my shoulder, grinned.

"Dance done heard this one fifty times if he heard me tell it one time. You maybe head outside for a smoke? Don't want to bore you."

"Keep on talking." Dance was laughing. "You just keep on talking, Bulldog. It's fine. I got to make sure you ain't planning to hang no fancies on it for these kids."

Bulldog ignored that. "...so Rube Lacy—fine player—handed me his guitar. He showed me how to make a chord, best blues chord ever. And James McCoy said, son, I wanna hear you strum that beat you been hitting the bench with, right here, on this guitar. You think you can do that? And I did. What we got to drink in here, Dance? I got a thirst, all that talking. I just wish Ches was here, listening to this. He always could tell my stories better than me. He had the gift of words."

"Farris got his share of the tip. He was a player. And he developed two things during those days in the park: a case of idol worship for Son House, and the understanding that what he really wanted was a guitar. Forty years later, when I was nine myself, I heard a song in a South London record shop, called 'Daisy Chain Blues,' and what had happened to the man who made me want to play guitar, happened to me. And that's a definition of family. It's not always about blood and DNA. Sometimes, it's about more than that, and less than that..."

We went through "Moody's Blues" three times. Third try, we recorded it; that was going to get sent overnight to the house musicians the Foundation worked with. Their rhythm section would have a few days to get it down, and this would give them time to get back to me with any problems or questions.

After that, the requirements met, we got down to what we'd come for. Two of Bulldog's and Dance's friends came by, one a bassist, one a trumpet player, and there was about an hour of some of the most perfect jamming I've ever been lucky enough to be part of, the bass doing a walking blues line, the trumpet as mournful and sharp as anything Miles Davis ever blew, Mac hitting the exhales on the harp as if he'd been working on them for a week beforehand.

We took a break, and Bulldog talked about Ches. He talked about how they'd come across each other, about days spent with

Bulldog talking and Ches listening, taking notes. He talked about what he'd told me back on Manassas Road, evenings where Sallie and Ches, brothers in every way except the blood, would let the old man doze and dream while they bought groceries, Sallie cooking and filling the house with the smell of whatever they'd picked up for supper, the two younger men sharing the washing up, sitting on the tiny front porch, looking out at the stars coming out one by one, in the skies over Ohio.

At that point, the women stopped being invisible and came up onstage to listen. Bree got behind me and rubbed my neck, her fingers light and sure, feeling me tensing up because something had come into Bulldog's voice, making it too damned close and too damned real.

Ches Kobel had been at our house a week ago, sleeping under our roof, eating Bree's cooking. It kept stabbing at me, getting crossed up in my head with Sara Kildare, tearful on the phone, giving me the news, and with my mother-in-law's voice, a woman who never gets agitated, saying flat and sure, *that boy simply shouldn't be dead...*

"Bulldog?" Tony sounded sharp, worried. "Are you okay?"

I jerked back to reality, turned, and felt my own heart stutter. Bulldog was leaning back, his hand over his chest.

"I'm okay, son." He didn't sound okay; his voice was suddenly thin, an echo instead of a church bell, and there was pain in it. "I just need my medicines, is all."

"Bloody hell!" I was up, out of the chair, cursing myself. It was past five, closer to six, and I'd spaced, completely forgotten, about not only my own meds, but Bulldog's as well. I'd promised Sallie he could stay home and not worry, because I'd make sure his dad took his pills. I could have kicked myself, being so stupid. "Hang on, I've got them right here. Dance, we need some water. Bulldog, which ones, the pills or the capsules? Or both?"

Katia and Dom had disappeared back behind the bar, and

106

come back with half a dozen bottles of spring water. There it was again, that feeling of cliché, of classic stereotyping, the women bringing the menfolk what they needed, staying silent, just outside the magic circle of what was going on. I really didn't like it, and if I hadn't felt so guilty over Bulldog's discomfort, I might have mentioned it.

I'd opened the worn toiletries case Sallie'd given me. Bulldog was leaning back on his stool, eyes closed; his breathing was steady and even, but he still had one hand on his chest and there were lines carved into his face, deep ones, that said *pain* to me.

"Here you go." Dom had passed me a bottle of water; I crouched down next to Bulldog, and put a capsule in his hand. "Here's the stuff for the chest pain. Angina, is it?"

He nodded, eyes still closed. "You take that capsule," I told him. "I've got some water right here. Do you need a Digoxin as well? Right, I'll get one out for you. Take that capsule first, though, get it working on the pain."

One pill, one capsule. He got them down, and I got a clinic on how to swallow a capsule about the size of an olive with no trouble at all: he tilted his head all the way back, stuck out his tongue and dropped the capsule right on the tip. Then he curled tongue and pill together back into his mouth. Just as he was about to swallow, he took a shot of water, gulped, and down it went. I damned near applauded.

Sallie'd warned me that Bulldog would get drowsy if he took both pills together, and he did. That wasn't a bad thing, since it gave us time for a dinner break, spectacular barbecue cooked and delivered from a rib joint just down the road from the Backroom. It seemed as if everyone in Ofagoula knew each other, worked with each other, got each other, right down to supper.

Bulldog woke up all the way after awhile, and had some ribs. I used my cell to ring Sallie, and let him know his dad had had his meds, and was fine. More jamming, more talking; Dom actually got into it, egging Bulldog on, wanting stories of the Yoruban priest who'd been dragged away from Nigeria as a slave. I think her own ancestors had gone through a similar thing, being dragged off by the slavers and fetching up in Jamaica. Whatever it was, she was about as close to curling up at a man's feet and listening to him talk as I'd ever seen her.

"...My father was with the Army, child—more blacks in the Army back then than most people know. We talking about Flanders, the First World War, before I was born; 809th battalion, Pioneer Infantry, all black men. They were mostly doing the building, construction work, roads and levees and bridges and that stuff. My daddy once said that by the time they got to France and got the 809th off the *President Grant*, those boys could put up a field hospital near as fast as a white soldier could clean and reload his gun."

We were all quiet, relaxed, listening. I was looking at Dom and I suddenly understood it.

That speech I was working on, the feeling that family connections didn't have to be blood or ancestry? I'd nailed it, and here was the proof, right in front of me. It was there in Dom's concentration, in Luke with his Strat in his lap, unplugged now, his hands quiet on the neck. It was there in Tony, with the connections he'd made to Bulldog and now with Dance, how he'd found the grandfather of his own tribe, those shit-hot monster barrelhouse piano players—he was right there, one of them. It was there in Mac, in his genuine interest, in the way his head was tilted forward to gather it all together, in the blues he'd begun playing back when he and Luke were straight out of school, and formed Blackpool Southern. And it was there, and would always be there, in the love between Bulldog and Ches, between Ches and Sallie, brothers and fathers and sons.

"Army let him out honourable when I was born, so that we

could move on up a ways, to Hattiesburg. They gave him an administrative separation—my mama had a hard time having me. But he stayed with the Army, my daddy did. Went right on back as a contractor. The C.O. at Camp Shelby, he worked with my daddy a long time. We did pretty good, even in the Depression…"

There were soft, strong fingers at the back of my neck, rubbing, finding the spots that hurt, trying to take the pain away: Bree, always there, never letting me down, never letting me fall, always giving me space to be who I am, to do what I do. I reached up, took one of her hands, and drew it around to me, up to my lips for a kiss.

"Right," I said, and got up. "Everyone done eating, then? Let's send Ches another tune, yeah? Because we've got just about another hour to play, and then we've got to head back to Cincy."

It's weird, looking back at it now, how mellow and laid-back I felt during that visit to Ofagoula. The weirdest thing about it was, there was nothing sounding any alarms or bells or sirens, nothing at all. We dropped Bulldog off, the limos took us back to the hotel, I made love to my wife, had a perfect night's sleep, no aches or pains. Airport, flight home, off the plane, ride home, all of it totally tranquil.

Bree noticed it, as well. Of course, it meant that she got to relax. She plays off my moods, mostly; fair or not, it's what we've always done, part of our particular pair bond, what makes us work as a couple, and always has done. She told me later that it was as if Ofagoula had dropped some sort of protective layer around my mood. The conversations, the stories, the music—she said that, while I was there, I was like a chrysalis: wrapped up, safe and sound.

We got home early in the day. That's one benefit of flying east to west, later to earlier; if you aren't too jet-lagged, you can get a lot done. And I wasn't feeling the lag this time, not at all. I was enjoying this odd mix of being peaceful and being energised.

I hadn't really given any thought to getting back into the City, but of course, Carla being Carla, I needn't have worried. There were two liveried drivers just outside the security point, holding up signs: *Sharpe/Hedley, Kinkaid/Mancuso*. I heard a tiny little "oh, wow!" from Katia, right behind me. I caught Bree's eye, and we shared a grin. If Tony did fetch up touring with Blacklight, Katia was going to get spoiled on all the small touches I take for granted. It was a nice thought.

We told Luke and Mac we'd see them in the morning—they were spending that night at a hotel, because Bree hadn't had time to prep the house for guests before we'd left for Ohio. We had the limo driver drop Tony and Katia off at their place, and headed home ourselves.

There'd been no call to Sammy, not this time. We'd only gone for a day, and anyway, Bree was making fretful noises about jonesing for a good meal of fresh fish. That meant a drive over to the Whole Foods market on California Street—Sandy, Kris Corcoran's wife, calls it Whole Paycheque, which for some reason Bree finds snorting-out-loud funny.

"Do you need me to come along?" There was a package on the kitchen table; Sammy'd been by to feed the cats, and taken delivery for me. "Because I will, if you need extra hands, but I really ought to work on the speech."

"No, it's cool. I'm a big strapping girl, I think I can carry a couple of lake trout and some veggies by myself. I don't need a roadie today. Besides, that thing on the table has the Hall of Fame's return address on it. You stay here and play with your notes. I'll get a few errands done—we're low on cat food and if we're out of town next week, I should stock up. I'm not going to want to think about it later in the week."

"Right. If you're sure, love, I'll do that."

"I'm sure." She leaned over suddenly, took my face between her hands and kissed me, tongue tip to tongue tip. That was a nice surprise—she doesn't usually initiate that unless there's follow-up in our immediate future. It always does something to the pit of my stomach, that gesture; Bree'd done that the first night we'd met. She'd apologised at the time, apologised for not being able to stop herself doing it, but in a strange way, that had sealed it in my head: together or apart, we'd been a couple since that first action, even if I hadn't accepted it or even really understood it straight off.

"Okay." I was grinning; her eyes were very green. That was a sure sign she was turned on, but it was going to have to wait, and we both knew it. Something to look forward to, later on tonight. "Off you go. I'll go over things and maybe I'll have some new stuff to read you when you get back."

Once the Jag's engine had faded, I sat down at the kitchen table, pushed the two male cats out of my way, and opened the package. It was an oversized bubble-bag, and it was what I'd been expecting: the return label had Sara Kildare's name on it. I tore open the top, and slid the contents out.

A notebook, one of those old-fashioned black and white ones with printed ruled lines on every page, fell out first. There were actually two of them, the first one looking well-thumbed, bristling with numbered sticky notes. The second one was obviously newer.

I arranged them one on top of the other, and let my fingers rest there. I was trying to get a sense of Ches, trying for something, I don't know what: a ghost, or a sense memory, anything at all that might be left of him. There was a very sour taste at the back of my throat. That notebook, the older one, had sat right here on the table, just a week ago. Ches had used it, jotting down things, thumbing back through the pages to find me tidbits. He hadn't always found what I wanted, either; after all, this book wasn't really supposed to be about Bulldog. It was about Sonny Boy Williamson and Son House and the movement of music up through the Delta, curling north toward Chicago, and then back down and out across the country and the Atlantic.

I sat for a few minutes, one hand on the notebook, remembering a bare week ago. The cover was cool under my fingers. I felt sick at my stomach. Ches was really dead, really gone. Nothing was bringing him back.

Simon had jumped back on the table, and was amusing himself with batting the envelope about with one paw. I'd have shoved him away, but I got distracted; something had rattled, inside the bubble-pack. I shook it loose, and caught it before it hit the table. It was Ches's thumb drive.

And suddenly, there was his ghost, a memory, sharp and clear: me sitting right here, in this same chair, asking him questions about Bulldog that he didn't have the answer to, him reaching into his briefcase and coming out with the tiny little computer drive, saying something about his laptop. And Bree waving him across, preoccupied with rubbing a wooden bowl with lemon for salad. What had she said? *"It's all booted up—just log in as 'guest' and upload whatever you want. I trust you not to infect my system."*

He'd actually borrowed Bree's desktop computer, in her kitchen alcove office. He'd sat right there, in Bree's Aeron chair, peering at the screen, muttering something to himself, typing something in...

It took me a couple of minutes of fumbling about to sort out how to access the damned thing. I've only recently got remotely savvy about computers; even though the band has been using them forever, I just wasn't interested, and I had other things on my mind. The murder of Vinny Fabiano, the Bombardiers' frontman, had pushed me into needing to deal with tech, because they'd used my basement studio to rehearse and record their new CD in, and that meant going digital.

112

So now I had a basement full of pricey gear, including everything I needed to send sound files back and forth to Luke, back at Draycote in the UK. I have to admit, it makes the international recording process a lot easier; saves a lot of work. And I was getting more interested in it, or at least better at using it, but I still wasn't up to speed. Bree's the computer person in the family, not me.

It turned out to be easy. The thumb drive was intuitive enough so that even a relative computer twit like myself could figure it out. I loaded it, read the instructions on the screen, did what it told me to do, and watched the screen flicker into display mode.

There was a directory there, with a little icon that meant a folder: *Moody Bio Project.doc.*

"Right." I'd said it out loud, talking to myself. The house felt emptier than usual, echoing; my own voice seemed to move around the high corners of the kitchen. "Okay."

So that's what had taken him to Hattiesburg. What had he told us, before we'd waved him off to the airport? *I'm off to Memphis for a day, then Hattiesburg… a research trip… a few facts I want to check on for the book…*

"Gordon Bennett."

I heard my own voice again, and nearly jumped. So he'd decided to do a bio of Bulldog. Between that trip to Hattiesburg and the icon I was staring at, it was obvious. Bulldog had come from Hattiesburg. He'd told us about it in Ofagoula, wonderful stories about life in the 1920s, clueing us in that not every black family in the South was a starving sharecropper.

I couldn't sort it out. Why had Ches been so secretive about it? He'd been providing me with information, helping me put together the best speech possible. Hell, he'd been the one to make the offer in the first place, opening up everything he had for me to pick info out of. If he'd decided to do a separate bio of Bulldog, why hadn't he said so? It didn't make sense.

I reached for the top notebook. First try at picking it up, I dropped it, and swore. For a moment, I thought it was the MS, because my fingers weren't steady.

It wasn't the MS. That pretty cocoon, that nice blanket of safety and calm I'd been wrapped in since Ofagoula, was threatening to dissolve around me. And I didn't know why.

The first thing I found, just inside the cover, was a printout. Bless Ches, he'd been well-organised; it was a one-page numbered index to the sticky slips. I read down the list: *number one, Son House, Robinsonville. Number two, Sonny Boy Williamson, early years. Number three, Albert Ammons. Number four, Bo Diddley-diddley-bo, box guitars.*

I hit Bulldog's entry at sticky slip number eleven. Ches had a good clean handwriting, and a nice crisp style. I know sod-all about writing. I'm a musician. But when I'm reading something, and what it's trying to get across to me is clear and easy to remember, I call that crisp.

"...*An amusing incident—one that seems almost inevitable in light of the times and the personnel—concerned a sunny spring afternoon in a local park in a town not far from Clarksdale, where James McCoy was trading licks with a couple of local players, Son House and Rube Lacy by name...*"

I read it through. There it was, the incident Bulldog had told us about; Ches had it down, every detail in its place, just the way Bulldog had shared it. Bulldog watching and fascinated, tapping those *bembè* rhythms out on the park bench without even knowing he was doing it, McCoy noticing. It was all there.

Another numbered sticky note reference got me to 1951. This story, I hadn't heard before, and it made me grin: *Sonny Boy Williamson recorded his second session for Lillian McMurry's Trumpet label on June 11, 1951. The session took place at Trumpet's studio at 309 Farish Street in Jackson, Mississippi, and the backing line-up that day would make any blues aficionado salivate: pianist Willie Love, session star Farris "Bulldog" Moody on guitar, Elmore James, Joe Willie Wilkins, and drummer "Frock" O'Dell...*

That was it, two numbered references that led back to Bulldog. There was nothing else, not another word.

I closed the book. It couldn't possibly be all. Something was missing. Ches had spent long hours down in Ofagoula, days and nights hanging with the Moodys, listening to every word, taking it down. I'd seen him do it. Even if he only used a fraction of what he'd got, he have got it down somewhere.

I turned back to Bree's computer. Her screensaver had kicked in—the Blacklight official logo—and I moved the mouse to get the screen back. It came back, the little icon folder blinking away: *Moody Bio Project.doc.*

I don't know, even now, why I was so edgy. But I sat there and looked at the icon for another few minutes. There was nothing in me that wanted to open the damned thing.

Showtime. I took a long breath, and clicked the mouse.

The notes weren't actually written, not as a book would be written. They'd been done in a sort of shorthand, a kind of code. I should have had a lot more trouble, sussing out what Ches was talking about. But I had no trouble at all.

Notes on LD's prison record; AWOL status 1920/21, re records, US Disciplinary B, Ft. Leavenworth. Dishon.Dis for desertion, double check Chicago source, Dixon/Duckworth; infant son abandoned, 1921—LD, SM work crew?

I scrolled down the page. My fingers were shaking so badly, I could barely get the mouse to work.

It didn't make sense. Bulldog's father hadn't abandoned him. He hadn't been AWOL, and he hadn't been dishonourably discharged from the Army, either. I could hear Bulldog's voice in my head, that big bell, telling Dom about how his father had gone back to work for the Army as a contractor, after Bulldog was born. That couldn't have happened if Salas had been in that kind of trouble. No damned way. And who the hell was LD? Who was Dixon, or Duckworth?

Rec. unavail—Lainey C, hospital. LD, meetings? Check w/old res; illegit. births/Army doc, children might know.

"John?"

I'd been so deep into it, I hadn't even heard Bree come in behind me. Her voice shocked me out of whatever nasty little trance I'd been stuck in; I jumped and jerked, so hard I knocked the mouse pad off the desk. I think I said something, I don't know what.

"What is it?" She was staring at me, her arms full of grocery bags. There was trouble in her face. No surprise there, because she'd seen it in mine; Bree plays off my moods, now and always. There wasn't going to be any lying to her. "What's wrong? John!"

I opened my mouth, closed it again, tried to swallow. I couldn't seem to get any words out, now. My throat had closed.

She dropped the bags, right where she was standing, and moved. I forget, sometimes, how fast she can go if she thinks I'm sick, if she thinks I need her. And I needed her, all right. I must have look like Death warmed over.

She read the screen over my shoulder, quiet, not saying anything. She read it again, and then a third time. I watched her eyes tracking the words, deciphering them, not believing them, her lips moving, reading again. Finally, she met my eye.

"Is this supposed to be about Bulldog?" The trouble in her face had got all the way into her voice, and her eyes were wide and shocked. "It can't be about Bulldog, John. What about everything he told us—about his father, and the tent shows, and his grandfather? This was Ches, writing this? What was he talking about?"

"I don't know. Or maybe I do." Out of nowhere, I was fighting for breath, and every muscle in my body was talking to me, just roaring away, as the stress and the jetlag and the shock of that

116

nice safe cocoon shredding around me came together in one huge rush of the MS, the disease doing what it does best, being opportunistic, taking me down hard. "Bree—listen. I need my meds, and a lie-down. And then I need you to ring your mum. I need to talk to her."

"Hang on." She'd got my meds from the stash she always carries with her, and a glass of water. "Here, take these. You want me to call my mother? Why not your own neuro?"

"Not about me." I swallowed the pills, seeing Bulldog in my mind's eye, him dropping the capsule on the tip of his tongue, curling it back, the capsules you weren't supposed to chew or break open, washing it down. I closed my eyes, wanting the idea that had come into my head to disappear, and knowing it wasn't going anywhere. "I need to talk to her about Ches."

Chapter Eight

"...One thing about history, personal history, musical history, world, family, whatever—you never know how much of what you know is real, and how much came from someone else's need to change the story. With family history, you've usually got some evidence. Things get passed down, generation to generation. There's photos. There's old letters, medical records, inherited genetics, anecdotes..."

Miranda came over for dinner that night. I was totally out of it when Bree rang her up; she'd taken me upstairs and got me into bed for a lie-down. My head was pounding with what I'd have sworn was a migraine, if I'd ever had a migraine in my life, and my legs and feet were shaky and tingling. Normally, under those circs, I wouldn't have heard a word; she'd have slipped out so quietly that I wouldn't have even heard her go. But this time, she stayed in the room, and rang her mum. She'd guessed I needed to know Miranda was coming.

"...Mom?" I was drowsing, catching Bree's half of the call. There was something dreamlike about it, words floating in and out of my awareness, and Bree's voice moving around in my head as I waited for the meds to kick in. "...yes, we're back—listen, are you on call tonight—come over for dinner—fresh trout—yes, it's important—I'd appreciate it—John wants to ask you about something—did you ever talk to that doctor in Cleveland—oh, man, okay—around seven—thanks, Mom—I wouldn't ask if it wasn't important...bye."

"...All musicians have got histories. It's a side effect, what happens when what you are is the same as what you do. I got to spend some time with Bulldog Moody recently, in his house in southern Ohio, making music, hearing his stories..."

I must have really needed the rest, because I slept for two solid hours. When I got up, the headache was gone way down, a sort of low-grade thump in the background, and my legs still hurt. I found myself hoping that I wasn't in for a full-scale exacerbation, or that, if I was, it happened now, and not next Wednesday at the Waldorf.

"...All right, I'll admit it—I got a rush from the stories, from the sense of connection between us. But knowing that damned near every musician I ever played with would give anything they owned to change places with me, that was an even bigger rush..."

When I came downstairs, the house smelled wonderful. Bree'd set the kitchen table and got some bakery bread out, with olive oil in tiny individual saucers, for dipping. She was sitting at her computer, with a notepad and a pen. She had her little drugstore readers on, the ones she says she needs for reading things close up, these days.

"Hey, babe. Are you feeling any better?"

"A bit, yeah." Something was flashing—I'd left the thumb drive plugged in, and it was blinking away. "How long until Miranda gets here? And how long until dinner?"

"Half an hour, give or take. I told her around seven. I didn't know how long you'd be sleeping." She was talking to me, but she wasn't giving me her full attention; that was on the screen. She peered at it, and made a note. "Are you hungry now? Have some bread, or there's salad—big wooden bowl, chilling in the fridge."

"No, it's good, I can wait to eat." I was right behind her, squinting, trying to read the screen over her shoulder. "Bree—what are you doing?"

"Trying to decode Ches's shorthand, before Mom gets here." She turned the Aeron all the way around, and looked at me. There was concentration there, in the crease between her brows, in the way her shoulders were hunched up. "Trying to see if he meant what I think he meant by all this, trying to make a little sense out of it. Mostly, I'm trying to wrap my head around it—what I think you think about all this."

I met her eye, and we locked up. It's not an equal battle, the pair of us trying to read the other one's eye; hers are muddy green, but they're easy. Mine are opaque, about as dark brown as you can get. If I want to hide something from Bree, I can do it, pretty much every time.

I didn't want to hide it, not this time. I'd been pushing away what I thought, the suspicion that had jumped off that damned thumb drive straight at me, for a couple of hours—long enough to sleep on it.

But I couldn't push it away any longer, and I didn't want to. I wanted to be wrong. I wanted Bree to tell me I was nuts.

"What do you think I think, Bree?" The big old clock on the kitchen wall said twenty of seven. Miranda was going to be here soon, any minute, maybe. "And what do you think, yourself?"

She didn't say anything. Instead, she handed me the notebook she'd been writing in.

Bree's got a sprawling sort of handwriting, most of the time; if she leaving me a quick note on the kitchen table, I mostly can't make head or tail of half of it. Where she suddenly gets tidy is when she's making lists. She'd written down some of the stuff from the bio folder on the drive, but she'd moved things around, paired things up, put them into an order that probably made sense to her.

One thing was obvious, straight off: in her head, this was a list. Her writing was clean, clear, precise. I could read every word she'd written.

Notes on LD's prison record. LD = Dixon/Duckworth? AWOL status 1920/21, re records, US Disciplinary B, Ft. Leavenworth.

"You think this LD is someone called Dixon? Or Duckworth?" Right—this was the way to approach it. It felt safe, it could almost have been a game, one of those brain teaser puzzle things in a child's activity book. Not real, no harm, no foul, no consequences... "That whoever this bloke was, he went walkabout from the Army, and got nicked for it?"

"Maybe. That much would be pretty easy to at least check, wouldn't it?" The kitchen was warm, safe, the way it always was. It smelled of lemon, and garlic, and trout. Everything was all right. "If you're really worried about it, I mean? Army records, well, they're there, John. They don't go anywhere."

Bree got up, and opened the oven; her voice was flat, too flat. Whether she'd picked up on my mood and my fear and was playing off it, or whether this was her own stuff, she was keeping hard control over it. Good. That kept it safe. *Not real, no harm, no foul, no consequences...* "Right," I told her, and watched her shoulders stiffen up. "I *am* worried, Bree."

"I know." She got the trout off its pan and onto a metal tray, ready to slide under the broiler. She'd arranged a bottle of olive oil and a saucer of sliced fruit—lemon, blood orange, lime—on the cutting board; she drizzled the trout with olive oil and began layering the sliced citrus, covering the fish with it. "So am I."

Dishon. Dis for desertion, double check Chicago source— Dixon/Duckworth again? Why Chicago?

"Chicago?" I glanced up at her. *All a game, not real, none of it.* It was all right. Ches had had a heart attack, and died of it;

121

Miranda would get here soon, and we'd have a nice dinner. She'd tell us that she'd let her imagination run away with her; she'd shake her head at me, and scold me for doing the same. She'd say she'd spoken with her cardio mate about Ches, that the cardio laughed at her, and that would be that. Ches had got hold of some wrong information, his sources had been wrong. He'd died a natural death, tragic and unfair, but natural. No harm, no foul... "What's odd about Chicago?"

"Because Ches wrote that, something about a dishonourable discharge, and then that thing about the U.S. Disciplinary Barracks, in Leavenworth. Leavenworth isn't in Chicago. It's nowhere near Chicago. It's in Kansas. I googled it."

"So you think something happened with this Duckworth or Dixon or whatever his name was, in Chicago. But whatever it was, it got him in trouble with the Army?"

"I don't know. But it seems reasonable."

"Right—give me a minute." I went back to reading. "Almost done, now."

Infant son abandoned, 1921—LD, SM work crew. LD = Dixon/Duckworth, SM = Salas Moody?

Salas Moody.

"Bloody hell." Something had gone down my back. "Oh, bloody fucking *hell!*"

"Talk to me." She was looking at me, not at the oven; behind her, I could hear sizzling and spitting from inside the big range, as the top of the trout broiled. "My mother is going to get here any minute, John. Please talk to me. You don't think Bulldog was telling the truth about his family. Do you?"

"How the fuck do I know!" For one black moment, I wanted to hit her. It wasn't safe any more—it wasn't a game. I'd spent half my life letting her keep the bad stuff in the real world away from me, making sure I had room to feel, breathe, do what I needed. She'd kept it all away; she'd kept me safe.

122

And now she was making me say it instead, forcing me to make it real, to say that the grandfather I'd made such a pure connection with, the man who'd given me my music, had lied and maybe worse. I heard myself—*shut up, Johnny, shut up, not safe to talk yet*—couldn't believe it, and couldn't stop myself, either.

"Look, Bree, do me a favour and belt up, would you? Just shut your fucking gob, stop talking for one minute, and let me think!"

Her face stiffened, went blank, smoothed out. I felt my own stomach twist up, hard and tight: Shit, shit, *shit*. She'd seen it in my face, heard it in my voice, all the resentment, all the panic. I'd wanted to hit her; in a way, in the only way that mattered, that was exactly what I'd done.

"Christ." I put a hand out toward her. "Bree…"

"It's all right." She'd turned back to the stove. Hiding from me again, the old patterns, the ones we'd been trying so hard to break… While I was trying to think of what to say, she dropped one of her oven mitts. We went down at the same time to pick it up, and I saw her hands were shaking. "I understand, John. This isn't pretty. I know how much you hate it. It's all right—"

"No, it's not all right." I was up next to her, stilling her hands under my own. "Look, leave the food for a minute, Bree, please. That's not important. What's important is that I'm sorry, okay? It just hurt like hell for a second, there. I wasn't looking at things and you made me do it. Knocked me off-balance, you know? It hurt and I wanted to kick the universe, and you were standing there instead. I'm not making excuses—just letting you know. I'm so sorry, love."

"Forgiven. Like I said, I really do know how much you hate this." She meant it, too; one small smile, as real in the right way as everything else we were talking about was turning out to be in the wrong way. The smile was gone a moment later. "There's more stuff—I mean, I wrote most of it out, trying to decipher it. There's one thing in there—something about Green, and a num-

123

ber. I don't remember it exactly. But if you don't want–"

"No, got it. 'LD, HPCem, soGreen, 49'—that it?" I hadn't got that far before, reading the actual screen; this bit was new to me. "Damned if I know what it means, though. Not a clue."

"Neither do I." She lifted her head; the trout was on a platter, the salad was about to come out of the fridge. "And there's the bell. Mom's a little early. Can you get the door? I need to mix a salad dressing."

My mother-in-law was here. There was the fish Bree'd wanted, and salad, and bread. Nice normal dinner, except for the chilly little cramp in the pit of my stomach, and the tension in Bree's shoulders, and the complete not wanting to know what Miranda was going to say to us.

The bell rang, again. Bree turned and looked at me; she had a cruet in each hand.

Right. Showtime.

I actually had one small hope left, about keeping things from coming real on me: a picture in my head, Miranda telling us we'd let our imaginations go nuts, telling us we were wrong, telling us there was nothing at all off about Ches' death. That hope went west as soon as I opened the door, and got a good look at her face.

The fact that Bree's dead easy to read must have come from her dad. Trying to read Miranda's like trying to get a fix on the Sphinx on the wrong side of a brick wall. She's got the surgeon thing happening, that whole trick of being friendly, polite, distant. Doctors like to inspire awe. They tell each other they're inspiring confidence in their patients, but that's bollocks. They like awe. It gets them back more than just all the dosh they spent, getting that degree in the first place.

It takes a lot to get any sort of mood off Miranda. The icy blonde colouring helps; it's about as effective as a nun's wimple, because she never seems to look any older, and she knows how to keep the professional mask in place.

Usually, when she's visiting and I'm the one meeting her at the door, we've got this ritual: I say her name, say hello, and step back out of her way. She waits until I do all that before she steps indoors. She does that no matter what the weather's doing—middle of a thunderstorm, she's still standing out on the front porch. It's as if she can't cross the threshold without an invitation.

I mentioned that to Bree, years ago, and she didn't believe me. So, the next time we had her mum over, Bree watched from just inside the front room, and saw for herself. Later on, curled up in bed together, Bree told me she thought maybe her mum was part vampire, because you have to invite a vampire in. I said I thought it was just her respect for boundaries.

Tonight, I opened the door and she walked in, no waiting for me. Her face was showing things, as well, and that was another difference: her mouth was tight, lips thinned out, and her eyebrows were drawn down together into a pale blonde vee.

So, yeah, not good, and there went any chance of not dealing with it. There was the voice in my head saying, *bad news, shit, bad news...*

"John." She came inside, and waited for me to close the door. Another difference, another wrong thing: all three cats adore her, and she adores them right back. They were wreathing round her ankles, trilling, purring, making plaintive little "please snog me" noises at her. She never even looked down. "I'm glad you wanted to get together tonight—I was going to wait until tomorrow morning, and then call you myself. Are you all right? You look tired."

"MS kicking up. It's not too bad. And yeah, I'm the wrong side of stressed, but that'll sort itself out after the induction ceremony is over. It's a really tight schedule. Mind the cats—you've got the entire tribe, waiting to get their tails stepped on." I took her coat.

"Bree's in the kitchen. She's got dinner waiting. Let's eat first, all right? You hungry?"

Miranda opened her mouth, but I held up one hand. "No, look, wait. I asked Bree to ring you up. There's things been happening, and I want to know what Ches Kobel's cardio bloke had to say, but let it wait until after dinner, Miranda, okay? Because she worked hard, putting a brilliant meal together, and it isn't fair to her, dumping all this on her. Let's eat first, and talk after. All right?"

She nodded. Another sign that something had rattled her off her usual balance; my mother-in-law is big on that whole verbal communication thing. So if she was nodding or shaking her head, instead of offering up spoken words, she really wasn't looking forward to talking. At least we could get a decent meal before whatever shit she'd found out could hit the fan.

So, of course, we walked into the kitchen, and Bree immediately made a total nonsense of everything I'd said to Miranda, out in the hall.

"Mom, hi, thanks for coming, are you hungry, here, sit." She barely waited for us to get into our own chairs. "Here, have some trout—it's pan-grilled, *au citron.* You told me you'd talked to Ches's doctor in Ohio. What did he say?"

"Right, okay." So much for that. I put both hands up. " I surrender. Bree, I told your mum it wouldn't be fair to you, to talk about it while we ate, but what the hell, if you're on, I'm on, as well. Let's get it over."

"I did talk to him, yes." Miranda got a forkful of stuff, chewed, and swallowed. "But I think John's right. We can leave the details until later—in fact, I'd rather do that. Even for a surgeon, this doesn't qualify as appropriate dinner table conversation. But I do want you to know this much: Stan Minkus was just as shocked by Ches dying as I was."

She looked at Bree, then at me, and I heard her take a deep breath. "He's going to ask for an autopsy."

126

Of course, that pretty much killed it for the rest of the meal. I've been doing supper table conversation my whole life. I was an only child, except for a month or two after my brother Matthew was born. I was just old enough to remember what our house was like after my mum went in to give him a feed and found him dead in his cot; after that, my parents must have wanted me there, in full view, for as much of our family time together as they could manage. So I got to listen to the flow of whatever my parents wanted to talk about, over sausages and chips, or whatever my mum had cooked up for supper any given night.

These days, the food's a lot better than I had growing up, but one thing's just the same: the supper table's still the place where we catch up on what's going on, small stuff, big stuff, stuff that matters to everyone, stuff that matters to just us. It makes sense, really: food is the other half of Bree's world. She says a good meal makes dealing with everything a little easier, and I'll tell you what, she's right.

But after Miranda dropped that bomb, that was it, total silence. Quietest meal I've eaten in years. There's something about the word *autopsy* that brings up some really ugly pictures in the brain. And when those pictures come attached to someone you knew, pleasant conversation is right out.

We didn't do our usual leisurely thing over supper, either. No taking time, no relaxing over it, none of the usual thing that happens at the supper table because Bree's fierce about food being a pleasure, not something to be rushed through. Tonight, we ate, Bree cleared the plates into the trash because you can't leave fish lying about when you've got cats, and we stacked the dishwasher. Miranda stayed quiet, and sat where she was; she's had meals with us often enough to know better than to offer Bree help with the clearing up. Bree's got her kitchen routines down, as precise as military manoeuvres. She lets her inner control freak out more in the kitchen than she does anywhere else.

Once that was sorted out, Bree went straight at it. She plugged in the electric kettle, got a pot of tea ready, set out a box of fancy little *petits fours* things she'd got at the Whole Foods bakery, and sat back down.

"Okay." She was looking her mum dead in the eye. "Why is this guy asking for an autopsy? What does he think happened? Doesn't he think Ches had a heart attack?"

"Well, he does and he doesn't." She must have seen the exasperation and impatience on both our faces, because she went straight on talking, not letting either of us interrupt. "Bree, honey, let me tell this my own way, and at my own pace, all right? Otherwise, you'll both be buried under a weight of medical jargon and this will take twice as long to explain."

We stayed quiet. Miranda had both hands around her cup, as if she wanted to warm her fingers. "First of all, Stan called me back yesterday. He's actually on vacation right now, so he was on Maui when he got the news. I got hold of him not long after that. He's cutting things short and flying back to Cleveland on the first flight he can get."

"Why?" I got up, and hunted out spoons. "Bree, have we got any lemons in the house—right, never mind, I see them. Why would he come back early? There's sod-all he can do, yeah? He can't bring Ches back to life."

She reached for the honey. "Obviously not, John. But he has to sign a medical request for an autopsy and he had to get permission, a signed release, from that boy's next of kin. Stan said something about a sister, but apparently she doesn't live in Ohio, so he was going to have some work to do, tracking her down and getting what he needed. He can't get any of that done from a condo in Hawaii."

"Ches's sister is called Paula, and she lives in Baltimore." I took a *petit four*; normally, I'm not much for sweets, unless Bree bakes them, but I had a strong feeling I was going to want a

128

mouthful of sugar as comfort food before Miranda was done telling us what she thought. "I was on the phone with Sara Kildare from the Hall, and she was actually at Ches's place when his sister rang up. I'll give you Sara's number, if you need it to get hold of Paula Kobel. Look, Miranda, tell it in your own words, tell it your own way, but tell it, yeah? Did Ches die from a heart attack, or not?"

"It's not that simple." She met my eye. "Yes, he had a heart attack. That's not the issue. You're asking the wrong question."

"Okay. Then what in hell should I be asking?" I was giving her back stare for stare. Bree was quiet, watching us. "You know, this isn't a game for me, Miranda. He was a friend of mine. I liked him. We had a connection, we had the music. He slept under our roof. He ate at Bree's table. And he's gone, out of nowhere. I want to know how and I want to know why."

"He had a heart attack, yes."

She reached out suddenly, as if her throat had gone dry, and tipped back a big mouthful of tea; lucky for her, it had cooled down to manageable. When she spoke again, she'd gone into something closer to her professional voice. I was suddenly very much aware that I was talking to Dr. Miranda Godwin, eminent surgeon.

"A couple of tourists found him where he'd collapsed. They called the paramedics. The EMTs showed up within minutes, took his vitals, and found no sign of a pulse or breath. They tried to revive him, without success. It was no use—he'd been dead a good fifteen minutes before he was found. The question isn't whether his heart stopped, John. It's what made it stop."

"But he had a bad heart." Bree hadn't so much as glanced at the *petits fours*; unusual, because unlike me, she does have a sweet tooth. "He told us that, Mom. He had same thing John has, the cardiac arrhythmia. He even took the same medicine for it that you take, didn't he John? I remember you guys comparing notes when we drove down to Ofagoula, that first trip."

"Yeah, same stuff. Digoxin. It's meant to slow down a stutter-ing fast heartbeat." Something was trying to get me to look at it, a fact, a memory, something. I didn't have a clue what it was, I just knew it was making me feel edgy and uneasy. "He also told me his own cardio bloke—Stan Minkus, is it?—had said there was no reason for Ches to not live to be a cranky old geezer of ninety or so. Was the doctor wrong?"

"No. He wasn't." Her voice was calm, flat and completely cer-tain. Voice of the expert speaking, but sometimes, it might as well be the voice of God. "Stan went over what he remembered of Ches Kobel's medical history and current status with me, when we were on the phone. He said that, except for the arrhythmia, Ches could have been the poster child for physical health. Excel-lent cholesterol levels—the good and bad numbers were both well within tolerances. He wasn't overweight. His lean muscle mass was close to perfect. He didn't smoke, only drank the occa-sional beer, limited himself to two cups of coffee a day. He avoided fatty foods, mostly, and was sensible about exercise. He ate minimal amounts of red meat, a lot of fish, and a good por-tion of his diet came from fresh fruit and vegetables. Stan said Ches wasn't even susceptible to seasonal allergies. Except for his heartbeat wanting to jump high and flutter occasionally, he didn't have a single thing wrong with him."

"But–" Bree's hands had woven together, and she was looking at me. "Mom, I don't get it. I just don't understand. Isn't the ar-rhythmia serious? If it's not, then why does John's doctor keep such a close eye on it?"

"It's not life-threatening, Bree, no. Not by itself. Especially not in this case, not according to Stan. Ches Kobel had what's known as lone atrial fibrillation—an irregular heartbeat that wasn't the result of any other primary cause. That's not all that common. Usually, arrhythmia is found in older people, but every

130

once in a while, you get someone who's healthy as a horse otherwise, still young, and has it. John has other health issues—the MVP for one thing—and he's in the age group where cardiac events are more common generally."

I was sorting it out in my head. She was right, of course she was; arrhythmia's usually there because there's something else going on with the heart. I've got mitral valve prolapse to deal with, and my bloke watches me for other stuff, as well.

"Then I really don't understand." Bree looked as bewildered as she sounded. "Are you saying Ches didn't die from his heart suddenly going too fast, out of control too fast, I mean?"

"That's exactly what I'm saying." Miranda looked tired, suddenly, and older. Not ageless anymore—out of nowhere, she looked like a woman at the upper end of her sixties, heading toward seventy. "He didn't die from an accelerated heartbeat. According to what Stan told me, the EMTs said there was no sign of that. Ches Kobel didn't die because his heart rate sped up, he died because it slowed too much to continue to support his basic circulatory function."

"Okay." My own heart was getting into the act, fluttering up high, making me dizzy. I could feel a fine sheen of chilly sweat, breaking out behind my ears, along the back of my neck. Bree saw it, and reached for my hand. "Then what did he die from? What do you think happened? What stopped his heart?"

"That's what we're hoping the autopsy will tell us." Miranda sighed, finally. "If I had to guess—and I wouldn't, not with anyone but you two, certainly not to be mentioned to anyone else—I'd bet on him somehow having taken a massive overdose of his medicine, just before he went for his run."

Chapter Nine

"...*Everyone out there, raise your hands: when you hear that three-two beat, what's the first thing that comes into your head? Come on, show of hands: Bo Diddley, right? Who Do You Love, Mona, Not Fade Away? Three-two, Bo really did that, put it out there, gave it to the public. It's classic, perfect, pure Bo...*"

"John?" Bree's voice was quiet, but she didn't sound drowsy. One more item, one more difference, one more thing to make today wrong. Far as I was concerned, today couldn't be over fast enough. "It's okay. It really is."

"I know." She wasn't any less sleepy than I was. My brain was going like the unscheduled train in Chuck Berry's *Let It Rock*; just thundering on down the tracks. I wasn't going to be able to stop this particular train; all I could do was to let it roll. "Sorry about that, Bree. I just don't seem to be up for it, tonight."

"...*But there's a twist, a slightly different take on it. And that's what I heard, when I was just turned nine. That twist was a splash of seasoning, a slightly different taste of a very different spice. Turns out it was Cuba my ears were tasting, Cuban salsa, but it had a bite to it that went all the way back to Africa...*"

"Don't apologise."

She was nice and warm, the curve of her body pressed up against me. Normally, I'd have had her on her back by now, getting her eyes to roll all the way back in her head, but not tonight. She settled herself against me. "You've got a lot on your mind."

I didn't answer that, just kissed the back of her neck. I had one arm draped over her, and that was going to have to do for tonight. Might have been tiredness, might have been stress, might have been the multiple sclerosis or age or just an off night, but for whatever reason, sex wasn't happening. A lot of what makes the mechanics for sex click on in the first place may be in the mind, but tonight, the mind was wandering and the rest of me wasn't cooperating, either. It doesn't happen often, that, but it does happen. I don't flip my shit over it any more—I'm old enough to know better—but it's rotten for poor Bree.

"*And that's what got me, just reached right off that record, 'Daisy Chain Blues,' three-two three-two, but with that difference. It got me by the throat and never left off making me hear it. Still hasn't. It's a drumbeat, not a melody: rhythm, as pure as it gets. And that's Bulldog Moody.*"

Right then, I was even less in the mood for talking than I was for sex. Bree was right, there was a lot going on in my head, and all of it was grim. I was glad we knew each other well enough for her to not take me having the off-night as some sort of commentary about her being doable. She knows me better than that.

"What time are Luke and Mac coming over?" She'd arched her back, letting me stroke it. Those light runs down her spine with the tips of my fingers, what she calls chills, she loves me doing that. Problem is, they're really tiring on the arm after more than a couple of minutes. But if I wasn't going to be offering up sex, the chills were the least I could do. She says they relax her, and anyway, I like touching her. "Should I set the alarm?"

"No need. Mac told me right round eleven." My arm was beginning to cramp. I squeezed her shoulder, very light, a longtime signal that my arm was giving out. "Maybe we can get back to normal life, once this induction's done with."

"I hope so." She was quiet a moment. "John—are you going to tell them about—everything? Ches, I mean, what my mother said, and what we found?"

There was moonlight, a long pale line of it, right across the foot of the bed. That meant we were having a night with no fog, something that doesn't happen very much in San Francisco in winter. I wondered if my mates from Blacklight were out on the town, hitting the streets in the clear moonlight. Maybe Luke would get lucky. I could see Mac clubbing south of Market Street, looking for a tasty little treat in a short skirt to bring home with him, Dom a few steps off to one side, making damned sure the tasty treat in question was a safe bet, not to mention making sure the treat was female. After all, this is San Francisco...

"John...?"

"Sorry, Bree. My mind was wandering. I haven't made up my mind yet. Do me a favour, though, and don't bring it up to them, all right? We don't really know anything, yet."

"No, of course I won't." She rolled over on her side, and faced me. She touched my cheek with the tips of her fingers; I love when she does that, soft, firm, right there, everything that says Bree to me, safe and warm, right there in my bed. "This is your call, all the way. I'll leave some food out in the dining room. That way, you guys can take a break from rehearsing and eat whenever you want. What's the plan for tomorrow morning? Is Tony coming over for rehearsal? Is it "Moody's Blues?""

"Yeah, it is. They're coming here; Tony's bringing the Bombardiers' sound guy. We'll be in the studio most of the day, trying for a good enough version to send out as a sound file to the house band at the Hall."

"I thought you recorded one, back in Ofagoula?"

"We did, but it's scratchy; the PA at the Backroom is quite a few years old. Not exactly high tech, and we didn't have a sound tech along. So we'll do another one, and send them both. That way, they can get the feel of what Bulldog's stuff is going to sound like, in there. The more we can prep them ahead of time, the better. The idea is to cut as much time off as possible."

"Kind of like catering—get as much of the grunt-work done up front as I can, and that makes it easier to give everything I've got to the actual event." She yawned suddenly. "Oh, man, I think maybe I'm finally getting sleepy. Hell, it's nearly three in the morning in Ohio, and I think I'm still on Ohio time. Poke me if you need anything, okay, babe? G'night."

So, right, maybe she was sleepy. I wasn't. For one thing, the nap I'd taken earlier was coming back to haunt me. More than that, my head was completely wired, trying to sort out the mess surrounding Ches Kobel, the new book he'd been planning, the bits he'd put into that computer folder, the heart attack his doctor—and Miranda—both said he shouldn't have had.

Miranda hadn't said it straight out, and I hadn't either, but we didn't have to. We both knew it: there was no way Ches had accidentally taken an overdose of Digoxin. Miranda knew because she'd been a doctor for forty years, and I knew because I take the stuff as well. It becomes habit, you know? Ingrained. You take your meds at a given point in the day, and that goes for damned near all your meds, not just the heart stuff.

With the heart meds, though, it's very specific. It's not a matter of *okay, right, my heartbeat's gone iffy, time to pop a few pills.* That's not how it works. You take a pill to regulate the rhythm and the rate, once a day, as maintenance. You don't gulp the damned things down like aspirin with a headache. That's why missing the proper time for Bulldog's dose had been such a stupid thing to do.

I could see Ches taking his every morning—that part was easy enough. I hadn't asked him, but him taking his just before his run every day, that made sense. He'd likely have done that to make sure he had extra control over his cardio rate while he was actively trying to get it steady at the high end.

But enough to kill him, by accident? Not bloody likely. I wasn't having it. And from what I could tell, Miranda didn't believe it, either.

From somewhere downstairs, I heard a long, discontented *meow*; one of the cats had probably climbed into the window seat in the kitchen and found the moonlight. That always seemed to get the cats going, that moon out there, nights when it was lighting up the house inside—you'd think they were wolves, or something, the way they wail at the moon.

Next to me, Bree sighed, and shifted in her sleep. I raised myself up on one elbow, glancing down at the tumbled mass of hair. It had absolutely no colour in this light, but I wasn't really seeing it anyway. My brain was clicking away, turning over, revving itself up the way my heart does, sometimes. Good. I wanted to think about things—I needed to sort it out, somehow.

There was a lot of rubbish churning about, but one thing kept pulling my attention away from Bulldog and Ches, and making me look at it: I was pissed off at myself, still, for lashing out at Bree the way I had. She'd done nothing to earn that sort of bullshit from me. It was the sort of thing I'd pretty much stopped doing, ever since my first wife decided that a heroin overdose was preferable to being tried for killing a journalist with one of my microphone stands.

Yeah, I'd apologised and yeah, Bree had forgiven me. What's more, she'd meant it. But I was still furious and shaken with myself over having done it. I don't like landmines, and we've got a lot of them, still, in our history together. I had the feeling that particular explosion had been all about one of those.

136

But really looking at why I'd snapped at her, sorting out what had triggered it, was going to have to wait; other stuff had priority right now. Tomorrow morning, I was going to lock myself down in the studio with Mac and Luke and Tony, and do everything I possibly could, to get a perfect version of the piece I'd written for Bulldog Moody. When that was done, I was going to have to finish writing the induction speech, as well.

Oh, Christ, that speech.

There were ugly little things, knocking about at the back of my head, making me wonder just how much of what I thought I knew about Bulldog—even more importantly, what I felt about Bulldog—were true. Not knowing was a huge barrier between me and wanting to write that speech. What if not one word of it was true? How was I supposed to write the damned thing, much less get up on telly and share it with the world, read it as if it were gospel, if I didn't believe it?

Bree shifted again, and murmured. I saw that her shoulders were twitching. She does that sometimes; she has nightmares, I've never known about what, but they must be corkers, because she mutters in her sleep. Sometimes, she wakes up yelling. Once, just once that I remember, she actually did say something I could make sense of, something about not leaving. It was right after one of the three trips I'd made back to London, to see my wife, so it was probably on her mind. I remember what she said, *don't leave, I didn't mean it, please don't leave.* Can't imagine what she thought she'd done to make me leave, but dreams are like that.

I did what I usually do, laying the palm of my hand against her cheek for a few moments. For some reason, that always seems to calm her down when she started all that thrashing and muttering, and it worked tonight. There was enough moonlight in the room for me to see her the corners of her mouth curl up in a tiny smile, and then her faced relaxed again, smoothed out, and she sighed. That particular noise sounded a lot happier.

I twitched a strand of hair away from her face—she didn't need to choke on her own hair in the middle of a dream, you know? She didn't move at all; fathoms deep. My own mind went back to the lists she'd made from the thumb drive.

Dixon, Duckworth. LD. Initials? L Dixon—was that the same as L Duckworth? Bree'd thought so. I wasn't so sure, but then, I was sure about fuck-all, except that Ches Kobel hadn't got any business dying of a heart attack, hadn't taken an overdose of his Digoxin, hadn't died naturally…

Don't go there, you don't want to go there, don't…

There it was, the thing I'd been pushing away. One huge sodding ugly taste of reality, looking at me like a bogeyman, peering out, saying *right, here I am and I'm not leaving, so you might as well stare straight into my face.*

When you come right down to it, there's only four ways someone can die. It can be natural, age or illness or the fullness of time. It can be accident, or misadventure, or whatever it's called: hit in the head with a flowerpot falling out a window, walking through the countryside with your nose in a book and not realising you're in quicksand, stepping in front of a lorry because your mind's elsewhere and you weren't paying attention. Or, maybe, accidentally taking too much of your heart meds.

I didn't believe either of them, not about Ches. I didn't believe the third possibility, either, because there was no way Ches had committed suicide. That was so ridiculous, it didn't even need looking at.

That left one other thing. The fourth option, that last way to die…

"John?" Bree's voice jolted me out of it. She didn't sound sleepy, not even groggy. She was wide awake, all the way awake. "John, what are you doing? John, stop, please, you're hurting me!"

I jumped about a mile. I hadn't realised my hand was still resting on her face, my fingers twined in her hair. I hadn't realised I'd tightened my fingers, catching her hair, pulling it. She'd twisted sideways, to ease the pressure. I let go in a hurry.

"Bloody hell! Sorry, love. Didn't realise I had hold of your hair." I bent down and kissed her. "Go back to sleep."

As soon as she closed her eyes, my mind went right back to where I'd parked it when she woke up. The more I looked at it, the uglier it got.

I didn't believe Ches had died naturally. I was in good company, there; his doctor and Miranda didn't believe it, either. And I didn't believe he'd died accidentally, because the only way that seemed possible would be talking myself into believing that he'd suddenly eaten a handful of Digoxin, after a decade or more of taking one at the same time every day.

Which left me with, what? Fourth option?

I bit back on the word that wanted out. I couldn't believe that, either. Ches had been alone when he died, hadn't he? He'd actually rung up Sara Kildare before he'd headed out on that last run, and he'd been fine. Sara had said he'd been excited about the jam with Bulldog, about the ceremony, about the whole thing. That sounded like the same mood he'd been in when we'd last seen him.

So that fourth possibility, the one with the ugly word attached to it, the thing I didn't want to look at? That wasn't possible, either. You can't take someone's life by wishing for it, and you can't do it from miles away, either. Even if the bloke's been digging in the dirt and finding out that the history you've been telling people for the better part of a century is all wrong, you still can't do it...

"John?"

I jerked my head. The moonlight was moving across the bed; it was partly on my face but full on Bree's, lighting her, making her look like she was made of mother of pearl. Her eyes were wide open, steady, on me.

Shit. Don't say it, please don't say it…

"You think Ches was killed." Her voice was absolutely flat, calm, certain. "You think someone murdered him. Don't you?"

It wasn't a question; she knew. I hadn't said a word about it, I'd been trying not to believe it, but she knew.

As soon as I acknowledged that, one unpleasant item fell off my to-do list. Here it was, the reason I'd flipped my shit and snapped at her, back in the kitchen: she'd known what I was thinking, and I hadn't wanted to be thinking it, so I'd tried to shut her up, as if maybe that way, I could shut my own thoughts up, as well.

"Yeah." I heard myself say it, and closed my eyes. "Yeah, I do."

It was out, and that made it real, made it possible. Once I'd done that, everything changed, and my last shot at just sucking it up, letting it be, doing sod-all to deal with it, went out the window. I swung both legs out of bed.

"What time is it, Bree?"

She sat up herself, and turned toward her night table; I have a bad habit of sleeping through alarms, so she gets sole custody of the bedroom clock.

"About twenty past midnight. Where are you going?"

"I need to use your cell. It's down in the kitchen, right?" I knew what I was going to do, what I was going to have to do, if I ever planned to have a decent night's sleep again. "Back in a few minutes."

That was all I said. But I'd have bet the royalties from the last Blacklight tour that she knew just what I was going to do.

I don't act on straight instinct, usually; intuition is much more Bree's thing than mine. But the sense that Bulldog was mine, blood of my blood, made that way by the music we shared, was driving me. I needed the air between us to be clear. I needed to know.

Bree's cell was charging, next to her computer. It was full

140

moon outside, but moonrise was over, and the house was beginning to get dim around me. The cats moved around my feet, Wolfling and Simon making soft sounds, Farrowen talking with that harsh thing Siamese do.

I held on to Bree's phone for a good two minutes before I did anything with it. I don't know what I was waiting for, maybe something, anything at all, to tell me not to do what I'd come downstairs to do. But nothing happened.

I flipped the phone open, and watched the digital display light up. I scrolled down the programmed numbers. She has a few people in her cell directory that I haven't got in mine. The one I wanted was eighth one down her list.

Right. Showtime.

I hit the call button, and listened to the phone ring on Patrick Ormand's desk at San Francisco's Homicide department.

At half past four next afternoon, I set my 335 in its stand, looked round at my mates, and told everyone I was off to do a quick local errand.

I'd worked it out with Bree, ahead of time. No one needed to know where I was going, and in fact everything I'd said was true. It was an errand, and it was local; I'd got Patrick to agree to meet me in the Fillmore, at a great little cafe just down the hill from the hospital where they keep all my specialists.

I was actually running short on sleep. When I first punched Patrick's number in, I'd been thinking I'd leave him a message. It was the middle of the night, you know? Any normal bloke would be long gone from his work, having a cup of tea, watching the late news, getting laid, doing something, anything at all, that wasn't his damned job.

But of course, Patrick being Patrick, he was planted at his desk and he'd picked it up on the first ring. That put me at a disadvantage, because all I'd planned to do was leave a quick message

141

on his voicemail, *hey it's JP Kinkaid can you ring me in the morning, need to have a word with you,* in, out, ring off, and give myself time to think about what I wanted to say when I actually did talk with him. And instead, first ring, click, and there he was.

"Homicide, Patrick Ormand."

Shit. I cleared my throat. "Evening, Patrick. You're working rather late, aren't you?"

"JP?" His voice sharpened up. "What's wrong? Is everything okay? You? Did something happen to Bree?"

"We're fine." I didn't have the words ready; I had to say something, though. "Look, I was wondering—any chance we could hook up for a quiet conversation? I need to talk to you about something, and it's tricky. Not here—I'd have you over for lunch, but we've got a house full of people coming in and out, and I don't want them in on this particular talk. It's a private deal, see, and I—"

"When?"

"Soon as you can manage." This was easier than I'd thought it would be. He hadn't asked a single hard question. "I've got a rehearsal for the Hall of Fame induction jam in the morning, but sometime after that, we could maybe meet up somewhere, unless you're too..."

"Do you want to come here?"

"No!" That probably sounded rude, but it was true. I had a very cold feeling, that I was somehow betraying Bulldog by ringing Patrick up in the first place. There was no way this side of hell I was having that talk at Homicide. "No, let's do a cafe, or something. I don't know what's near you, and I'd need to take a taxi—Bree knows I'm ringing you and she knows why, but I'm not having her drive me. Maybe somewhere in between? There are a lot of Starbucks in the City."

"I can come to your neighbourhood." Crisp, clear, still no questions. That should probably have been reassuring, but it wasn't;

all my inner alarms, the little sirens that seemed to have Patrick Ormand's name all over them, were pinging away, and I wasn't sure why. "Do you have a place where they know you, where we can talk without being interrupted?"

"Interrupted by who? What, you mean, fans or groupies or something?" That actually got a grin out of me; too bad there was no one but the cats to see it. "I'm a sideman, Patrick, not a frontman. People really don't recognise me all that often. Now, if you were trying for a quiet uninterrupted conversation in a public place with Mac, that would be different. You'd get very thankful for Dom being there, after about two minutes, believe me. How do you feel about Mediterranean food? Kebabs and that lot? There's a good place we use, Persian food, regular spot for when Bree doesn't want to cook, just off Fillmore on Sacramento. Of course, I'm buying..."

So we'd set it up. Patrick hadn't asked a single question, not after satisfying himself that Bree and I were both okay. And for whatever reason, all my interior wires were humming like a tube amp turned up too high.

I couldn't sort it out. Not only had he not asked any questions, he'd jumped at my suggestion for a meeting. I looked at it, thinking: *right, John, you're imagining that.* I might have been, easily; my reactions to Patrick Ormand have been pretty muddled since we first had to deal with him.

But not this time. He'd cut me off in mid-sentence, jumping ahead, suggesting where to meet.

So I couldn't make sense of it, and that cost me a good hour's worth of kip. I might have nodded off earlier if I'd gone back up to bed, but there was Bree. So, right, I was a coward about it, but either she'd crashed, in which case I didn't want to risk waking her up again by tossing and turning myself, or else she was still awake, reading me like a book, knowing what was going on in my head even when I didn't. Truth is, I was more put off by the second possibility than the first one, and that's even though I know what a light sleeper she is. But I had the feeling I didn't really want her knowing why those wires I talked about were humming so hard.

So I was short of sleep, and not at my best next morning. Things were tingling and jabbing, especially an ominous jabbing little tremor, moving up and down my right leg. I spent most of the session working out "Moody's Blues" sitting down. If I was going to have to a nice walk up and down the hill in Pacific Heights later in the day, standing about holding a guitar for four hours first wasn't the brightest move.

Things were slightly uncomfortable between me and Bree. Nothing serious, just an odd little mood; I hadn't offered anything about what I'd set up with Patrick, not beyond the bare fact that I was meeting him, and she wasn't going to ask.

That's on me, that reluctance of hers; it's my fault, and I know it. She has this belief that if she asks me to do anything or not to do anything, it's all going to come crashing down round her ears. I get why she feels that way, that it goes back to her asking me not to go back to London to take care of Cilla when she'd had cancer and me going anyway, but that was nearly thirty years ago. Still, it's grown over the years, that fear; there's times I think she's waiting to ask me something she knows I won't possibly be able to refuse.

So she was staying silent, because I hadn't offered. And I was staying silent, because I was feeling guilty; I knew she wouldn't ask and I was counting on her not asking, because I didn't want to discuss it yet.

But of course, I was going to have to deal with the strain between us, and soon. With everything going on, I couldn't really afford to let it stretch out.

Bree being Bree, of course she didn't take it out on me or on the rest of the band. She'd told me she'd get a buffet lunch together and she did, food out on the sideboard in the dining room. She'd kicked the cats out and closed the doors, come downstairs to the basement studio, and waited for a break in the music to let me know she was going out.

"Hey, Bree." Luke had spotted her standing in the doorway before I did. "Need help with something?"

"No, nothing. I just came down to tell John that I left lunch out in the dining room, and to make sure the cats don't hide in there when you're done eating. But thanks for asking." She wasn't really making eye contact with me, or Luke, or anyone else. "If anyone wants coffee, the espresso machine's on the counter next to the fridge, and cups are above the sink. And if you want to just stack plates on the table, I'll get them in the dishwasher when I get home."

"Oi! Hang on a minute, Bree. You off shopping?"

I got off my stool, and put an arm around her waist. There was something in the way she was standing, the look on her face, a sort of distance, that worried me. I really don't like it when she seems remote from me. I brushed her ear with my lips.

"I'll tell you about it later, I promise." It was barely a whisper, and no one heard it but Bree. I felt her relax in the circle of my arm. Ridiculous, that what I thought, or said, or did, should have that kind of power to affect anyone else...

So at just about ten past four, I waved everyone toward the back garden with stuff to eat and drink and listen to, and took myself off to meet with Patrick.

Of course, he'd got there before I did; pure Patrick, always out after the advantage. There was a bottle of Pellegrino on the table, and some toasted triangles of pita bread in a basket. He'd obviously been there a few minutes.

"Hey, JP."

"Hey. Sorry to keep you waiting. Am I late?" I caught the waiter's eye, and nodded him over. They know us quite well, at

Cafe Houri. "Afternoon, Khalil—no, Mrs. Kinkaid's not with me today. Had time to look at the menu yet, Patrick?"

We ordered a round of Houri's excellent Persian food. I didn't plan on bringing up why I'd wanted to have this little face-to-face in the first place until after we'd finished. Luckily, Patrick didn't seem to be in any big rush, himself. We ate, we made small talk about food and politics and movies. We didn't say a word about anything that mattered until after Khalil had cruised by and taken our plates.

"All right." The restaurant had emptied out; we had about half an hour before they closed to prep for the dinner crowd. Patrick was watching me over the table, those dirty-ice eyes of his completely unreadable. "You wanted to talk to me about something? It must be something important, for you to call me after midnight. You said you guys were okay, right?"

"Yeah, we're fine. It's not about us, not really. And it's not major—just, important to me." It was tricky, meeting his eyes. "I ought to tell you, before I say anything else, that this is confidential. Completely confidential, just between the two of us, not official business. That needs to be clear."

"Are we talking about the commission of a crime?" Both his eyebrows were all the way up, but he hadn't got his predator face on, not yet. He wasn't hunting, he just wanted to know. "Because if we are, I may be the last person you should tell. I can't promise to conceal evidence or knowledge of a crime, JP. I'm a law enforcement official."

"Yeah, I know that." My throat had gone dry on me, and I reached for the Pellegrino. "I don't know whether there's been a crime done or not, Patrick. If there has been, it didn't happen anywhere near here. Would that make a difference, it not being on your turf? If there was a crime?"

He opened his mouth, and shut it again. He looked completely confounded. Satisfying as that was, it wasn't much help. I was

146

having enough trouble of my own, working out what I wanted to tell him, without having to wonder what was safe to tell him. But right now, it was his move.

"JP—look. Let's try it this way. You have something you want to tell me. It may or may not concern a crime. If a crime has, in fact, been committed, it wasn't in my jurisdiction. Is that accurate?"

"Yeah, it's accurate." Another mouthful of sparkling water, down the pipes. At that point, I wasn't sure whether I was thirsty or just stalling for time. "It's not complete, though. There's more to it, before I even get to details."

He was watching me, steady on. "Such as?"

"Ches Kobel is dead. You didn't know that, did you?"

I saw his face change. He didn't show a lot of feeling past the sudden thinning out of his lips and lines deepening around his mouth, but that was enough to show the reaction. He'd met Ches, as well; he'd hung with him at the Geezers gig at the Great American, drunk with him, talked music with him.

"Yeah, I didn't think you knew. Here's the deal, Patrick: I think there's been murder done. I don't think there's any way to prove it. And I have to tell you, straight up—I don't want to prove it. I don't want be right about this, not about it being murder, not about what I think happened, and really not about why it happened. I want to be wrong, all the way wrong. I want you to laugh in my face for being such a suspicious berk, is what I want. But I've got the feeling you won't."

The words were out, in one nervous explosive rush, and that was it. I couldn't take them back. But I wasn't committed, not yet, except by how much I needed to know the truth, how much not knowing was going to mess with my head. Whatever I told him from then on was going to depend entirely on what he said next.

Just then, he wasn't saying anything, he was processing. You could see the wheels and gears, meshing and moving, putting it

147

all together. Across the cafe, Khalil had parked himself in the doorway to the kitchen. We were the last patrons of the lunch hour, and they were getting ready to close.

"You think Ches Kobel was murdered." It was really peculiar. This was exactly the sort of thing that should have had him salivating, the smell of something wounded and guilty just upwind. But he wasn't eager, not at all; he was just being cautious. "And you aren't going to tell me why you think so, or how you think it happened, unless I promise I won't act on it in my official capacity. Because you don't want to believe it?"

I nodded.

"Okay." He said it, completely matter of fact. "It's a deal."

I just sat there, gawking at him like an idiot. He looked serious, intent, and I suddenly got it, he wasn't done talking yet.

"The problem is, I don't know what you want from me, JP." Khalil had moved out, closer to us; if Patrick was aware of it, he wasn't saying so. "I've said I won't take any official action. Now that you have my promise, what do you need from me? What is it you think I can do?"

I gave him the entire story then. The way I saw it, he'd sworn he wouldn't act on it, and in a weird way, that promise committed me to telling him. I hadn't asked him for it lightly, and he hadn't given it lightly. That much of a concession from him demanded as much from me.

I've said it before, Patrick's a fantastic listener. That comes with being a copper, of course, but it's more than that with him. The bloke takes information seriously, no matter what he plans to do with it.

So he listened, no interruptions. And when I finished, Khalil had brought back my change, and Patrick and I were both on our feet. I reached into my jacket pocket, and pulled out Ches's thumb drive.

"Here. Take it." My eyes were stinging. I'd done it, and no

148

turning back. I had a moment of hating myself, just wanting to fucking kick myself in fourteen places, wondering if I was ever going to be able to meet my own eye in the mirror again. Because it didn't matter what he did with whatever he found out. What mattered was, I hadn't been strong enough to keep my damned mouth shut. Any way I looked at it, this was an act of betrayal, of disloyalty. "The notes Ches made, for the book he was doing about Bulldog, they're all on here."

"You still haven't told me what you want me to do, JP. I know what you don't want—but what are you expecting from me? To find out what all this means?"

"That's it." Bulldog, damn it, why had I done this? Why couldn't I have left well enough alone? "I just want to know, Patrick, okay? Because I've got to stand up in front of a few million people next Wednesday and read a speech about Bulldog Moody's life. And right now, every word feels wrong. I feel like a liar. I have to know. I just hope I'm wrong. And you, well, you're a cop. You can get your hands on official channels, that lot. All-access. I just—I need to know, all right?"

"Sure. But there's one more thing." Still no predator, there. "I get the feeling you don't like me. I also get the feeling you don't trust me. So why do you keep asking me for help? Why tell me in the first place? Just making use of the obvious tool for the job?"

I stood there, staring at him. It was a damned good question. What's more, it was a question I'd never stopped to ask myself, or even think about. And I wasn't going to think about it now, apparently, because I just opened my mouth, and let it rip.

"I don't like you very much, no." Oh, bloody hell. "At least, not when you're doing your Big Bad Wolf thing. I didn't like you jerking us around in New York, back when you were investigating Perry Dillon's murder. I didn't like you looking at Bree like she was Little Red Riding Hood, like you couldn't wait to lick her blood off your lips. And yeah, I didn't much like you hanging her out for Terry Goff to shoot at, back in Cannes. But I also owe you, both times. Because I know damned well you could have put Bree away for ten years if you'd wanted to, aiding and comforting a murderer, whatever the legal term is, and you didn't. Bree's not in jail, she's free, and Terry Goff didn't shoot her. She's alive, and she's with me. And yeah, you fucked that up right royally, and we both know it. But you covered her when the shooting started. So I owe you, for my old lady's sake."

"And?"

Bastard. Of course, he was going to make me say it. Of anything I couldn't stomach about Patrick Ormand, this little trick of his—twisting down the last screw for maximum power tripping—was right up there, near the top of the list.

Ah, fuck him. Couldn't live without it, couldn't he? I locked eyes with him, and said it.

"You want it, mate? You've got it. I don't like that you fancy Bree. I hate that you're ten years younger than I am. I don't really get warm and fuzzy when I remember her half-naked in the pool, with you a few feet away. Watching you dance with her used to make me want to use the guitar for something Les Paul never designed it for."

The son of a bitch was actually grinning. Oh, right, he was banking it down, but it wanted out. That smug little shit...

I kept talking. If it was going to be out, might as well be all of it, you know?

"But when you say I don't trust you, you've got it wrong. I might not trust you if I thought it was about something you wanted—I don't see you letting anything get in your way, then. But for something like this, information, fact and reality and the rest of it? Truth is, there's no one I'd trust more. And that's not exactly a love-note from me, either. I just think it's the way you're made. If I asked you to find something and you tell me you've done it, you wouldn't be lying to me. I don't know how I know that, but I do, all the way down and bone deep. And right now, this matters to me more than damned near anything else. Bulldog Moody, this is my life here, what I do, what I am. It matters to me."

I stopped, not because I'd finished, but because I'd lost all control over my voice. One more word, I'd have been in tears. And there was no way I was giving Patrick Ormand that kind of advantage.

There was a long uncomfortable silence. Patrick broke it.

"When do you need the information? I gather there's a serious time constraint here. I can take four days and go hunt things down, that's not a problem, but when do you have to have it? Before the induction?"

I nodded. I still had no voice.

"I'll do my best." His voice was still absolutely matter of fact. You'd have thought we'd been talking about the food. "I'll keep you posted. And by the way, JP, just so you know? I'm not hot for Bree. I like her more than I like most people, but then, I like you almost as much. It's a pity the sentiment isn't returned, but I certainly understand your reasons. I'll check this out, make some calls. Thanks for lunch."

Chapter Ten

"...I want to talk for a moment, about the effect American blues had in some places a long way from America."

A few years ago, when I finally admitted to myself that nothing in the world was going to make my annual MRI anything other than completely miserable, I developed a trick.

It's a technique, really, and a damned useful one. It started off reserved exclusively for the whole MRI experience. The older I got, the more I felt I needed a way to get through being stripped naked, shot up with dye, and shoved into a metal coffin to have magnetic pulses banged off my skull, so that a bunch of chirpy MRI technicians could tell me not to move while they monitor what the multiple sclerosis is doing to my brain and body as time goes by.

What I did was, I worked out a way to focus my mind on something cool and calming. I call the process going Zen. It's a sort of trip, into deep inner space.

"...Now, I'm a few years younger than most of the UK guitarists who were weaned on American blues. I'm talking about the greats:

Clapton, Page, Peter Green. They were already doing sessions or in working bands before I was old enough to get out there myself. There's a lot more, but you don't need a full list. Most of them are already members of the Hall of Fame anyway..."

That whole going Zen thing worked out so well that, these days, it's become my technique for getting through anything that smells too much like shit. I've tried explaining it to Bree, and I think she gets it—she can't seem to do it herself, though, more's the pity. Since most of the time, what she flips her shit over is about me, you'd think she'd be able to take that cue. But it doesn't happen.

"...For a lot of us blue-eyed types, the history of the music we played was purely a head trip. We all knew our Robert Johnson, our Reverend Gary Davis, our Muddy Waters. We all knew the licks, we had them down bone-deep, the same way we could all play Johnny B Goode in our sleep. All Chuck's children were out there playing his licks, but before there was rock and roll, long before, there was the music out of the Mississippi Delta, following the players north to Chicago and Minneapolis and New York like a river of sound..."

"John?"

"Mmmm." I was nice and relaxed, Bree between me and the bed, her looking up into my face and my fingers laced through hers. The past half hour had been brilliant; all the sex that hadn't happened last night had shown up tonight, and we'd just had a hell of a ride. So there we were, feeling the best kind of lazy I know.

I managed to lift my head enough to touch her cheekbone with the tip of my tongue. She had a lovely glaze of sweat, salty and perfect, pure Bree. "How you doing, love? Am I too heavy? You had enough of me for tonight?"

"...And for a lot of us, that timeline and that geography became almost mythical, a sort of Camelot. Everyone knows about Graceland. But not everyone knows about Hattiesburg or Rosedale or

Clarksdale or Sundial Records. It's like a secret handshake amongst us English white boys, an entrée into a very exclusive private players club: who's your main man? John Lee Hooker? Son House? Me? Oh, mine's Bulldog Moody..."

"Nope. You're just right." She meant it, too. I know the stereotype: after a raucous belly-bump, women are supposed to want to cuddle and men are supposed to want a good long kip. We don't go that road, me and Bree. Yeah, I do get sleepy, that's just physics, but I like staying right where I am for a few minutes, after the big bang. There's something miraculous about the way her curves fit with my angles, head to toe. "John? Did you—oh God, what are you..."

Whatever she'd meant to ask, it went straight out of her head for the next fifteen minutes or so; I made sure of that. That's the other thing about not falling asleep, the energy I do get back is something I can use to take her places.

So I took her where I wanted her to be and watched her rippling like piano music, the full scale, up and down until she was limp and peaceful. Side by side, bits of us touching somewhere, that's when the cuddling kicks in. It's got nothing to do with sentiment—it's about her being too drained to do anything else but cuddle until her battery recharges. Since it's her battery we're talking about, not mine, she makes the call.

"John?"

"What, love?" She had her back to me just then, lying on her side, and I lifted her hair off her neck so that I could nibble. I've got a thing for her neck. "Mmmm, you've gone completely salty, lady."

"Sweat, you mean? Well, you ought to know—it's your fault." There'd been laughter in her tone, but it faded. "John—I don't want to kill the mood, but..."

She stopped, and I sighed. Damn.

"Right. You want to know what happened with Patrick."

She didn't say anything, but I felt her nod. I'd known this was coming; I'd promised her before she'd gone out that I'd tell her about it. She wouldn't be asking me, otherwise. The problem was, I wasn't sure how much I wanted to tell her. Bree knows I've got issues about Patrick Ormand, especially where she's concerned. That wasn't what was making me back away from having to tell her.

Just because it wasn't a problem didn't make me giving her the conversation word for word any easier. Basically, if I told her just the way it had gone down, I was going to feel like a total berk, and that's not something I enjoy. Feeling like a berk without any help is bad enough, but knowing I'd put my foot in it by losing it, and throwing a tantrum that was really just barnyard jealousy, that was even worse.

"Okay." I touched my tongue to the spot just behind her right ear. I was probably hoping I could distract her, because that spot's one of her on switches. If I'm being honest with myself, I probably was looking for a way out of having to dish.

She didn't take the bait, though; if anything I was doing was turning her on, she had it under control. I gave up, and gave in.

I think I've said it before, Bree's not a great listener. She gets impatient with people, or something twigs her own frame of reference and there she is, interrupting, jumping into it. She can derail a conversation, completely change its course, in a matter of seconds. I'm her one exception: when she's listening to me, she's giving me all her attention. Mostly I love her giving me that space—makes it easier to sort out what I want to say. There's usually no one else I'd rather talk to, and I can tell her damn near anything, just let it out, let it flow. There are times I've done that and wanted to kick myself afterward, when I realise that something I've said hurt her.

Tonight, I picked every word I said. I gave her the meat of it, the substance. I let her know that Patrick had wanted to know why I kept coming to him. And I was straight up about the way the talk had gone when I'd made it clear I wasn't going to ask him unless he promised to keep it unofficial and off the books; the inner censor, the one in my head, didn't seem to have any problem with letting her know that particular part of the exchange, pretty much word for word.

"So he's willing to just get the information? He actually agreed to not take any official action about it? That's really cool." She'd sat up, her hair swinging around her shoulders. I'm glad I have enough money to not have to think about what heating our house costs; Bree sleeps nude, and watching her hair not quite covering her upper half is one my own personal pleasures. I'd pay whatever it took to keep her out of pyjamas; I never grow tired of it. The few times she's had flu and couldn't get warm, she's worn pyjamas. Damned flannel passion-killers…

"I want some water. Did you remember to take your meds? Are you thirsty?"

"Yeah, I did, but I wouldn't say no to a glass of water, if you're offering."

I watched her head off toward the master bathroom. The view from the rear was every bit as nice as the front look. Bloody hell, I was getting turned back on. Nice to know I could still get there at my age, and with my dodgy health, but I had no idea whether Bree would be up for it. After all, it was late and I'd already given her a workout tonight.

She came back to bed, and curled up next to me; her lids looked heavy, very sated and sleepy. Right. So much for a second round. Of course, her being ready to nod off, that had its own upside; it meant I didn't have to tell her about the rest of that conversation with Patrick Ormand.

"You look ready to crash." I kissed her, but the goodnight I was going to offer up didn't get said. Instead, she laid her palm against my cheek, a mirror gesture for the one I'd used myself, last night, when she was thrashing in her sleep and talking under her breath.

For some reason, that got to me. And just as I was digging it, liking the realisation that whole mirroring action had left me with—*you're a jammy sod, Johnny my lad, lucky as it comes, yeah?*—she spoke up.

"Thank you for trusting me enough to tell me about what went down between you and Patrick. I know you didn't want to." Her voice was quiet, so soft I could barely hear her; she left her hand where it was a moment longer, resting against my cheek, and then moved it off me, and snuggled down under the covers. "Goodnight, John."

"Bree?" Damn, damn, damn. No choice, not now; she'd just kicked my legs out from under me. If I didn't tell her all about it, I was going to feel a complete fraud. "Bree, love, look. You haven't heard all of it. There's—well, there's more."

"Okay." She had her back to me, but she spooned, rubbing against me. Damn the girl, this was going to be tricky. "What was it?"

I told her. I'm not really sure where that convenient censor in my head had got itself off to, maybe it was having a cigarette break or something somewhere, but I told her what Patrick had asked and I told her what I'd said, as much of it as I could remember. I gave it to her word for word. And yeah, I felt a complete prat. But she got the truth.

I thought she might melt down over it, give me hell—after all, I'd given her cause, and there's plenty of women who'd be mortified, hearing their old man confess to having had that sort of conversation about them with another bloke. But when I was done, she was right where she'd been, up against the bits of me I'd mentally put away for the night. And when she finally said something—the silence went on too long for my taste—she didn't sound narked. She didn't sound tired, either.

"You blew up at Patrick Ormand because you thought he was

hot for me." She wriggled suddenly, right up against my groin, and right then, she lost her shot at telling me she was too tired. Just as well she didn't seem to want to tell me that, anyway. "You actually said that to Patrick Ormand, about me? In a *restaurant?* You're not kidding, John? You really did that?"

"You're damned right I did." I turned her over and pinned her. She arched her back, and I bit her neck, and she snatched a kiss up at me. I pulled my face back, laughing down at her. "And you're loving it. Crikey, look at you, you're damned near purring. Not quite the reaction I thought I'd get, but I'll take it, believe me."

"Why not take me instead?" My lips were moving down off her throat, pushing the hair out of my way. She was keeping both hands at her sides, letting me do whatever I wanted to do, and she'd gone breathless. "Much more fun."

We slept in next morning, not oversleeping, just not setting the alarm. The rest of the band weren't due to show up until early afternoon—Luke had promised his daughter Solange he'd stop off at one of the state universities and pick up some information for her, and even though he could have done it by phone, he'd told us he fancied a look at the campus, whether it was likely to appeal to Solange. Personally, I suspected he wanted a few hours out of the basement studio, but either way, we had the morning free, me and Bree.

We must have been thoroughly knackered from all that rowdy sex, because we slept until nearly ten. A quick snog before showering, dressed, and downstairs to find Bree putting together batter for these muffins she makes, with soft mouthfuls of candied ginger in them, and all sorts of spices. Even the weather out of doors was good.

"Morning, baby. There's coffee dripping. These are going in as soon as the oven preheats—ten minutes until breakfast, okay?" She finished stirring the batter—she doesn't use any of her fancy stand mixers for muffins, she says the batter's supposed to be lumpy, otherwise they're pancakes. "Oh, and your phone beeped, a little while ago."

"Where is—oh, right. Thanks." She slid it across the table to me. I flipped it open; one missed message, sent about ten minutes earlier.

"*(beep) John, this is Miranda. I just heard back from Stan Minkus. He's spoken to Paula Kobel in Baltimore, by phone, and there's not going to be an autopsy after all. Ches Kobel was cremated Tuesday morning.*"

It was right around then—the moment when I realised that, no matter what dirt or truth or whatever Patrick Ormand managed to dig up about how and why Ches had died, there wasn't going to be any real way to prove it—that I tapped into a whole new level, a whole new meaning, of going Zen.

I rang Miranda back, straightaway. I don't know, maybe I made a noise, but I must have done something to clue Bree in, because she stopped stirring the muffin batter, and stared at me. I remember thinking she looked the wrong side of silly, with that big wooden spoon just hanging there in space, dropping batter back into the bowl, *drip drip drip*.

Miranda picked up on the second ring. "John?"

"Yeah, it's me." Bree was still staring, not stirring. I mouthed her mum's name at her; I can't imagine why I thought that was likely to get her to relax, because it didn't. She seemed to get tenser. "Thanks for letting me know. How'd you find out, about him being cremated?"

"Stan got a call back from the sister in Baltimore." Miranda sounded odd, crisper even than usual, and I suddenly found myself wondering if it was anger I was hearing. "She hadn't heard the phone message until after she got back from the cremation, in Cleveland. The number Stan got, from the woman at the Hall

159

of Fame—what's her name? Sara something or other?"

"Sara Kildare." I was watching Bree; she'd put the bowl and the spoon down on the table, and headed for the coffee pot. She was reaching for cream, and a spoon—that meant she was making me a cup. She drinks it black, no sugar, herself; she says she likes her caffeine honest, not all tarted up. "What about her?"

"Nothing, except that the phone number she gave Stan was Paula Kobel's home number, not her cell phone." Her voice sagged, suddenly. "So Paula Kobel had no idea there was any question about the cause of her brother's death until she got home to Baltimore and found the message on her answering machine. And by that point, it was too late."

"Okay." Bree'd set the coffee down, and I took a mouthful. "Look, Miranda, I've got a question. Even if Ches hadn't been cremated, how likely was it that this Minkus bloke would have found anything?"

"That would have depended entirely on what Stan was looking for." She'd sharpened up again, Dr. Miranda Godwin, all her flags flying. It's amazing, what getting someone started on their own speciality will do; I've sometimes wondered if I do the same thing, when I go on about music. "And before you ask, John, yes, I do have a fairly good idea what that would be. Do you seriously want me to run down all the possibilities?"

"No point, is there?" Bree'd gone back to the stove. She was dropping batter into the muffin tins. The kitchen smelled like coffee, and ginger, and some spice I couldn't put a name to, mysterious and rich. "Even if he'd been bunged full of rat poison, there's no way to prove it. Right? No way at all."

"No way at all," she agreed. "So that's that. Hug my daughter for me, please, John. And if I don't see you before the show, have a nice trip to New York."

We rang off. And right then, that whole new Zen thing began to kick in.

160

It was very weird. It wasn't that I was blowing off that heart attack, Ches meeting up with a chilly death out there near the lake, with the gleaming glass roof of the Hall of Fame museum behind him. I was still convinced, just as certain as I'd been before, that he shouldn't have died, that he'd been helped along. I still wanted to be proved wrong, just as much as I had before. I still needed to know, just as badly as I had before Miranda's call, and maybe even worse.

But Ches was gone, gone completely—there was nothing left of him but ash. Stan Minkus could throw a wine and cheese party, he could get Miranda and every pathologist in Ohio together, they could sift through those ashes from now until the day after forever, and they wouldn't be able to find anything. The only way I was going to know for certain, or at least enough to take the weight of being in the dark about what had really happened off my mind, was by way of an entirely different person sifting through very different ashes.

It was all down to Patrick Ormand now. And no matter what he found, it wouldn't change anything. He could change his mind, go back on his word, decide he had to play Great Detective and follow the blood trail, and it wouldn't make one penny's worth of difference. He couldn't prove anything; all he could do was gather his information, make his best guess, and tell me. It was out of his hands, out of my hands. He could find out, I could find out, but it didn't matter. Neither of us could do anything about it.

The pressure was gone. In the meantime, we were leaving for New York Saturday morning, I still had the rest of the speech to write—not to mention tailor it down to a workable six minutes, maximum—and there were rehearsals to deal with.

There was also some business we needed to take care of, nothing to do with Bulldog or Ches Kobel or the induction, purely Blacklight-related. I'd known it was coming, just not when, and it was something I was looking forward to. But for now, it was all the way at the back of my mind.

I'd been expecting Luke and Mac early afternoon, but they surprised me by showing up a good half-hour early. The muffins had come out of the oven a few minutes earlier, and I'd eaten one, still warm and crumbly. Bree got the door, and Mac and Luke came in together.

"Morning. Or is it afternoon already?" I was wiping ginger crumbs off my lips. Something was going on; they both had that look, what I always think of as their band-business faces.

"No, it's still morning, for about another ten minutes. But we want a huddle with you, before Tony gets here." Mac had stopped in his tracks, sniffing. "My God, this house smells gorgeous. What's that spice?"

"Bree made gingerbread muffins for breakfast. There's a couple left. If you're very, very nice to her, she might let you have one." The light had gone off in my head. "Are we talking about having Tony along for the *Book of Days* tour? That what the huddle's about?"

"That's it, yeah. We've got Ian and Carla ready for a conference call, if we can use your phone for it." Luke was sniffing the air, as well. "Are there enough of those left for me? Those muffins, I mean?"

I got the details of what they had in mind out of them while they were stuffing themselves with the leftovers from breakfast, with Bree hovering round the table, making sure they got blood orange marmalade and maple syrup and coffee. It was all straight up, nothing fancy. The three of us had agreed it was a good idea, back in Cincy on the way to Ofagoula. I'd mentioned it, at the hotel, and Tony had made cautiously approving noises; just as importantly, so had Katia.

So Mac and Luke had put the idea to the Bunker Brothers, Blacklight's rhythm section, Calvin Wilson and Stu Corrigan.

According to Mac, they'd both been enthusiastic to say the least, and that meant getting Ian and Carla into the loop. Carla would handle the arrangements and PR stuff—this would be the first time Blacklight had toured with someone who wasn't a member of the band since my first quick European tour with them, back in 1977, before I'd been formally asked to join. Ian had the figures ready for Tony, damned near down to the penny, and he'd be getting the contract together. All it needed now was the formal offer out on the table.

It was Bree who thought to ring Tony's house and get Katia on the phone. After all, as she pointed out, this wasn't a matter of springing a big surprise on Tony; Katia was his wife, and she had a right to be there when the offer was made. Bree sounded really fierce about it, and I knew why.

"Want a touring mate, do you? Someone to go shopping in Milan with?" I shot her grin, and she went pale, her way of letting me know I'd scored a hit. "No, you're right, love. Katia ought to know. Ring her up, by all means."

So when Tony and Katia arrived, we had Ian and Carla already on the line, with the speaker phone turned up. Everyone settled round the kitchen table, and Ian made Tony the offer.

Basically, Blacklight has a nice straightforward policy about this sort of thing. If someone just sits in with the band for a song or two during a show, that's a jam, and that's how it stays; there's no money involved. But a tour—or in my own case, for someone joining the band as a member—that's different. It's equal shares, split between all of us.

And yeah, the Bombardiers do the same thing, but we're not talking about similar numbers. That got made very clear when Katia, who handles Tony's finances the way Bree's always handled mine, started asking the big questions.

"So, how big a tour are we talking about?" Ian had laid it out, the basic 'we'd like to extend an offer...' deal. Katia was taking notes, electronically I mean; she's got this fancy toy, sort of half cell phone and half palm device. "What kind of numbers would Tony be seeing? And would there be a base guarantee on the numbers?"

"He'd be seeing the same as everyone else in the band." Ian sounded very crisp. We'd probably got him away from dinner or a nice night in front of the telly or something, since it was just about half past nine at night in London. "Equal shares is official Blacklight policy, and always has been. Equal shares would work out to six points, in this case."

"Six points of what?"

"Of the net." That was Carla. "Ian, do you need the 2005 tour numbers? Because I've got them up onscreen."

"No, that's all right. I've got them." Ian cleared his throat. "Right, here we go. Let's say Tony had been with the band on the 2005 tour. His take—this is in dollars, of course—would have been $2,653,070.23. That's figuring for six points of the net take, but not including the merchandising. That brings in a lot of revenue, the merchandising does."

"Two mil–" Katia's voice had gone very faint. Tony looked as if he'd been hit with a rock, just completely gobsmacked. "Two— you said million? Two million dollars?"

"Two million, six hundred thousand and some change. But remember, that's just an example, not a hard number. We're talking about the *Book of Days* tour, and that's going to be bigger— has to be, since we'll be supporting a double disc. So the money on this one's going to be higher, even split six ways instead of five, and even considering the tour costs are going to be higher than 2005." He gave a good long sigh. "And don't get me started on the tour costs, all right? We're working that out, believe me."

"Right." He'd just brought up a point I wanted to know more about myself. "Ian, what are we looking at for starters, this tour? Have we got anything solid yet?"

164

"Yeah, we do. We're starting the booking first of the month, that and the rental at Shepperton. Studio H, this time, the big soundstage; Nial already has the word out to the staging crew. The way this one's planned so far, it's looking to cover about 50 dates, arenas, call it about the same ticket scale and cost, just for starters."

"So revenues should be about 30% higher." Mac always seemed to have the math right there in his head. It was habit with him—back in the early days, Chris Fallow, our brilliant manager, had made him and Luke take classes in economics and financial management. Damned good thing, too. "A thirty per-cent increase for starters, that'd make each of our projected shares of the tour about $3,800,000, if my sums are right. Tony? Sorry, mate, did you say something?"

"No." His voice was just about as gone as Katia's had been. He cleared his throat, and tried again; he still looked blank with dis-belief, and I found myself wondering if he'd ever stopped to think about the kind of money a band like Blacklight takes in during a major tour. "Unless you're talking about that soft squishy popping noise. Pay no attention, that was just the top of my head explod-ing. Holy shit, guys, are you serious? Nearly four million dollars?"

"Give or take a few hundred thousand." Carla was back on. "My math matches up with yours, Mac. That's the basic con-firmed for now—and when I say confirmed, I mean guaranteed, under the standard contract clauses, and not including the per diem. But if the tour gets extended, of course that number goes up. That's always a possibility. So what's your take, Tony? Do you want to run this by a lawyer first, or your manager? I'll need to know pretty soon, the sooner the better, in fact. The people in the London office will need to get the contract together and I'll need the lead time to get the PR stuff organised. Blacklight's never toured America with a hired gun before."

"Besides, the stage setup for this one's not like anything we've

165

ever done before." That was Luke. "We'd need more lead time for adding keyboards even with a simple set, but this one isn't simple, it's new to all of us. Very revolutionary. So yeah, soonest is best."

"Lawyer, manager, um, sure, no problem." Tony had his voice back; he was grinning, and bouncing in his chair. "I think, right now, that I can say yes to this. I do need to run it past the rest of the Bombardiers, but that's just to let them know. We're not touring or anything at the moment, so I wouldn't be letting them down. And our record label doesn't get a vote. So put me down for the tour and send me the paperwork. Or actually, send it to Katia. And then let me know where I need to be, and when, and I'll be there."

So that was that, a nice done deal, no complications or issues to deal with. Ian and Carla both made the appropriate *happy to have you aboard* noises, we rang off, and headed downstairs to rehearse "Moody's Blues" for the Hall of Fame show. When we left the kitchen for the basement door, me being the good host and being the last one down the stairs, I looked back and saw Bree shoving Katia into a chair and lighting up like a Christmas display herself. I hadn't heard those two make noises like this since Bree had shown Katia her engagement emerald.

I followed the others downstairs, grinning to myself all the way into the basement studio. Blacklight was getting Tony and his amazing barrelhouse piano chops along for the ride, and Bree was getting her best friend to hang out with. She'd never done a European tour with me before, and something told me that, on her own, she'd have found it got pretty boring after a week or two, with no one to keep her company. Between living on the other side of the world and hiding away from my working life until my first wife died, Bree wasn't close to the other band wives. Besides, as glamorous as it sounds to most outsiders, playing rock and roll is my job. It's my work. And doing my job, my work, I do it right, which means I'm busy.

But with Katia coming along, Bree was going to have someone right there to wander with, sightsee with, have meals with while I was off in an arena somewhere in Berlin or Lisbon or Prague, bored half off my skull during one of the endless soundchecks our sound bloke, Ronan Greene, loves to make us do. So right now, I couldn't imagine any better way that conference call could possibly have ended.

The enthusiasm about Tony signing on for the tour got into the music that day. We ended up not only rehearsing "Moody's Blues" until I was completely satisfied with it, but also a couple of songs from *Book of Days*, as well. They were songs Tony'd never played; "Remember Me," the one I'd written in my head onstage at Frejus last year, after we'd nearly lost Mac to a racist sniper called Terry Goff, seemed to particularly hit all Tony's buttons. He got into it hard and fast, coming up with some viciously edgy piano lines for the breaks into the verses.

We'd been downstairs a good two hours before we got forced into taking a break. Bree came down and stuck her head round the edge of the studio door. Since she rarely interrupts me when I'm downstairs, I stop when she does, because her being there means whatever it is, it's important.

"John?" She was holding my cell. She keeps it upstairs with her when I'm working down below; it gets rotten reception downstairs and I probably wouldn't hear it over the guitars and whatnot, anyway. "Call for you."

I raised an eyebrow—*who?*—but she stayed quiet. That meant that whoever was on the line, Bree was thinking it might be something I didn't want anyone else to know about.

I set the guitar back on the stand—I'd been playing my Zemaitis, Big Mama Pearl, just to give her a workout, but she's an extremely heavy axe, and I was just as pleased to have a rest. I nodded at the band. "Back in a tick," I told them, and followed Bree out.

167

She surprised me. Instead of heading upstairs to the kitchen, she went out the back door of the garage, and into the rear garden. By the time we'd made it over to the lawn chairs, both my eyebrows were up.

"Katia's still upstairs. I thought you'd rather have this be private." She wasn't smiling. "It's Patrick Ormand. He says he's calling from Hattiesburg."

Chapter Eleven

"...In autumn of 1971, I went to see something called the American Folk Blues Festival, at the Royal Albert Hall in London. I was twenty years old, and I'd been doing live gigs and sessions for a few years. I was a veteran."

It took me a moment of getting my stomach to settle down, before I could really give my attention to that conversation with Patrick.

"...The Festival was a sort of travelling show all over Europe—it had been going on since the early sixties, bringing American blues legends to Europe and letting people hear what the blues were all about..."

It was nuts. I'd asked him barely one day earlier to look into things. Last I'd heard, he was going to make a few phone calls. What in hell was he doing in Hattiesburg, Mississippi, assuming Bree had heard him properly?

"...That show at the Albert Hall is one of the things I remember best about those years—the memory of it shines. It was everything I'd hoped it would be, up to a point. There was one crucial thing missing.

169

I'd seen the occasional blues gig, a single player, but this? Jimmy Reed, John Lee Hooker, Bukka White—the performers list looked like the guest list at the backstage door in Blues Heaven. If you were lucky, if you hit every note right in this life, St. Peter would give you an all-access badge. That's how good the line-up was."

"Oi, Patrick." I'd taken the phone, and sat down on one of our garden chairs. Bree settled herself into another one, watching me. "Is everything all right?"

"I'd got a fantastic seat, eight rows back from the stage. I remember watching every move everyone made, telling myself to remember the licks, the fingering, how it was done..."

"Hey, JP. Everything's fine, if you happen to like the weather in Mississippi. I don't, much." He sounded perfectly normal, but of course, his voice never gives much away. Cops are good at hiding things, and Patrick was brilliant at it. First night we'd met him, investigating a murder in my dressing room backstage at Madison Square Garden, he'd hid what he already knew and he did it so well, he'd snookered us completely. I'd never forgotten it, and I wasn't about to.

"I thought you were going to make some calls." It was windy, even with the high fences round our back garden; Bree's hair was lifting up at the ends, and the fruit trees and climbing roses were rustling and moving about. "That's what you told me, anyway. So what the hell are you doing in Mississippi?"

"Chasing down your information." His voice was totally neutral. Infuriating git. "For starters, in about half an hour, I'm going to be meeting up with a nice old woman. I'm probably going to get stuck drinking stuff I thought I'd never have to drink again after I left the south—mint juleps, for pity's sake. Her name is Cassandra Chenery. Does that name ring any bells, JP? She was born and raised in Hattiesburg."

"...Here's some synchronicity, between then and now: That 1970 tour, Bulldog Moody was supposed to be playing. I went to the show

170

thinking he was going to be there, and I had a plan: I was going to stand outside the backstage door and wait for him to come out. I'd introduce myself and tell him I was a blues bloke, that we had that in common, that even though I was a skinny white kid from South London, on the inside I was really a black Delta blues player. Complete and total fan boy, I was..."

"Cassandra Chenery?" I caught Bree's eye; she was still watching me, her hands in her lap, not saying anything. "Can't say it does. Why should it? Who is she?"

"She's the daughter—the legitimate daughter—of a woman named Elaine Chenery. According to Cassandra, her mother was a nurse, a volunteer—she worked on the local Army base after the First World War. And she says no one ever called her mother anything but Lainey."

I was quiet. There'd been something peculiar about the choice of words, the way he'd emphasised "legitimate" daughter. But something else was pinging at my memory, something from that thumb drive, something Ches had written. *Lainey C...*

It came straight into my head, all of it, as if the entire line of broken shorthand had just been sitting there right behind my eyes, waiting for me to look at it again. *Rec. unavail—Lainey C, hospital. LD, meetings? Check w/old res; illegit. births/Army doc, children might know...*

Illegitimate births. Children might know.

"*...so I sat there, waiting for Bulldog Moody. I watched Jimmy Reed, and Bukka White, I got my first taste of zydeco with Clifton Chenier playing, but all the time, I was waiting for Bulldog Moody. And he wasn't there. The show went on, it finished, and I went out of doors and waited by the backstage door until someone with the tour came out, and I asked, where's Bulldog Moody? Turned out he'd had a heart attack, a small one, about a week before the tour started, and he'd had to cancel.*"

"JP? You still there?"

171

I came out of it, and realised I'd been staring at Bree. She'd gone very pale. There must have been things going on in my face, thoughts she could identify.

"Yeah, I'm still here. So this girl—this nurse. She was called Lainey, Lainey Chenery? I don't know much about the south. Was Lainey not a common name, or something? The name, I mean. Was it unusual back then, 1920 or whenever? Because if it wasn't, then I can't sort out why it should mean anything."

"Yes, it's unusual. Back then, it was usually Ellie—hell, it still is, or at least it's the one I've come across most of my life. And I'm from the south, sort of, even if a lot of delta types like to excommunicate Florida from Dixie membership."

"Right." And of course, there was the main thing, the big thing I'd only just thought about: this woman, Lainey Chenery, Lainey C? She was there, she was from there, Hattiesburg, the place Ches had told us he was going to for research...

"That thumb drive note, about Lainey C—it seems to fit." All of a sudden, Patrick's voice wasn't quite so neutral anymore. There was a note in it, the sound of him smelling blood. I could see his face, picture it in my head: Patrick Ormand, sniffing about. "But I'll know more once I talk to Cass Chenery, or at least I hope so. I'll call you when I'm done."

I opened my mouth, and closed it again. For a moment, there, I'd had no voice. "Sounds good. Keep me posted—do you need some dosh for this, by the way? Money, that is? We can wire you what you need. And by the way, you never answered me. What in hell are you doing in Mississippi? Last we talked, you said you were going to do this on the phone."

"Well, I had the time off." There he was, neutral again. "I decided to take it. I get restless sometimes. I'll let you know what the trip cost me, once it's over. And don't worry, I'm not going to be proud about it—the flight out here wasn't cheap, what with it being a same-day booking. Remember, JP, I can't bill you for my

172

time or work on this, even if I wanted to. I'm not a licensed PI. But you'll get a bill for expenses."

I stayed quiet. I wanted a real answer, and I'd sussed that waiting him out was the best way to get it.

"I called a few old friends down south." I'd been right; me staying quiet had forced it out of him. "Local police people, a couple of army guys. They did some fast checking and got me a few facts, some names, some dates. Those particular facts and dates mostly had to do with things that happened in Hattiesburg, a long time ago. So I decided to head out here."

Bree was still watching my face, her hands in her lap. I smiled at her, a real smile, and watched her face relax, loosen up. She still wasn't ready to offer up a real smile of her own, but she did lose the edge off that lost, tight look. That was a look she could lose all of, as far as I was concerned; seeing it there brought back memories of our early days together, when she was still a baby, really, and I was still married to someone else. She used to get that look too often, then.

"Right," I told Patrick. "You said mostly to do with Hattiesburg. What were the parts that weren't?"

"Some information from the Chicago police, old stuff. An incident from 1938, to do with an armed robbery, about a guy named Charlie Duckworth. And military records—there was that thing about Leavenworth, on the thumb drive." I could almost hear him shifting at the other end of the phone. "Look, JP, I need to head out. One thing every good southern boy learns early, it's to never keep a lady waiting. I'll let you know what I find out."

The phone clicked. He'd rung off.

We sat in the garden for a while, just hanging out. I wanted to process some of what I'd got out of Patrick, and I wanted to talk it over with Bree, as well. Sorting them out in my head first seemed important. Fortunately, Bree wasn't about to push, or nag about it. She doesn't, not with me.

I ran it through my head a few times, end to end, trying to make some sense of it. After a couple of minutes, I got up and stretched; my legs were shaky, and sore from the weight of the Zemaitis.

"Patrick called in a favour from a few of his mates," I told her. She nodded, looking up at me, staying quiet. She knows the difference, between me starting a conversation and me thinking out loud; we've been together so long, of course she can tell. Right then, she knew it was me just thinking, no conversation required. "Apparently, cops in the south all drink beer together or something. Anyway, he rang up a few of them, and they got him some gen about the woman Ches mentioned on his thumb drive, Lainey C. Remember?"

She nodded, staying quiet, watching, listening. We've got most of our cues down pat over the years.

"Patrick's found out who she was." The breeze was picking up, chilly and stronger. "She's got a daughter who's still alive, a woman called Cassandra Chenery. He was just heading over to get drunk with her, and pump her about her mum."

"Get drunk with–" Bree stopped suddenly. Right, she'd remembered that I was still in thinking-out-loud mode.

"Yeah, get drunk with her, or something—he mentioned mint juleps. He also got hold of some people in Chicago. There was something Ches wrote, about checking Chicago—I don't remember what it was, exactly. Do you, love?"

"Sort of." I'd asked her a direct question, finally, and so here we went, genuine conversation. It was pretty obvious she'd been biting her tongue, wanting to jump in and talk it out with me. "There was something about notes on this LD guy's prison record, about him going AWOL right around the time Bulldog was born, about him being in the records at the Disciplinary Base at Fort Leavenworth."

"I remember that, yeah." *Dishon.Dis for desertion, double check*

174

Chicago source, Dixon/Duckworth; infant son abandoned... "And there was something about a Chicago source. Seems Patrick got hold of them, as well. He said there were records, about a bloke called Charlie Duckworth, and an armed robbery. Sounds major, doesn't it? He's going to follow it up and let us know if we need to send him some cash."

"Good. I just hope he remembers we're out of here in two days." She'd turned her head toward the house. "And here come Luke and Tony."

"Back to work for me. Here, hang onto my cell, would you? I'm expecting something from Carla, some contact numbers for the blokes in Traitors Gate—we're supposed to be jamming with them after their induction segment, and we need to synch up on the set list." I kept my voice down. "Bree?"

"What?"

"If Patrick rings back, come get me. I don't give a damn if we're in the middle of something, just come get me."

She nodded. I didn't have to say it, because she already knew; I had a very strong feeling that the nice old lady with the mint-flavoured booze was going to have something we needed to know.

It's a sign—or a testament, or whatever, I'm not really sure what the right word is—of just how much of my attention was locked up with what Patrick was doing in Hattiesburg that I sleepwalked through the rest of the afternoon's rehearsals. Usually, if what's happening is music, I'm right there, all of me.

That day, nothing was business as usual. I gave my phone back to Bree and went back to the studio. Turned out I'd been gone longer than I'd realised, because everyone else had taken a break, hit the loo, had a bite to eat, and got settled back in. They were powered up and ready to go, just waiting for me.

We went straight back into rehearsal, "Moody's Blues" and a

couple of old Willie Dixon and Robert Johnson standards, just to keep loose and make sure we had a few things on the roster come Wednesday at the Waldorf. My guitar was a major part of those particular songs; I can play the standards in my sleep, bottleneck, slide, whatever.

That was lucky for me because, in a way, that's what I did: play in my sleep. I just couldn't put all my attention into it—part of my head refused to go. I kept circling round some of the stuff Patrick had already found out, and what he might be finding out.

I know it's probably pants, but the picture in my head was straight out of *Gone With the Wind*. I kept seeing a big white plantation house, with a porch swing and pillars out front and hunting dogs asleep on the lawn, while Patrick and an old woman sipped cold drinks and talked about—what?

That was where my imagination set up camp, pitched a tent, parked the car. What did Cassandra Chenery know?

We played, played more, rested, started again. From the blues stuff, we somehow got back into playing a few numbers from *Book of Days*. Tony ran a few riffs, classic barrelhouse stuff, and that just naturally segued into a thing Mac had written, called "Hammer It Home." The song's got very angry pissy lyrics, you could take them as being about sex or politics or personal relationships or anything you wanted. And Mac grabbed a microphone and went into it.

"*...every time the big man tries to nail you, every time the jackboot finds your door...*"

So of course, Luke lit up like the Christmas display on Regent Street, amped his Strat as hot as it could go, and ran with it. He's a shit-hot guitar player, especially when he's getting musically bitchy—he holds the axe against his body like a lover he's not planning on letting out of his arms before morning. I just

176

grinned, and laid back; on that song, Luke does the front stuff, and I do the rhythm and emphasis stuff. He makes the killer noise for it.

"...every time your self-respect has failed you, when you think you can't take anymore..."

I have a drum machine down there, luckily, because the song has a major backbeat, and we were definitely missing the Bunker Brothers being there. It occurred to me that what I really wanted were a few more players down there, giving the song what it really demanded. Tony was doing his best to cover the bass, slapping out a low dense thing on the piano's bottom end, muffling it with the soft pedal, but it wasn't bass.

"...You don't have to take it, you don't have to buy it, you can make that nail your own, just hammer it home, I tell you hammer it home..."

We played it twice, and recorded it on the Korg; I made a mental note to myself, to burn CDs for everyone. It was pretty clear that asking Tony to come play for *Book of Days* was likely to be one of the smartest moves Blacklight had made in a long time. It was a pity our manager, Chris Fallow, wasn't alive to cheer us on over it. He'd have approved.

"Tony, that was brilliant, man." Mac was bouncing on the balls of his feet. Nice for Dom to have the day off, and Mac was thoroughly energised. "Is it possible to bring that low voicing up an octave, when we have the full band setup going? Because you might run into Cal's bass line, if you keep playing the punch at the bottom. But if upping it an octave is going to lose the power, we'll have to sort it out..."

Everyone was talking, noodling on their instruments, Mac

177

running the lead vocal, Luke trying out harmonies, experimenting with different voicings. The conversation moved around my head; some of it was directed at me, and I answered, and nodded, and adjusted. But the whole time, there was this question, the main thing, niggling away at me: who in hell was Charlie Duckworth? And why would an armed robbery in Chicago in 1938 have anything to do with Bulldog?

I just couldn't make any sense of it. There were all those initials on Ches's thumb drive, tantalising little bits of information that weren't quite enough to go on with: LD. SM. Dixon/Duckworth. Lainey C. Military records, an AWOL, a dishonourable discharge. An armed robbery in Chicago in 1938. Someone or something called Green. None of it made sense. None of it had to do with Bulldog...

It was nearly three hours later before we stopped for another break. This time, Bree came down to tell me that Dom had shown up, and that Carla was on the phone for me.

"Right." I lifted one eyebrow at Bree, and she shook her head. It was so slight, I doubt anyone not looking for it would have twigged, but the signal was clear enough to me: she knew what the raised brow was asking, and here was my answer: *no call from Patrick.* "Anyone want some supper? Because it's gone seven, and I want food."

I watched everyone head upstairs, while I took the cell out into the garden. It was dark, and chilly, and a bit damp.

Carla had names and numbers for me: the lead singer and guitar player for Traitors Gate, and their manager's number, as well. Carla seemed to think I already knew the blokes in the band—after all, their lead singer, Gregory Carver, had been onstage with Mac for benefit stuff, Amnesty International, Doctors Without Frontiers, a few others. Plus, the guitarist who'd founded Traitors Gate in the first place, Winston Dupres, had been a sessions bloke in London in the late seventies. But between living in

America and the timing in general, I'd somehow managed to miss ever even seeing them live, much less meeting them. Even at Live Aid, we'd played Wembley at the same point they'd been onstage in Philadelphia.

"Look, Carla, do me a favour, would you?" I was taking as much shelter as I could, staying near the back door. "I'm out of doors right now, it's cold enough to freeze the bollocks off a brass monkey, and there's fog dripping down my neck. I've got nothing to write with and a house full of people upstairs. Once we ring off, can you ring the cell back and leave the numbers and what-not in my voicemail?"

"Sure. They're all expecting you to call—I spoke to Winston Dupres myself, and he was practically dancing at the idea of meeting up with you and Bulldog in New York. Seems he's a fan."

"A fan of Bulldog's?" The fog had come in fast and thick; I'd been able to see across the garden two minutes ago, and now it was buried in a white damp mist. "The bloke has taste."

She sounded amused. "Actually, a fan of yours. Bulldog too, but I got the feeling it's mostly you he wants to meet. He was all excited about playing with you. He had suggestions for the big jam at the end of the show—it's going to be a 'Back to the Blues' themed thing. Do you want me to leave the flight information for Sunday in your voicemail, too? Because I've booked everything, hotel, limo, flights. I sent the itinerary to Bree's email, but some backup's probably a good idea, right?"

"Right." That was pretty mind-blowing, actually. The West In-dian guitarist who'd founded Traitors Gate, and kept it going for twenty five years without ever once letting the band move away from the blues and into the drum machine synth-pop rubbish of the eighties, was a fan of mine? "And yeah, I'll ring Winston Dupres. Um—Carla, where are they, actually? Because for all I know, the bloke lives in Johannesburg or Cairo or something, and

I don't want to wake anyone up to talk about the blues at half three in the morning, fan or no fan."

"He's in London, or at least, his number is. So he's probably socked out right now. But he says he's going to get to New York early—you're all at the Waldorf for this. Anyway, I'll leave those numbers in your voicemail. Let me know if there's anything else you need, okay? And if I don't talk to you before the show, safe travels and I'll see you at the induction ceremony on Monday."

By the time we'd said goodnight, I was damned near soaked through with fog, and shivering. I headed upstairs, hearing the phone beep, Carla leaving me the long message with the numbers for Traitors Gate. I'd get those later; right now, what I mainly wanted was a dry shirt and a hot meal.

We shooed everyone out around eleven, and locked up for the night. There's something comforting about the nighttime ritual we've got; it's evolved over the years into something I find myself looking forward to, that whole half hour of winding down, getting the cats sorted out and put where they're supposed to be, powering down lights, setting the house alarm, deciding whether or not we want a last cup of herbal tea, shutting down the computers, plugging in the cell phones to recharge.

We'd got everything done, and Bree was actually out the kitchen door and heading for the stairs, when I plugged my own cell into the charger. I've got one of those flip phones, where the display is dark unless you give it a function to process. Plugging the charger into the power supply counts as a function.

The display lit up, little clear black letters across a pale green screen. *New messages, 2.*

"John?"

"Shit!" I picked the cell up, flipped it open, pressed the listen to messages option. "Hang on."

"*(beep) Hey, JP, it's Patrick. I have some stuff I need to talk to you about—I got dumped right into your voicemail, so you're probably*

180

talking to someone. Anyway, I'm getting on a plane for Chicago to-morrow, and after that, I'm probably going to Kansas. Phone'll be off, mostly. Would it be possible for us to hook up in New York? Because I don't know if I'm going to be able to get the whole story confirmed before Wednesday. Leave me a message and let me know."

Chapter Twelve

"…I want to take a minute—really, just a minute, because I only get six of them for this entire speech—and talk about the enormous impact American blues has had on rock. I began as a blues player, and basically, everything I play has the stamp of the blues across it. And that's exactly as it should be, because rock and roll wouldn't exist without Robert Johnson, or Son House, or Albert Ammons. It's not just guitar—it's drums, and piano, and bass, and every instrument any rocker's ever used…"

"Patrick? Shit! Patrick?"

I took a long deep breath, to stop the urgency that wanted into and out of my voice. Bree, across the breakfast table, kept her eyes aimed at my face. She'd talked me out of ringing Patrick Ormand back last night, when I'd got his voicemail, pointing out that Hattiesburg was in a different time zone. Since Patrick was probably knackered from all the mint juleps and time changes and plane rides, waking him up at half past three in the morning would be a crap way of saying thanks for all the hard work he was doing.

"…There was Stax Records, too, all that soul out of Memphis. I'm *not forgetting them, believe me, because how could I? Rufus and Carla Thomas, Booker T, they aren't forgettable. Soul, funk, Memphis blues: there's another link, another connection back to the Delta..."*

Of course, Bree was right, and of course, I'd listened to her. But being considerate cost me some kip, and at my age, with the MS, I don't need any help sleeping badly. This morning, I was achy and edging on pissy, and it took all my self-control to not take it out on poor Bree. I wanted to bite something.

"The Mississippi Delta gave us Elvis Presley, and that showed all of us blue-eyed wannabes that we could touch that sound, that heartbeat. Without American blues, I'm out of a job, and I'm not alone. Hell, without players like Bulldog Moody, I wouldn't have the privilege of inducting the strongest musical influence I ever had into the Rock and Roll Hall of Fame, because there wouldn't be any rock and roll..."

"Patrick, this is JP. I was on the phone with Carla when you rang me yesterday. Look, we're going to leave your name at the Waldorf for the induction ceremony. The audience is guest list only, so we're adding you to our table—Carla's getting you a hotel room as well, so ring her up, you've got her number. If we can't hook up on the phone before then, we'll see you at the Waldorf ballroom Monday night, all right? And by the way, if you get anything you think I ought to know straightaway, ring me any time, day or night, I don't give a shit what time it is."

Today was the last day of basement rehearsals before we got on a plane and headed east, and Bree was busy at the big kitchen island. Between wanting to make sure the crew had a decent lunch ready when we broke for lunch, and wanting to leave stuff for Sammy to defrost when we headed home again, she was going to be stuck in the kitchen for awhile. Good thing it's her favourite room, outside our bedroom.

"The ceremony's supposed to kick off at eight on Monday night, but they usually start a few minutes late. Just show them

183

picture ID at the door to the ballroom, and you're in. If you get there early enough, they serve a passable dinner. Whatever happens before then, we'll see you there. Safe travels, mate."

I rang off. Bree was chopping herbs and fresh spring onions out of our garden; she does this thing she calls a frittata, with eggs and herbs and artichokes and tomatoes and whatnot. I quite like it, but it looks to be a lot of work, so I don't ask her for it often. But when Luke had stayed with us right after I'd got my MS diagnosis, Bree had made it for him, and ten years later, he not only remembered it, he'd damned near begged Bree to make him one.

"No luck getting Patrick?" She was cracking eggs into one of her big plastic mixing bowls.

"Just his voicemail. And yeah, it's going to drive me round the fucking twist, waiting to talk to him." I glanced up at the kitchen clock—the band was due in about ten minutes. "Bree, have you seen that notebook I was using? The one with the phone numbers Carla left me—oh, right, never mind, got it."

This particular phone call, to Winston Dupres of Traitors Gate, was one I actually wanted to make. It had certain echoes of my meeting Bulldog, getting to introduce myself to a damned good guitar player who, according to Carla, had the same opinion of me. The big difference was the role reversal; this time, I got to play elder statesman. Very odd feeling.

I tried the London number first, and got dumped straight into *the party you are trying to reach is not at present within the service area* voicemail, this time in a metallic female voice with a posh London accent.

"Oh, bloody hell, not again!"

"What's wrong?" Bree was rubbing two of her flat fry pans with fresh garlic and olive oil. "Bad news?"

"Not really—I'm just frustrated. Seems to be my day for wanting to talk to people, and getting snotty little voicemail messages

184

telling me to piss off. No luck with Winston Dupres." I glared at the cell for a moment. "Isn't the technology supposed to make life less frustrating?"

"Maybe on another planet. John, didn't Carla say he was heading to New York a day or two early?" It was really funny—Bree was alternating between talking to me and doing what she always does when she's working with food, which is singing under her breath. The result was a weird sing-song lilt to everything she was saying. "Would it make sense to try getting him at the Waldorf? Because if he's on a plane right now, leaving him a message at the hotel would work just as well, wouldn't it? He'd get it as soon as he got in."

"Yeah, it would. Ta, love." I hunted around the page of numbers I'd scribbled down: Winston Dupres number in London, Traitors Gate's lead singer Gregory Carver's home number just outside Boston, Sara Kildare's cell, my longtime European guitar tech, Jas Wilhelm, who was planning to fly in from Liverpool just so he could get me set up properly for the induction ceremony... "I can't believe I didn't write down the Waldorf's main number. I'm a fucking idiot—oh, wait, it's on the next page over, never mind. And stop grinning at me, lady, or I'll thump you."

"Yeah, right." The pan was apparently hot enough for the frittata; she glanced at the clock, muttered something under her breath, turned down the flame on the big range, and poured the egg stuff into the pan. There was a noise like a startled adder, and the entire kitchen was suddenly full of the most glorious smell imaginable. "Sure you will."

"Save me a mouthful of that, will you? It smells like paradise, and I'm hungry." I lifted one eyebrow at her; I'd seen her roll her eyes. "And what was that crack in aid of, not to mention that rolling of the eye thing you just did?"

"Just that you're always promising to put me over your knee, and you never do." She shot me a look over one shoulder; her eyes were hooded. "One of these days, I'm going to have to figure out how to annoy you enough to get you keep that promise. Can I help it if I'm curious?"

"Yeah, well, we'll see about that tonight." Things were suddenly standing to attention down below; if Mac and the rest hadn't been due in five minutes, I'd have got her round the waist, turned the stove off, dragged her upstairs and provided whatever she said she wanted. "Delighted to oblige. Right now, I've got to make this damned call. Believe me, if I didn't, you might find yourself having some trouble sitting on the plane tomorrow. That is, if you're serious about being curious."

"Really?" She was holding the heavy pan in one hand, away from the flame, staring at me.

"Really. In fact, you're on, lady. Let's see if I can get you to ask me to stop. Serves you right for provoking me." I met her eye, a straight steady stare, and watched a muscle in her throat jump and flutter. Life looked to be getting really interesting, suddenly; no idea where she'd suddenly come up with wanting to play that sort of game, but I wasn't arguing with her. "Actually, Bree, plan on that. And no complaining about it later, yeah? Your idea, not mine."

Winston Dupres hadn't got to the hotel yet. The desk staff were polite and close-mouthed; that was fine, because you want that from a five-star hotel staff. If you're famous, you value your privacy more than most people do. The last thing you want is your hotel telling people you don't know and probably don't want to talk to that you're in residence.

The tone of voice got less distant once I told them this was JP Kinkaid of Blacklight, I'd be checking into the hotel myself tomorrow, I wanted to leave Winston a message, his cell number was off and out of the service area. They unbent enough to tell me he was expected later today, and did I want to be connected to his hotel voicemail?

I was just ending the call when our doorbell rang, and the last

186

morning at home before the induction ceremony kicked into high gear, beginning with frittatas for everyone. The entire band, plus Katia and Domitra, had shown up at the same time, so I got everyone indoors and waved them into the dining room, stopping to pat Bree's bottom lightly on the way. She went very still.

I leaned in close. "Later." I mouthed it, up against her ear.

That led to a really funny moment, in an "I know a secret and I'm not telling" way, once everyone was settled in. Bree hadn't mentioned she was going to make frittatas, and the noise Luke made when he saw what was sitting on the warming tray was enough to get Mac's attention. He took a mouthful, and I watched his eyes go wide.

"God, this is fantastic." He headed into the kitchen, where she'd begun a second pan. "Bree, angel, what is this egg thing? And is there any more of it?"

"There will be in a minute." She turned round and glanced at him over her shoulder. He gave her a good long look.

"Do you know, Bree, you look quite yummy this morning. You're even paler than usual, and you've gone all glowy, and rather secretive-looking. Nervous, apprehensive—hell, you look practically virginal. The blushing bride look suits you, angel. Johnny's probably going to thump me for saying so, but really, you look like you've swallowed a budgie. What are you smiling about, the pair of you?"

"Nothing." I swear, when it comes to matters of sex, Mac doesn't miss a damned thing. He's like one of the cats, sniffing out catnip. "There are ginger muffins on the table, and I remembered Dom's mango juice from last time. Go eat."

We got about two hours worth of work in before Bree came down to tell me I had a phone call.

I knew, straight away, that it wasn't Patrick Ormand on the phone; I'd told Bree to come get me for that call, to interrupt us if she had to. And she didn't, just hung out in the doorway for a minute, letting us finish the number we were doing, a nice funky slow version of Robert Johnson's *Key to the Highway*. That was just for fun—we had no plans to play it at the ceremony. Eric Clapton and Keith Richards both do stellar versions of it. No point tackling a number on live telly, if you can't better it or bring anything really fresh to it.

"Oi." I set the chambered Paul on its stand, put the slide down, and stretched. "Is that for me?"

"Winston Dupres, calling from his room at the Waldorf." She handed me the phone. "I'll be upstairs getting packed for the trip, John—I don't want to have to do it tonight. If you want to give me the phone back, come upstairs and get me, all right?"

"Yeah, I will. Everyone want a break, then? I'm going to take this outside."

That phone call was really cool, at least as far as it went. Winston Dupres still had the lilt of the Caribbean in his voice—he sounded like a male Domitra.

"JP Kinkaid speaking."

"JP Kinkaid? That's really you, is it?"

He sounded incredibly pleased. He also sounded indecently young, and that was nuts, because he had to be pushing fifty, or at least in his mid to late forties. There was something about his voice that made him sound like a kid, though. Maybe it was enthusiasm, or good health, or maybe it was just that lilt. "I finally get my chance to speak with you, and we even get to go raise hell at this induction ceremony together! How cool is that? And why oh why have we not played together before, ever?"

"It's pretty damned cool—at least, I think so." I knew, straight off, that I was going to like the bloke. "And you know, I was wondering about that whole not playing together deal myself. So far as I know, the only gig we ever both played was Live Aid, and Blacklight was onstage at Wembley while you were scorching the Philadelphia crowd. Not exactly one of those 'arms round each others waists and bow to the audience' group moments, was it?"

"No, but now we fix that, don't we? We get to play. We will leave the whole crowd begging for more, come Monday. Tell me, please, will you introduce me to Farris Moody? Because that man, he was one of my idols, and I want to meet him. When I was told he was being inducted this year and so were we, I rang the Hall of Fame, and they gave me to a woman named Sara Kildare–"

"I know Sara," I interrupted. "Very nice woman."

"Yes, she seems to be very nice, but I would have loved her much more and all the way to forever if only she had said, yes, Winston, of course you may have the honour of inducting Farris Moody. And instead, she told me you were doing it, but you know, that is really all right too, because this way, I get to finally meet you both."

"I tell you what, I'm really looking forward to this." I was grinning. "Winston, listen, we're going to be jamming for the show's finale. Did Sara tell you about it? It's a back-to-the-blues deal."

"She told me that, yes. There is a packet here, that they give you when you check in to the Waldorf, for the bands. It seems we will have two songs, one short and one we can jam on until we shake the paint off the walls, if we want to do that. Blues, as you said, and since Traitors Gate is the main inductee this year, we have first choice. But you know, mostly what I want is for us to play together. What would you like to play, JP? Do you have anything in mind...?"

By the time we rang off, we'd settled on the obvious choices: "Little Red Rooster" as the first of the two at the show's end, and "Daisy Chain Blues," the first song I'd ever heard Bulldog play, for the closer to run the evening out. I'd promised Winston I'd get the rest of the band working out an arrangement, and got his email address so that I could send him the sound file; he'd promised he'd work on it with Traitors Gate as soon as it got there.

Heading back into the basement studio, I was about as relaxed and cheerful as I'd been since those first bad moments of reading Ches Kobel's thumb drive notes. Looking at it, no surprise, not really, you know? The musical programme was sorted out. The speech was mostly done. Winston and I had got on so well, we might have been best mates half our lives. The multiple sclerosis was behaving, at least to where it was only twinges and stabs, rather than a full-scale exacerbation.

And later tonight, once we finished up and got everyone the hell out of the house, I was going to take Bree upstairs, kick the door shut behind us, and see just how serious she was about getting adventurous in a way she'd never asked for before.

One of the coolest things I'd seen in a long time was the look on Katia's face when we got to the Waldorf Saturday night, and she got her first taste of what to look forward to on the *Book of Days* tour.

Blacklight doesn't usually stay at the Waldorf when we're in New York; Carla always books us up around Central Park, near Columbus Circle. I'm not sure why, but it's become a tradition. At our age, traditions are like nice old comfy shoes, something you don't give up without a fight. Even though Carla's a baby in terms of the band's age—she's in her late thirties—she gets that.

But it made sense for us to be at the Waldorf this time. Just get into the lift from our suite up in the tower, and straight into the Grand Ballroom for rehearsals and the induction ceremony itself.

We were met at the airport by a pair of stretch limos with liveried drivers. Even with the background fret of wanting Patrick to ring, I was in a very mellow mood, very cock of the walk satisfied. We'd had a hell of a night.

"This is so cool." Katia and Tony were sharing our limo, and Katia had found the cooler with champagne in it. "Bree, you never told me you got to travel this way. Limos and bubbly, is that normal?"

"Well, I haven't done a lot of travelling with the band. I probably take a lot of this granted, though."

She shifted in her seat. I found myself wanting to smile, because I knew why. My doing.

I don't know how long she'd been thinking about what we'd ended up getting into last night, but once she decided to get into it, she was all the way in. We'd got very experimental, me letting her tell me exactly what she wanted. Problem was, I got quite enthusiastic myself, and I'd got carried away. Between the MS and the fact that I'm skinny, it's easy for me to forget that I've been carrying ten-pound guitars for most of my life. Most of the physical strength I've got is in my arms and, well, there you go.

Mind you, if she'd asked me to stop, I would have. No questions asked. But she hadn't. She seemed to be feeling it around the edges this morning, and it was having that whole 'bloke in charge' effect on me. It was a damned good thing it was Tony sitting opposite, sipping champagne, and not Mac. Mac would have taken one look at Bree squirming in her seat and me looking smug, and known exactly what had happened last night.

"Damn, this is good champagne." Katia took a sip of her bubbly. If she'd noticed anything, she wasn't saying. Personally, I doubted she had; her attention was pretty well taken up elsewhere. The limo was moving slowly, which was no surprise. New York traffic doesn't part like the Red Sea just because you're in a limo. "Veuve Cliquot, no less. You guys really know how to do it. What's so funny?"

"Nothing. Bree's right, though. We do take this sort of thing for granted. Have you never been to the Waldorf, Katia? It's quite a nice hotel."

"No, I haven't, and I can't wait. I mean, the Waldorf!" She finally seemed to notice Bree moving around in her seat, trying to get comfortable. "Bree, are you okay? You seem kind of twitchy."

"I'm fine." Bree reached out suddenly, and took my hand, and held on to it, hard and tight. That had a very weird effect: it drained all desire to strut straight out of me. There was something about it, the gesture itself, the way she seemed to need some kind of reassurance, that just knocked me out. You'd have thought the last thing she'd have needed was reassurance.

What killed me was that nervous look, that and the need for my touch. It made her look about seventeen years old. I could see the girl I'd met all those years ago looking out of her eyes, the girl who'd apologised to me for not being able to resist kissing me just before she'd reached out and offered me a mouth that tasted of strawberries, just before I'd fallen in love with her. I put one arm round her shoulders and pulled her close, just holding her there.

And of course, Sod's Law being what it is, my cell went off. I said something rude under my breath, and fumbled it out of my pocket.

I had a bad moment, just before I looked at the caller ID. I'd been desperately wanting a call from Patrick, some information, anything at all, before I saw Bulldog again. The suspicions at the back of my head were like that ugly dark stuff you pass laws against, the stuff big factories sneak out the back way and into clear streams, hoping no one will notice. My feelings about Bulldog were being polluted, tainted. Bree wasn't the only one who wanted some reassurance.

But this would have been a really bad moment for Patrick to be ringing up. That wasn't a conversation I could imagine having in a limo, not with Tony and Katia sitting a few feet away, listening. If it was Patrick, I was going to have to tell him I couldn't talk right now. When I saw Carla's name and number in the ID box, I let my breath out, and opened the phone.

"Carla?

"JP, oh good." She sounded rushed. "Listen, I'm afraid I just did something a little high-handed. I'm pretty sure it's what you'd

192

want me to do, but I thought I'd better check. I've booked eve-ryone—you and Bree, the Mancusos, Luke, Mac, Dom, the whole Blacklight contingent, basically—into suites at the Wal-dorf Tower. You know, the very fancy suites on the top dozen or so floors of the hotel?"

"Sounds good to me." Bree had a hand resting on my thigh, very light, but there it was again—she seemed to need to have some part of us touching, somehow. I covered her hand with my free one, and smiled at her. I watched a tiny smile tremble up, and instead of meeting my eyes, she cast her own down. That just about eviscerated me; last night seemed to have left her shy of me, after all these years. "What's the problem, Carla?"

"Nothing, except that when I talked to the hotel, they told me the Foundation had booked Bulldog and Sallie into one of the regular rooms, downstairs in the hotel. And that just didn't seem right to me, JP, honestly. I mean, it's his party, right? Monday night is all about him. Shouldn't his room be at least as good as yours?"

"You're damned right it should." We were into midtown. "Not the Foundation's fault, they've done their standard thing, but I want this done properly, everything top of the line. Good call, Carla. Can you handle it?"

"I already did." There was relief in her voice. "I told them to put Bulldog and Sallie in the best suite they had available, and Blacklight Corporate would cover the difference. Is that okay?"

"No. I mean yeah, the best suite available thing's spot on, but it's not Blacklight's do, Carla, it's mine. The band shouldn't be hit with the bill. This one's on me. When it comes back to you, move it over, will you? Get it off Blacklight Corporate and over to my personal credit card, all right?"

"I will. Oh, and you have a rehearsal set up first thing, ten o'clock tomorrow morning: Bulldog gets in around nine tonight, and you two start out the day. The production company liaison called—really nice guy named Jesse—and asked if you could be down a few minutes early, to give them time for set-up. They also wanted to know if you wanted the whole house band, or just the rhythm section."

"Just the rhythm section, please. Can you let them know? So I'll plan on being down in the Grand Ballroom at around five of ten tomorrow. I just hope the house band knows they aren't sitting in on the acoustic lead-in, that's just me and Bulldog. Want me to tell Bulldog tomorrow's schedule? That would save you having to ring him."

"Oh, would you? Thanks, JP." She sounded apologetic. "I'm afraid it's going to be a long day rehearsing for you. The rest of the schedule is at the hotel, in a packet they're supposed to give you when you check in. You've got that hour with Bulldog and the rest of the band for your part of the ceremony, then the other bands get their time, and then you get back for the show-closer, and that rehearsal is going to go on for a while, I'm betting. You do get a decent break in the middle of the day, but still—long day. And Jesse said they wanted the extra time to get you all familiar and comfortable with the marks and the tech set-up, and getting everyone placed, especially with the house band in their usual spots for the closing number. Oh, and by the way, your interferon is in the fridge in your suite, so nothing to worry about there."

"Good to know, because I'm taking it a day early this week. Look, Carla, we're just pulling up at the Waldorf. Are you already here? No point talking on the phone if you're upstairs in the hotel."

"No, I'm still in Los Angeles—there's shitloads of stuff I need to clear off my desk. I'm taking a redeye tonight, so I'll be there in the morning. Ian's already checked in, though, so if you need anything, you're covered, just call him on his cell, or check at the desk for his room number. Have a great dinner, and say hi to everyone."

Even if I'd been expecting the rest of the trip to be a stone drag, the look on Katia's face when she got a look at their tower suite would have been worth the cost of the plane ride. Carla'd told the Foundation that Blacklight Corporate would handle our bookings, and of course she'd put us in what the Waldorf calls "Premier Suites," good-sized suites with gorgeous views out over the city. Katia followed the concierge in, and I heard her make a stunned little noise. We were right behind her, Bree still clinging to my hand.

It was right about then that I realised something: Bree was tense as hell. I couldn't sort out why. After all, she'd made a point of asking me to do what I'd done last night. But now, for some reason, she wasn't willing to meet my eye. As soon as I realised that, everything—wanting Patrick to ring up, the insane schedule we were on, the induction itself—faded and became less important. What I suddenly wanted, needed, was to get her alone, reassure her, let her know it was still John and still Bree, make sure we were okay with each other.

She'd been to the Waldorf before, just once. Back in the days when my first wife was alive, Bree had spent most of her time trying to stay invisible around my world. Guilt, believing she'd broken me and Cilla up, whatever: I'd never understood her reasons, not back then. But one of the few things she'd come along for with no argument was Blacklight's own Hall of Fame induction. She'd got a lot more comfortable touring with us, now that Cilla was dead and Bree and I had got married, and we don't stay in two-star hotels.

Besides, we'd stayed at Claridges for a full week, in their priciest suite, when we'd gone to London on honeymoon; that had cost an indecent amount of money, but it had been worth it. And on the 2005 tour, we'd mostly stayed at the Four Seasons. So she was used to top of the line hotels.

But the Waldorf—it's not just the opulence that gets to you, is

195

it? The place has got some history to it, as well. That gives it a sort of quiet elegance, self-assurance, something, I don't really know what to call it.

Katia followed the concierge in, with Tony at her heels, and us right behind. She stood there, looking around the suite, from the antique furniture to the chandeliers. There were fresh flowers in a crystal vase on the table, and more champagne chilling in a silver bucket. The bed—you could see it through the open doors—looked like something you'd expect to find at Versailles, or something.

Like I said, I'm used to it. The truth is, I don't notice that sort of detail, not without reason. Maybe I'm spoiled, or maybe it's just because I've done so many gigs in so many cities in my life that all I really notice about a hotel is whether the beds are comfortable, and whether the hotel is convenient to the venue for whatever show we're playing. The first US tour I'd ever done had been as a member of Blacklight, and they were already a star act then, staying at the best hotels.

Really, except for a couple of short stints round Europe when I was starting out, I'd never done it any other way. So I miss the fine points. Right now, though, I had good reason to notice the details: Bree wanted her best friend to be digging this, and I wanted whatever would make Bree happy.

"Wow. Oh, wow!" Katia slid her own hand into Tony's. She looked completely blissed out. "You know what? I could get used to this. Oh wow, are those Belgian chocolates…?"

We left them settling in, and followed the concierge along to our own posh digs. I tipped the bloke, closed the door behind him and finally, I was alone with my wife.

"Bree?"

Silence, not one word. I walked straight across and got both arms round her. She was tense as hell, just rigid, and her eyes kept looking everywhere, sideways, mostly down, anywhere that wasn't at me. That scared the shit out of me, for some reason. It wasn't like her. None of it was like her.

"Bree, listen to me, all right? And look at me. I said, look at me. Please?"

There was something glinting on her cheeks: tears. What in sweet hell was all this...?

"Bree." I tilted her face down to mine. "Talk to me. What's the matter? What's wrong?"

"Nothing. I just—I feel–" She sniffed, and stopped. The eyes started back down again.

"Oh, no, you don't. None of that, lady—talk to me, not to the floor."

She looked at me, finally, but I could see the effort it took, and I suddenly got what was going on. "Gordon *Bennett!* You're not feeling embarrassed, are you, or ashamed? Because if you are, stop. I had a brilliant time. Didn't you? Because if you weren't digging it, why didn't you tell me to stop?"

"You did? Really?" She was biting her lower lip. "I feel as if—I don't know—like I'd put you—I don't know–"

"Jesus, Bree, stop that! What, it wasn't obvious, how much I was digging it? Why do you think I got so carried away? Hell if I thought you'd be up for it, I'd toss you back over one knee and do it again, right now."

Her eyes went very wide. I grinned, and kissed her hair.

"I did say *if*, didn't I? Seriously, love, we can play at anything at all, anytime you like, or we can not play at all. And yeah, I know you're not supposed to be able to teach an old dog new tricks, but I'm not a dog, am I, I'm a cat. I'm sorry I got carried away; don't know my own strength, sometimes. I think we'll save any encores for days when you haven't got to sit in one place too long, all right?"

She laughed out loud at that. She'd relaxed a good bit, but not all the way. I didn't know why, but there was a voice in my head saying, *right, remember, nearly thirty years together but in a lot of ways, she's as old-fashioned and virginal as they're made, you just be careful Johnny, this is new territory and it doesn't matter that she asked you to take her there, you need to take things easy…*

"One thing." I was choosing my words. "If you do decide you want another go at it, you've got to not be afraid to tell me when to let up. Some sort of signal—a safe word, or whatever it's called. We'll work that out together. This is new territory for me as well, love. It isn't just you. Thing to remember is, I'm not inside your skin, and the last thing I want to do is damage it. I've got quite fond of your skin over the years. All right? Are we good?"

She opened her mouth, but whatever she was going to say stayed where it was. In my pocket, my cell suddenly buzzed.

Restricted number. Caller: Patrick Ormand.

Chapter Thirteen

"...So, where have we got to? Starting out in a Nigerian village called Ife-Ile, through the slave trade to the Caribbean and into Cuba, to bembè drumming and tent shows for a whole different religion, to a public park in Lyon, Mississippi, through sessions and gigs, the man moving along with the music from south to north to east and back south again: Bulldog Moody, moving like a river flows back to the sea..."

"Finally!" I got the phone open fast. "Patrick?"

"Hey, JP, good, you're there. I was starting to feel as if we'd be playing telephone tag until the ceremony."

If he'd been running around, or was feeling jetlagged, none of that was obvious in his voice. He sounded just the way he always did when he was sitting at his desk. There was no clue as to whether he was tired, or even what time zone he was in. There are days I'm halfway convinced he's a robot or something. I'd like him better if he was a bit more human.

"JP?"

"Yeah, still here." Bree was at the door to the suite; our luggage had arrived, and she was busily waving the redcap in, and

199

digging out money to tip him. "Hang on, let me find a chair; I've been on my feet too long, and the legs are dodgy."

"Sure. Take your time."

Actually, there was a chair about a foot from where I was standing. But I wanted the redcap gone before I got one word deeper into this particular conversation, and of course Bree knew it. She'd got the luggage in, slid a folded bill into his hand, and had him back out in the hall before I had time to change the phone from one hand to the other.

"Right." There was an ice bucket full of Perrier on the table, more evidence that Carla's got no equal when it comes to doing her job. Tony and Katia's suite, there'd been the identical silver bucket, but theirs had a bottle of pricey champagne in it—I'd noticed that myself. Not in our room, though. I'm an ex-boozer, and keeping the supposed temptation all the way out of my reach was part of the deal. So our room had water, not wine, and there was no way the hotel had known to do that on their own. Bree would phone downstairs if she wanted some bubbly. "Sorry about the phone-tag thing, but we've either been locked down in my basement studio rehearsing, or else we've been in the air. Where in hell are you, by the way? And have you got anything new?"

"Oh, yes. I've got plenty." Something came into his voice, and coloured it. I knew what that was, too: interest. He'd got hold of something and he was savouring it. "The picture got a whole lot clearer over the last day or two. Oh, you asked where I am? Right now, I'm in a motel near Greenwood, Mississippi. It's right on Highway 49. Great little truckstop diner, just down the road— they make amazing pancakes and gravy."

"Glad to hear it." I thought about strangling him, just a nice wistful moment. "Look, Patrick, just dish, will you? What have you got? I'm in rehearsal all day tomorrow and I've got to finish writing the speech. Half a tick, I'm going to put this on the speaker phone; Bree's here, as well. Right. Talk to me."

He sounded nice and crisp, suddenly. "I'm going to. I went to Chicago, and sat down with some very old incident files in the police archives. The date in question was August 27, 1938—an African-American male in his early forties was arrested while trying to commit an armed robbery at a South Side liquor store. He was pretty liquored up himself, and he botched the robbery. Shot the owner, not fatally, just enough to piss the guy off. The name he gave the police was Charlie Duckworth."

I was quiet, remembering Chas's notes. It was really bizarre, the way those bits of shorthand had carved their way into my memory: *Dishon.Dis for desertion, double check Chicago source, Dixon/Duckworth...*

"Duckworth wasn't exactly the brightest bulb in the rack." Patrick's tone had changed—I could hear an edge of contempt. There was amusement in there as well, and it jarred me. It made me remember that I was talking to a cop. No one can show the level of contempt that a cop can, when he's confronted with a dumb criminal. "They'd been looking for a guy with that name on an ADW charge, about four months earlier. So they were rubbing their hands over putting down two cases for the price of one, until Charlie Duckworth announced that he wasn't Charlie Duckworth. That wasn't his real name."

He stopped. Very dramatic, that pause was. Deliberate as hell. He wanted a reaction, and I gave him one. After all, I'd asked him to do this, to find out. That fact that I dreaded knowing the truth meant fuck-all. And there weren't any safe words, not for this.

"What was his real name, then? And what's ADW?"

"Assault with a deadly weapon. And his real name was Lucius Dixon." No mistaking it, not now. There was a cold satisfaction in his voice. "In fact, he had dog tags to prove it. Apparently, when they pulled him in for the robbery, he protested that his name wasn't Charlie Duckworth, it was Lucius Dixon, and they had the wrong man. He proceeded to throw a set of dog tags on the table to prove it. Lucius Dixon, he told them. From Hattiesburg, Mississippi. The cop handling the arrest, an Irishman named Murphy, wrote it all up, a lot of detail."

Dishon.Dis for desertion... "And?"

The word came out as more of a croak than anything else. I wasn't trying to play games with Patrick, not really, or even be dramatic. It was just that my throat had gone dry as a bone; planes have a way of doing that to me, no matter how hydrated I try to stay. Bree, who'd come back in and curled up on her side on the loveseat on the other side of the table, was listening; she watched me while I unscrewed the top on the Perrier and took a long chug of it. It was nice and cold. "Right, that's better. What happened next?"

"Well, they did the obvious thing, and ran the tags." Patrick cleared his own throat. "Did I mention that Lucius Dixon, aka Charlie Duckworth, wasn't too bright? Stupid as mud. He seemed to think the cops would see the dog tags, apologize for inconveniencing him, and send him on his merry way. Of course, they ran the tags and found out all about Lucius Dixon. Turned out he really was Lucius Dixon, and that was his bad luck, because Lucius Dixon was listed as having gone AWOL from the Army about eighteen years earlier. Seems he'd slipped away back in 1920, when he was working on a road crew out of Camp Shelby, down near Hattiesburg. The army doesn't like AWOLs and it really doesn't like it when one of their people commits crimes against the civilian population—it's very bad publicity for that whole 'be all you can be' deal."

"What happened to Lucius Dixon?" Bree eased the weight on her hip. "Was he sent to Kansas?"

"Yes, he was—that's the army's disciplinary base at Ft. Leavenworth, not the federal prison. Lucius Dixon got twenty years hard labour, and died there. They never let him out again. He was lucky they didn't execute him. That could easily have happened."

"Okay." The picture was fleshing out fast, and I was bracing myself. I couldn't shake the feeling that I really wasn't going to like what came next. "So what's the connection?"

"I'm coming to that." He paused a moment, as if he wanted to find just the right words. "About that AWOL incident. The man in charge of the crew was reprimanded, really more of a light slap on the wrist; apparently, the man in question was very highly thought of by the command at Shelby. Clear so far?"

"Yeah." There was a sick feeling at the bottom of my stomach. *LD, SM work crew?* Answers, right, I'd wanted those, but I hadn't expected that I'd know what he was going to say next. I didn't want to be right, I didn't want to know, but there wasn't any way to turn back now. "The bloke in charge, the head of the crew…who was that?"

"A former member of the 809th Pioneer Infantry Battalion, the black division of engineers during the First World War." Patrick had gone quiet, suddenly. It was almost as though he didn't want to tell me, didn't want to cause the regret, but that was bollocks, it had to be bollocks. He'd never even met Bulldog. "Name of Salas Moody. Moody reported Dixon's desertion at the time— that's in the records. He might have got severely reprimanded for it, might even have lost his benefits, but he didn't. People slipping away from the work crews on the county roads wasn't uncommon. And besides, Moody was highly respected. He'd done very good work for the army for a good long time."

He paused. There it was again, that sense that he was choosing every word as carefully as he could. "There was another circumstance mentioned in there, another reason why he probably didn't get any flak over it."

Out of nowhere, literally a bolt from the blue, I got hit with a huge wash of memory, clear and sharp and more than a little spooky: The Backroom, the club in Ofagoula, Dom sitting and listening, all of us listening to Bulldog talk about his father, his life, his family, the day we played until the day was gone and the stars came out over Ohio, and we played for Ches. I could hear Bulldog, sharp and clear, talking to Dom, curled at his feet and listening: *"...My father was with the Army, child—more blacks in the Army back then than most people know. We talking about Flanders, the First World War, before I was born; 809th battalion, Pioneer Infantry, all black men."*

Bree got up suddenly, wincing a bit, and moved to my side. She knelt down, knees on the carpet and her face against my hip, just being there, resting there, consoling, supporting. She's something special, my old lady is. And I'm damned if I could tell you, even now, why I suddenly was having trouble meeting her eyes.

"Okay." *Infant son abandoned, 1921...* "I've got all this so far. Lucius Dixon worked under Salas Moody. They were both in the Army. Dixon went walkabout in 1920. What I don't understand is what in sweet hell any of that has to do with Bulldog."

"It connects, JP." He paused, and Bree suddenly covered my free hand with hers, and squeezed. She'd heard the regret in his voice. "It connects through a woman named Elaine Chenery. She was a nurse at the Camp Shelby base hospital. Her father..."

His voice trailed off, and I heard a yawn. So he actually did get tired, just like a normal human being? Good to know.

"Sorry—I'm a little sleep-deprived right now. Her father was a doctor at the same hospital. There wasn't much about her in the official hospital records—little notes, just small things. She seems to have stayed very low-key. There's one note in her file that I found interesting, though: she was off on the twenties version of official sick leave, for almost six months. No details about that, except that the leave was signed off on by her father. What I did get, about that and everything else to do with Lainey, I got mostly from her daughter Cass."

204

"Patrick?" It was very strange; Bree's voice was normal, casual, but her hand was stroking mine, rhythmic and soft, and she was kneeling by my knee. I felt my stomach twist up on me. It was an unintentional parody of the pose she'd been in last night, just before I'd met her eye and said *right, lady, here we go, you wanted this and you've got it,* just before I'd got both hands on her and taken us both to new places, down the road she'd pointed us towards. "It's Bree."

"Hey, Bree. How are you?"

"Fine." She leaned back, letting her shins take her weight. "That leave of absence—did it correspond with the date of Bulldog's birth? Did it overlap, I mean?"

"Yes, it did. And according to Cass—my God, that woman is the kind of old-school Southern gentry gossipy belle I thought was extinct fifty years ago—there was some sort of scandal attached to that leave of absence her mother took from nursing. Cass told me she remembered how, when she was a little girl, the other women in town would whisper behind their hands whenever Lainey walked by."

"She was pregnant, wasn't she?" I heard myself say it, the first time I'd said it out loud. *Rec. unavail—Lainey C, hospital. LD, meetings? Check w/old res; illegit. births/Army doc, children might know...* "That leave of absence, six months—she'd had a child. It would fit. Oh, damn it!"

"It wasn't just because she'd had a child out of wedlock." Patrick's voice was neutral. "Yes, that would have been a scandal, certainly. But if Cassandra is right, Lainey's child was fathered by none other than Lucius Dixon."

I closed my eyes. It didn't matter that I'd been expecting it; I wasn't about to believe it.

It wasn't possible. Bulldog, son of a felon, a thief, a robber, a deserter? It made no sense at all. What about genetics? If Cass Chenery was right, then where had he come by that amazing talent? If he had no blood connection to that Yoruban priest, to that line of drummers, how had the child of nine, the little boy in the company and care of the father who wasn't his father at all, sat in that municipal park in Lyon, Mississippi, and been enough of a natural player to earn his share of the day's take in Rube Lacy's porkpie hat?

"There's another thing—that mitigating circumstance I mentioned, why Salas Moody wasn't reprimanded for letting one of his work crew desert. Salas's wife was pregnant herself; there was something in the records about her having a bad time, and Dr. Chenery actually setting up a consultation at the Moody home. His wife was too sick to travel." He paused, just for a moment. "JP? I'm sorry."

He was, too. He meant it. I tightened my hand round Bree's, and held it a moment. The speech, I thought, all of it was no more than fantasy, a load of bollocks. What in hell was I supposed to do about it? Was I supposed to just suck it up, pretend none of this was real, stand up and lie in front of the television cameras and a ballroom full of the industry's top players? And how the hell was I supposed to look Bulldog in the eye tomorrow?

"Do you want more?"

"Yeah, I do." I felt as if my answers were coming from light years away. There was still a lot I didn't know, and I was going to need to know before I could jump to conclusions. Maybe that's all I was doing, jumping to conclusions. Maybe that was all I'd been doing all along. "For one thing, how did she come across Lucius Dixon? I mean, if all that was true and she'd got booked for a baby, how did the white nurse hook up with the black worker in the first place? Did that happen much? Because I'm finding that a bit much to swallow, Patrick."

"Did it happen much? God, no. In fact, that's probably why Dixon jumped and ran." All the emotion had gone out of Patrick's voice; he was remote as the back end of the Milky Way, just

206

reporting. I had a moment of hating his guts, just a moment, but it was a bad one. Must be nice to go through life, never letting anything touch you, or affect you, or matter enough to hurt you. "He'd have certainly been lynched. This is Mississippi in 1920 we're talking about. A black field worker didn't get himself a baby on a gently-bred white girl, not if he wanted to be alive at the end of the day. If Dixon had half a brain, he'd have jumped the road crew and headed north as soon as Lainey told him she was pregnant."

"Did Salas Moody adopt Lainey's baby?" Bree had gone down the same road I had; I could see it in her face, hear it in her voice. "Why would he do that, Patrick? I mean, what connection did he have with the Chenery family? Was it through the army base? And by the way, you said Cass was Lainey's legitimate daughter. Did Lainey marry someone with the same name? How did Cass come to have her mother's maiden name? I don't get it."

"I asked her that myself, about the family name. Cass's father was a local man who ended up getting stabbed to death in a drunken brawl—all that was right there in the town records, easy to find and confirm. Bill Calley wasn't the nicest guy in the world—Cass was a little purse-lipped on the details, and I didn't press her, but she said that as soon as he was dead, Lainey went back to using her father's name, and Cass took it too. I got the impression Calley beat both women on a regular basis. A real sweetheart, Southern-fried."

"She had a weakness for bad boys, didn't she? Poor Lainey." Bree had stood up, and was stretching. I watched one hand go absently to her bottom, rub lightly, stop...

I reached out and pulled her over to me, and sat her down on my lap, my arm round her waist, holding her there; I could feel the heat of her, against my thigh. I couldn't see her face, though. She was keeping her eyes hidden. We were back to being shy, apparently.

"You didn't answer Bree's other questions." I let my hand slip round and up, tweaking lightly, and heard her draw in her breath. "Did Salas adopt her baby, and what connection did he have with the Chenery family in the first place?"

"That's part of what I don't know for sure yet. But I'm hoping to get more tomorrow. That's what I'm doing in Greenwood—following Lucius Dixon's trail. The actual military records are very spotty—there was a huge fire back in 1973, at the National Personnel Records headquarters. It destroyed most of the army's personnel records for the first half of the century. But my buddies in Kansas managed to dig up a couple of things on Dixon. The most interesting thing is that he had a half-sister, much younger than he was. She was the one who claimed his body, after he died in prison."

"Is that why you're in Greenwood? Seeing his sister? She's still alive?" Bree's voice jumped. She'd had both hands folded in her lap, but my own hands had got busy, she was squirming, and she'd sunk her teeth into her lower lip.

I was ready to ring off, myself; Patrick had given us a lot to process. And yeah, I was planning on processing it. But that was going to have to wait until later.

I'd taught Bree an acronym, back in London, when we'd gone on honeymoon: KORWIGH. It stands for *knickers off, ready when I get home*. And yeah, maybe it was because I was pushing away dealing, but right now, I was home.

"That's it, Bree." Patrick had caught something, probably the movement in Bree's voice. "His sister is still alive, and she lives here in Greenwood. Her name's Lillian, and I'm seeing her tomorrow. She's going to show me her brother's grave."

If you've never seen it before, the first sight of the Grand Ballroom at the Waldorf is pretty damned impressive.

I think I've mentioned before, Tony and his mates in the Bombardiers are touchy on the whole subject of the Hall of Fame. It's like any other honour, from the Academy Awards to the Grammys: if you get picked for it, you're likely to have a better reaction than if you get passed over. And in this instance, getting nominated is the same thing as getting picked for it. It's not a competition. You're in, or not.

Blacklight went in the first year we were eligible, and the Bombardiers, well, it's like their bassist, Kris Corcoran, likes to say: *it'll be a cold day in hell when that happens, so don't forget your sunscreen.* They're touchy about it if it happens to come up in conversation, but since I mostly forget about Blacklight being in there unless there's a new exhibit or something, it's not usually an issue.

Tony had only ever seen the room on television, watching the occasional induction ceremony. He swears the only reason he ever sees the show is because Katia makes him watch. I do my best not to roll my eyes at him: *Yeah, right, whatever, mate. Try it on the dog.*

"Holy shit!" He craned up and around, staring at the galleries, at the ceiling four floors above his head, at the whole painted jewel of a room. "This place is fantastic."

"Not bad, is it? It's even got halfway decent acoustics." Luke had come in behind us, Strat case in hand; he was a bit heavy-eyed. "Are we the first ones in? Any sign of Bulldog? JP, you look as if you slept for about three days without moving. Well-rested. Ready to rock and roll?"

"Yeah, well." Truth was, I was actually short on sleep. Just then, thinking about the reason, it took some self-control to keep the grin off my face. I was remembering Bree last night, holding on to me like a drowning woman with a life preserver, her drifting off, me waking her up, putting her through it, watching her ripple, letting her fall asleep again, waking her up, starting over...

We'd been through it four times before she cracked, started crying, and said the magic words—*please stop*. Of course I'd stopped; like I'd told her, it was her call. We'd cuddled like a pair of newly-weds, and we'd both slept like babies. I'd been feeling guilty, wondering if maybe I'd hadn't taken it too far and put her through too much while she was still off-balance, but I was pretty sure, now, that she hadn't minded. She'd actually woken me up in a way she hadn't done for the better part of a dozen years. Luckily for both of us, my own batteries had recharged. Whatever that look I'd thought I'd seen on her face was, it didn't seem to be there now. She had a glow on this morning, and she wasn't shy.

They were both staring at me. Ah, sod it. I felt the grin coming, and just let it come. "Yeah, excellent night. I like the beds here."

There must have been something in my voice, because both pairs of eyebrows went all the way up, and Tony pursed his lips up, as if he was going to whistle. If either of them wanted to say anything, though, they didn't get the chance. The ballroom doors were being pushed open. I glanced over Tony's shoulder, saw who was coming in, and froze in place, not moving, barely breathing.

Bulldog came into the ballroom behind Sallie, who was carrying his father's Byrdland case, moving slowly.

They stopped. Bulldog stood a moment, looking around, taking it in. He had one hand up to his chest, as if he was having trouble getting air, or as if something hurt. I felt my own heart ramp up into arrhythmia, and a cold chilly sweat broke out along my hairline.

I'd seen Bulldog Moody, played with him, got him his meds, less than a week ago. And for a moment, just a really bad breath of time passing, I didn't recognise him.

A week, less than a week. In the space of that time, the man I knew had gone, disappeared, been swallowed by someone else. The man who'd sat with me at the Backroom in Ofagoula, trading good-natured jabs with Dance Maxwell, listening to me finger-picking "Daisy Chain Blues" and throwing the *clave* chucks

210

that took a standard blues number and turned it into something new and immediately identifiable as his, had hit a wall, and the wall was time. Out of nowhere, he'd grown old. And there was something else, something was wrong...

"Bulldog? That you?" Mac had come in behind him. "Good morning. Hello, Sallie, how are you?"

I was still standing right where I'd been. I don't know how to describe it, except that I could see the change, feel it, damn near smell it. Bulldog had wilted—that giant frame was sagging at the shoulders. I'm not a fanciful sort, but for a moment, watching him turn to say hello to Mac, it seemed to me that there was some sort of cloud around him, something dark and cold. Whatever it was, it went down my own back...

"Johnny?" Mac had come up, and I hadn't even noticed. He was looking worried. "You've gone chalky. What in hell, you're swaying! Are you okay?"

"Yeah." I shook myself out of it. "Yeah, I'm fine."

Bulldog was moving, coming towards me. He looked as if his legs were about to give way under him. Sallie was behind him, one big hand hanging on to the Byrd case, the other one ready to slip under his father's elbow if it was needed.

"John." Bulldog looked at me, the big bell of a voice quiet, a bit dull. He lifted his head, finally, and his eyes, the brown eyes that were so much like mine, that had seemed to seal that link between us, locked onto mine, and shifted away. I honestly thought my heart was going to stop, break, something.

He knew. And he knew that I knew, as well.

It was all there, impossible to miss; I saw the knowledge in his face, guilt, understanding. He couldn't hold my gaze, that straight-staring giant of a man, grandfather of my tribe, the purest immediate bond I'd ever felt with another human being besides Bree. He couldn't meet my eye.

Something had got to him. He was broken.

211

"Right." I got the word out, closed my eyes, waited. All the time, I was mentally talking to my heart: *stop racing, just stop doing that, calm, easy, deep breaths, get through this, you've got to get through this, you can do it, stop racing, just stop that, behave yourself...*

"Morning, Bulldog. Hello, Sallie. Flight all right? Hotel making you comfortable, then?" It was amazing, my own voice coming out normal. "Sallie, here, let me get that, there are guitar stands already set up onstage."

Whatever Bulldog had seen in my face, it had stopped him talking. He followed me to the stage, where the PA layout we'd be using for "Moody's Blues" had already been set in place. There was a small Baldwin upright set up for Tony, and a mic for Mac's harmonica, and the drums and bass for the house band were ready to go. I'd brought my 335 along with me for the show, as well as my Martin and Little Queenie; I'd already spent fifteen minutes with Jas, my guitar tech, so my axes were tuned, tweaked and ready to go. There were two stools set up as well, with a guitar stand next to each. One stand had my 335 sitting on it; the other, waiting for Bulldog's Byrdland, was empty.

I don't know what it was that hit me. I just know that I looked at my guitar, then at that empty stand, and I just felt a wave of love, connection, something.

Whatever Ches had found out, whatever Patrick was finding out, all that stuff about Bulldog's personal history—did I really give a rat's arse about that? He was what mattered, him and the music. And if he wasn't Salas Moody's child, if he wasn't the grandson and great-grandson of those drummers, those priests, what the hell did that have to do with anything? However he came by the music, it was his, and no one out there did it better. Wasn't that what mattered?

"Bulldog, here, do you need Jas to do anything about the Byrd?" The words came out in one explosive rush. "That's my

212

guitar tech. Did the Byrd settle much during the flight? Jas is brilliant with hollow-bodies, you can trust him with it…"

"It's good. Doesn't need anything, John." He'd settled onto his stool; Sallie got the Byrd out and handed it carefully to his father, and Bulldog got the guitar on his knee, tuning it, slow and careful. I thought I saw one hand shake, just the faintest tremble, but it was gone so fast I couldn't be sure. "Guitars, they aint like people. Time makes guitars better and better. Us, well, time just chews us up and spits us right on out again."

"I know. Believe me, Bulldog, I know." His speech—there was something off there, a kind of slurring. He was having trouble forming words, as if he'd had a stroke, or something. My own dad had gone down with a stroke; coming on top of his heart trouble, it had killed him.

So maybe I was off my nut, thinking all that rubbish I'd been thinking about him. Could it be he'd just had a stroke, and all the rest of it, that was my own head, my own stuff? Had I read it entirely wrong?

I got my slide out of the 335's case, and got onto my stool. I couldn't talk, not just then, because there was a hard lump in my throat. He was so old, so tired, so frail, and I couldn't see it and realise it without the cold little thought: I was heading down that same road myself.

Like hell I was. I thought back to last night, Bree warm and vital in my arms. I thought back to the way she'd woken me up, the way I'd responded, the pair of us laughing. I wasn't all that far down the road yet. I still had some good years. And what's more, I had Bree.

We went through "Moody's Blues," just the pair of us opening the number. I forgot about everything and got into playing, sitting there with Bulldog as he nailed it, just perfect, the unique style of rhythm with its Afro-Cuban backbeat getting the solid seamless mesh with what I was doing, talking to the wail of my slide on the 335's strings. For a few minutes, it was just me and

Bulldog and no one else in the world, father and son, brothers, whatever. Musicians.

The rest of the band came in halfway through,, hitting their marks, synching up with us. I'd been so deep into playing, I hadn't even noticed the house band's rhythm section arriving, but there they were, bass and drums, and there were my mates as well, Luke running a really talkative line on the Strat, blues because that's what this was, but also his own signature, and that signature of his is greased lightning, rock and roll. Mac's harmonica came in, wailing and teasing, sexy as hell.

But the real surprise was the piano. It was absolutely killer. Tony seemed to be channelling every great boogie-woogie and barrelhouse player he'd ever listened to: Albert Ammons, Meade "Lux" Lewis, Pete Johnson. His hands were dancing up and down the scale, taking it high, taking it low. The rest of us went with it, just flying.

We went through it twice. We probably didn't really need to do that—after all, we'd hit it stone solid perfect the first time, and everyone knew their cues and their marks. Besides, there was a lot of rehearsal to come, including Traitors Gate and the Back to the Blues show closer that was going to need all of us. No matter how spontaneous they may sound, big complicated jams take a lot of work.

I insisted, though. Looking back, I wonder if I was just trying to keep the music close, keep it happening. Because there was magic in there, and if we were making magic, the real world couldn't get in and mess things up. Or maybe I was just afraid of it all, afraid of talking to Bulldog, afraid of trying to finish the speech I'd worked so hard on and knowing that it was based on air, afraid of hearing from Patrick again, afraid of looking into Bulldog's face, knowing what I knew. I couldn't do a bloody thing, not about anything. Christ, at that point, I wasn't even sure I was doing a halfway decent job of hiding what I knew.

Turned out I didn't have to worry about talking to Bulldog. We'd got done what needed doing, we'd got it done in the time allotted by the production crew—they're good people, very good at what they do—and we were clearing off, making way for Traitors Gate to rehearse their bit. But Tony hadn't even finished rippling out the last bit of tiara music on the piano, closing out the number, before Sallie was onstage, taking the Byrd and setting it in its stand, and helping his dad up.

"Bulldog?" I forgot about not wanting to talk to him. "Can I help?"

"No. It's okay, John, Sallie's got it." He sounded tired in a way I hadn't seen from him before, the weariness of age. It scared the hell out of me. "Old bones and airplanes don't deal together, truth to tell. There's a nap waiting for me upstairs. You tell me when I need to be back down here, I'll be here."

"Bulldog?"

I put a hand out to him. I don't know, even now, what in hell I wanted to tell him. I don't know whether I wanted to reassure him, or lie to him, or blame him, or what. Everyone else had gone quiet; out of the corner of my eye, I saw Mac's face twist up. Knowing Mac, that was probably sympathy. I used to think there was nothing to him but sex and politics, but I was wrong about that. Over the last couple of years, I'd got to know him a lot better than I used to. He's a surprising bloke.

"It's okay, John. I just need a little rest. You can talk to me later, you think you need to." Bulldog turned his head towards me, and I saw that the whites of his eyes were yellowed and damp. "And John?"

I said nothing, just listened, waiting. He waved the arm that wasn't resting on Sallie's around, taking in the ballroom, the musicians, the gear, the occasion.

"Thank you for all this. For everything," he told me, and went.

215

Chapter Fourteen

"In the end, it's really about family. Not just the blood lines, or the genetics, or that kind of ancestry. Because I see myself as a child of Bulldog Moody. I love the music he has in him. I have it in me, as well. He and I have a connection that's got so much more going on than DNA..."

Considering how smooth the rehearsal with Traitors Gate and the house band was, it really wasn't fair that I ended the day in a snarling pissy fight with Bree.

My wife had been out all day Sunday. No surprise, since I'd basically shoved her out the door. Hell, this is New York, and there's a lot going on: shops, food, the park, all that. Besides, this is my job, and there's no need for her sit there and watch me rehearse. I mean, if I worked a straight job in an office somewhere, or down a sewer, I wouldn't expect to have my old lady with me all day long, would I? Poor Bree would be bored off her nut.

That fight Sunday night—okay, so, Bree was right to get narked. I let myself get more physically tired out than I should have, just because I didn't take the breaks I usually take. That was my fault, at least mostly; I'd promised Bree I'd remember to do it, so that made it worse. It was standard, programmed into our relationship since the day of the diagnosis, when we learned what to expect from the disease: her telling me to remember to rest, and me promising I would. Mostly, I did.

The thing about MS is that you can't argue with it. It's got certain realities, certain things that set it off. You can't pretend it isn't happening, and you can't talk your way out of it, either. An exacerbation is going to kick your bum good and hard when it comes, and if you're smart, you figure out early on in the diagnosis what triggers the damned things, so that you can do your best to simply avoid them. For me, the triggers are stress, other autoimmune issues, and tiredness. Standing about in one place too long triggers it. So does concentrating so long that my muscles tense up. That's the sort of stuff Bree trusts me not to do.

That day, I fucked it up completely. It was a double mess-up, because we'd decided to risk doing the interferon shot a night early, since I didn't expect to get to it until way too late Monday night, and anyway, I couldn't exactly stop and premedicate while the show was going on.

So, we weighed the options and decided to do it Sunday, to give me flexibility for resting and premedicating. And of course, I forgot to do either. On shot days, I take masses of acetaminophen, five times during the day; it cuts back on the pain-based side effects. This time, I blew it on both counts.

I realised just how badly I'd blown it along about half past three, when my left hand, fretting a diminished seventh chord on Little Queenie's neck, began tingling. The tingle became a jab, a hot little stab of pain, and then numbness.

"Shit!"

I stopped straight away, shaking my hand, rubbing it, trying to get the sensation back so that I could get back to playing; just then, the hand wasn't good for anything at all. Everyone else

217

stopped as well. That was a lot of people; we were rehearsing "Little Red Rooster," getting all the stops and cues down, with everyone but Bulldog. Sallie had called down about an hour earlier, to say his dad was sleeping, he'd had his medicine early because he was having some pain, but would be down when he woke up.

"Sallie—is he all right? Does he need anything?" I was remembering Bulldog, one hand to his chest, little furrows of discomfort between his eyes, catching his breath. I remembered the huge pills I'd had charge of, when we played Ches Kobel's memorial in Ofagoula. "Did he have an angina attack?"

Sallie sounded worried. "That's what it was, Mr. Kinkaid, yes. He been having that three, four days past. Doctor told him nothing to be done, just take his stuff, be careful what he eats, rest when he needs it. The meds, they make him want to sleep. You saw that, Mr. Kinkaid."

"Yes, I did, and I know all about it. Let him sleep; we'll rehearse around him. We're doing 'Little Red Rooster' right now. Your dad can play that one with one hand tied behind his back—we played it together, the first time I came down there with Ches…"

I stopped, because my voice had caught. The memory had come back, Ches curled up listening to us, watching us play guitar, trading licks, Bulldog talk about the past…

"Mr. Kinkaid?"

"Yeah, still here. Look, Sallie, let him sleep. Just, ring me up if you need anything, or if he needs anything, all right? I'm right here, downstairs."

"I surely will, Mr. Kinkaid. Right now, though, there aint nothing but sleep he's needing."

So I went back to rehearsing. One cool thing was, I got to trade riffs with Winston Dupres, and that was one of the high spots in a day with some interesting ups and downs. When

218

Winston and his vocalist, Gregory Carver, showed up in the ballroom, it didn't take any time at all to know that I'd just met another kindred spirit.

I'd seen pictures of Winston, of course—people in the business know what other players look like. So I'd known he was mixed race, a Dominican mother and a white French father. Thing is, last picture I'd seen of him, he'd had short hair, so I wasn't expecting grey-streaked dreads hanging down his back. I wasn't expecting the grin, either—most celebrities have a habit of posing for things looking solemn, or portentous, or just plain grim. Traitors Gate was no exception. Their last CD had them posed on the back cover, scowling. I had a good reason to remember it; the CD had gone toe to toe with Blacklight's last CD, the two of them trading the number three spot on the charts for a month.

"JP Kinkaid!" Here he came, a lanky bloke with long beaded grizzled dreads, and a grin that lit up the room. I waved at him, he saw me, and the next thing I knew, I was being crunched in a hug. "I will be completely damned!"

"Blimey, I hope not." I got myself out of the hug—I'm not a hugging type—and shook his hand. I was grinning back at him. So was everyone else in the room; there was no way not to. It was contagious, that grin. "Not completely, anyway."

"Metaphor! That was a metaphor!" He saw Mac, waved, and yelped. "Malcolm! We're here!" Mac waved back. He looked very amused, himself, and I knew why. Winston Dupres was amazing.

I don't know how or where he got the energy he had, but it lit up the entire ballroom. You had to respond to it; it would have been impossible not to. He just sort of vibrated, you know? Everything he did, even standing still, he seemed to be bouncing on his feet. Only person I've ever seen come close to that level of energy is Mac, and I wonder how long Mac can keep it at this level, at his age.

Winston had got the sound file I'd sent, of "Moody's Blues." He and the rest of the band had talked the hotel into letting them use one of the business conference rooms, grabbed some acoustic instruments, and spent a couple of hours getting it down. Solid pros, these blokes were; not too surprising, considering that Winston was an old session player. That's the thing about the sideman head space—you get it bred in the bone, getting the song down as fast and completely as possible. Otherwise, you end up getting sick to death of hearing and doing the same song, over and over.

I had a very peculiar thought, while Winston and I were trading slide riffs on "Little Red Rooster." It turned out he was forty-eight years old, or would be for another three months; his birthday was the same day as Bree's. And him being younger than me, being healthy, all that energy he had, how fit he seemed, that was all the stuff I resented the hell out of in Patrick Ormand. For some reason, though, Winston didn't press a single one of my buttons.

We got deep into playing, working out "Little Red Rooster," seeing where my slide talked to Winston's and where it rubbed wrong. Everyone else hung back until we'd sorted that out, and then it was Luke's turn, playing a wailing lead guitar, very evocative of the sixties, meshing it perfectly. After that, the house band's rhythm section, drums and bass, came in, getting the timing down, and then, finally, Mac and Gregory Carver, trading their vocals.

That was one hell of a moment, two of the longer-lived and hotter vocalists in the business doing their thing. They went for an interesting back and forth, a call and response style, instead of trying to harmonise. That made sense, since their vocal ranges were similar. The result was a killer vocal, hotter than the surface of the sun. There were going to be women watching all over America who'd be twisting in their chairs. It was fantastic.

By the time Bulldog came down, we were ready for him. We'd

got all the bugs out of "Rooster," and were ready to get him into it. Once that was taken care of, we'd be ready to rehearse the full jam on "Daisy Chain Blues."

When I looked up and saw him coming through the ballroom doors, I saw Bree and Katia right behind him, and I suddenly realised, I was dizzy and aching. I'd been playing for about five straight hours. I hadn't eaten anything since a room service breakfast ten hours ago. I'd grilled Sallie about Bulldog's meds, and promptly forgotten all about taking my own. I was in deep trouble. Bree was going to kick my arse.

And now, we had to finish the rehearsal, and I couldn't stop; the ceremony was tomorrow, we still had to rehearse "Daisy Chain Blues," and we had to talk to the tech people from the production company, make sure that was all sorted out. Bree was going to flip her shit entirely.

Right then, I started bracing myself for some major marital unpleasantness. It was likely to hit me after rehearsal; Bree never gives me shit in front of other people, especially not in front of my mates. If she's narked at me and there are other people around, her usual thing is to get very remote, far away. I hate that, and she knows it.

She came in right behind Bulldog. She stopped in the doorway to talk to him; she looked shocked at the sight of him, at how tired he seemed. She put a hand on his arm, and he patted it. Then, sure enough, she headed over to me, looked around for signs of dinner, and of course, there weren't any.

"Hey, babe." She kissed me, and her voice was casual, but her head was tilted. *Damn.* "Have you had dinner?"

"No, not yet." *Come on Bree, not now.* "I was about to suggest we ring up catering and get some food."

Of course, that pretty much sealed it, because she knows me. If I hadn't had dinner, I probably hadn't stopped for lunch, either. And if I hadn't stopped for lunch, I'd probably missed all my meds. I watched her mouth thin out. She wasn't going to rip me a new one in front of other people, but I was going to catch hell later.

"Then we'd better get some dinner organised." Her voice was chilly enough so that Tony and Katia, who know her very well indeed, both flinched. "Did you guys not stop for lunch either?"

"Forgot." No point in not admitting it. *Come on, Johnny, minimise the damage.* "I'm sorry, love, I'm a prat. Forgot my meds, as well. And I just remembered, the interferon's still in the fridge. I haven't had a chance to get offstage. Where've you been all day, then?"

"We went to the Met. There's a fantastic exhibit on baroque jewelry." Katia had come up onstage, and was kissing Tony. "Baby, aren't you starving? Because I want some dinner. Bree and I had lunch at the Petrie Court, but that was hours ago. I can't believe you didn't stop to eat!"

"Yeah, well, we're musicians." Tony kissed her right back. "We're all insane. You knew that when you married me."

"He's got a point." I tried catching Bree's eye, but it wasn't on. She'd gone distant on me.

Right around then, I began getting upset, myself. I mean, I'd apologised for it, in front of the band, and yeah, all right, I'd blown it, but it wasn't the end of the world and she was acting like a damned diva. "Look, I need to take a food and meds break, all right? And I need to nip upstairs and get my stuff out of the fridge—"

"I'll do that." Chilly and remote as Jupiter's moons, no thaw at all. I was in deep, deep shit. "You might as well stay here. Katia, can you get them some food ordered, please?"

Bree was out the door before I could open my mouth. Mac gave a long, low whistle.

"Crikey, Johnny, the girl's seriously cranky. You're in for a nice bit of hell after hours."

I shot him a look, and he belted up. He was right, Bree was going to nail me. But I was damned if I wanted to think about it now, or talk about it with Mac or anyone else.

The Waldorf's catering staff brought in a parade of covered trays about twenty minutes later, and we finally got some food. I hadn't realised quite how hungry I was, but I didn't get to enjoy that dinner. I was far too edgy. And Bree didn't come back down.

We went back to work and finished the first run-through on "Daisy Chain Blues." Bulldog looked just as exhausted, just as old, just as broken as he had when he'd first walked in on Sallie's arm and nearly stopped my heart for me, but that didn't show in his playing; hell, I was aching all over myself, but it didn't show in my playing, either.

He must have been as wasted as he looked, because he seemed even less up for conversation than Bree was. I found Winston tugging my sleeve, and remembered that I'd promised to introduce him to Bulldog. So that was a nice moment, but Bulldog still wasn't up for talking. It was just as well, because we still had a lot to get done, and it was getting late.

We went back to work, straight into the closer. We linked up, me and Bulldog, the Byrdland kicking out those rhythmic chucks that were pure Bulldog Moody, my 335 handling the slide work. We got it first try, perfect, the two of us playing like a single straight, even heartbeat. Winston and Luke came in together behind us, and that was kickass, two guitars working like a handshake.

This was one hell of a band we'd got together. It was so good, I could almost ignore that everything, from stabbing hamstrings to throbbing jaw, was in pain. And it let me push back the scene with Bree I knew was coming. The fact that she hadn't come back downstairs, hadn't stood there and made damned sure I ate, hadn't fussed over me like a mother cat with one kitten, spoke for itself: Hell to pay, waiting upstairs.

It was close to ten when I slipped the guitar strap over my shoulder, and set the 335 back on its stand. It took some serious effort; both arms and shoulders had joined the pain party. No point in putting it off any longer—it was time to face an entirely different kind of music.

"I'm off. I'll see everyone back here in the morning." *Right. That's if Bree doesn't kill me.*

"'Night, Johnny." Mac looked up, and caught my eye. "And best of British luck, mate. From the look of things, you're going to need it."

In a way, I'd actually worked myself up to hold up my end in a good clean row. Keep it short, keep it sharp, get it over, get my meds, and hopefully not go to bed angry. And Bree being Bree, she doesn't change much; no matter how what else is going on, her first thought is to make sure I'm okay, that I've got what I need. Hell, she's a doctor's daughter and a patient's wife. She doesn't give me shit when she knows I'm not doing well. That's not her way, at all. My health comes first, and always has done, since the day she'd nearly been sent to prison as a teenager for stealing heroin for me, because she was afraid I'd die without it.

So yeah, she was going to make me squirm over breaking my promise. I knew that much—if she hadn't come back down to check on me, she was seriously pissed off. But she also knew I had that shot to give myself, so she'd give me hell tomorrow, you know? Not on a shot night.

What I wasn't expecting was to let myself into the suite, and find her on her cell. She looked up when the door opened.

"Patrick, hang on. John just came upstairs." Her voice was shaky, and so were her hands; she wasn't bothering about covering the speaker on the phone. Her face was a mess, clogged with tears, blotchy and swollen-looking. "It's Patrick Ormand. Did you eat?"

"Yeah, I did." There were tear tracks down her cheeks and her eyes were puffed, half-closed. "Bree, what the fuck, were you crying? You don't need to cry—just chill, will you?"

"Why don't you not tell me to chill, John, okay?" She sounded as if her teeth were clenched, but they couldn't have been. Her voice echoed, clear and furious, all around the suite. "We both know you aren't going to tell me to chill later, when you react badly to the goddamned shot because you forgot to goddamned premedicate or take a single rest break all day, don't we? We both know you aren't going to get condescending and patronising at half past three in the morning, when you're shivering with fever and I'm half out of my goddamned mind over it, trying to keep you warm and worrying that you're going to have a goddamned heart attack. We both know you aren't—"

"Stop it." I sounded like ice water, and it stopped her midsentence. "That'll be enough of that, Bree. I'm not saying you're wrong, but this isn't the time for it, and I don't need you piling it on. So just belt the fuck up and give me the bloody phone, okay?"

"Fine." She tossed the phone at me. "Works for me. What fucking ever."

She turned on her heel and walked out. The doors to the suite weren't designed for slamming, but they might as well have been.

"Oh, shit!" I sat down hard, holding the phone. "*Shit!*"

"JP? You there?"

He'd heard that last exchange; the only question was how much he'd heard. It was a good thing I was as off-balance as I was; otherwise, the idea that Patrick Ormand had been listening in on me and Bree fighting would have made my skin crawl. "Yeah, I'm here. What's going on? And why'd you ring Bree, not me?"

"Well, I did try you first. Yours didn't even ring—I got dumped right into your voicemail, and left you a message. So I called Bree's number, and she said you were pretty wrapped up in rehearsal. Are you done for the day? Have you got a few minutes? I don't want to take you away from anything important–"

"No, it's fine, we've powered down for the night. Hang on a second, will you? I need to get my meds out of the fridge. It's a shot night and I forgot to take any painkillers today. Having the damned needle be full of ice-cold meds would pretty much put the lid on it. Right, never mind, Bree's done it."

I settled down on the fancy sofa, one eye on the door. It was half past ten; she had to come back soon. If she hadn't come back by the time I was done with this call, I was going to ring her—no, I wasn't, because I was talking to Patrick on her cell. My own phone was in my pocket, probably with the red message light blinking. Shit, shit, *shit.* "Okay. What have you got? More about Lucius Dixon?"

"I'm afraid so." He sounded gentle. "About Lucius Dixon, and about Salas Moody's wife, and a couple of other things."

It was the tone of voice that did it. Out of nowhere, I found myself remembering, seeing a backlit image of my own brain on a lightboard, being given a diagnosis I didn't want to hear. Something in his tone was ringing those bells, loud and clear: whatever this was, I wasn't going to want to hear that, either. My throat was dry.

"What do you mean, you're afraid so?"

"I pretty much tied this up today, after I met up with Lillian Jackson. I'm afraid it looks pretty conclusive, even though you'll never be able to prove it. I'll get to that in a minute. Lillian took me to her brother's grave. He's buried in the Hudson Park Cemetery, just down Highway 49. Simple little stone: *Dixon, 1900-1952.* Life and death on a piece of rock, about as bare bones as it gets. Lillian's as poor as dirt, and the army wasn't going to spring for carved marble angels and an 'in the everlasting arms' inscription on a fancy headstone for a convicted felon and an AWOL. The grave's not very well tended; she's pretty elderly, and lives alone. Can't really expect much else from the poor woman."

"Probably not." I was shivering, maybe because it was getting late and my nervous system wanted its interferon, maybe because Patrick sounded detached, almost ironic, and it was creeping me out. The door to our suite wasn't opening, either. Where in sweet hell was Bree…? "So he died in the stockade or whatever they call it, and his sister went to Kansas and got his body back, and had him buried in Mississippi. What's that got to do with Bull-dog? You said you were afraid this was conclusive. Conclusive of what?"

He was silent. The soreness in my jaw had settled in, good and hard, and I had the beginnings of a spectacular headache, coming up behind my eyes. "Patrick? Talk to me."

"When she claimed her brother's body, the prison hospital also signed out on his personal effects. Not much, an old cheap guitar and those famous dogtags of his." He took a breath; he seemed to be picking his words pretty carefully. "There were also letters."

I started to answer him, but there was a click, and I jerked my head up. Then the suite door was opening and I was on my feet and heading straight for Bree, gathering her in, kissing tears off her face, holding her, mouthing *I'm sorry, I messed up, I'm so sorry love, I'm an ass, I'm sorry* into her ear, while she leaned against me and shook…

"JP?"

"Yeah, I'm still here." I kissed Bree. "Give me a second—Bree just got back. Hang on, all right? Just hang on."

I've never claimed Patrick Ormand can't be tactful; he's actually quite good at it. He'd heard that last bit, heard Bree storming out in the first place. I don't know whether his cell phone reception was good enough for him to pick up me grovelling at my wife's feet for being a shirty berk, but truth is, I didn't give a rat's arse if he had. I was too busy realising that she'd been gone less than fifteen minutes and I'd spent every one of them thinking

227

she wasn't coming back. Right that moment, I was so relieved at having her prove me wrong, I had no attention to spare for anything else. I wasn't thinking about Bulldog, or Ches. Patrick could damned well wait. And to do him credit, he waited.

"God, love, you scared me." I finally let go of her, and chucked her under the chin, one knuckle, and lifted one eyebrow. I wasn't bothering keeping my voice down. "You all right?"

"I am now." She was still shaky, still tearful, but she had her voice back. "Patrick? Are you still there?"

"Yep." Total detachment, total patience. "Still waiting to finish reporting to JP, though."

"Sorry about that." I pulled Bree down on the sofa next to me, one arm round her. We pretty much never fight, but when we do, I tend to fall the hell apart. And when the fight gets bad enough for her turn her back on me—Christ, there's nothing worse. I wasn't risking her even getting up and leaving the sofa, much less the room.

"Okay. You said Lucius Dixon had letters, that the army gave his sister Lillian letters when she claimed his body. Did she remember what they were about?"

"She didn't have to remember." Detached, patient; something went down my back. "She still has them. Or, rather, had them. Now I've got them. Nice little stack of letters, ten of them, stretching over two years, preserved nice and careful. All printed, too—I think the writer probably wasn't sure how well her boyfriend could read. Lillian handed them over to me."

"Who..." I stopped, and tried again. Bree'd got hold of my hand. I'd pushed the aches and pains away, holding on to her fingers, clinging to them like a rope from ship to shore. I didn't want the answer; besides, I already knew it. Only one thing Patrick could say. "Who were they from?"

"Lainey Chenery." Flat as a damned rock, that voice was. "To the father of her baby boy. The first one was written in summer

228

of 1921, the last one is dated Christmas 1923. She was keeping him informed about what was happening, from right after the child was born through the child's adoption by a black family who'd just lost their own newborn daughter, until she finally gave up, because Dixon never wrote back."

"And he had them when he died, what, thirty years later? He saved them. Oh, man." Bree's eyes were wet, and her voice had gone soft. Myself, I was remembering something Patrick had said last time we talked, about Salas's wife having complications with her own pregnancy. "He never answered her but he saved those letters, all that time. He must have taken them along with him every time he moved, every city, every town, everywhere he went. I wonder how long it took for those letters to catch up with him? I wonder who made sure he got them?"

"My money's on Salas Moody." It was mind-blowing. Lucius Dixon had cut and run, probably two seconds after he found out the pretty white nurse he'd been rogering had come up pregnant, and he stood to get lynched. There would have been no way for Lainey to know where he'd gone. That meant the letters had to have been sent on by a go-between, someone who not only knew where Dixon was, but who knew Lainey and her family, and had their trust.

It all added up to Salas Moody. Add him and his wife taking the baby after their own daughter had died, and that gave Salas all the reason in the world to play middleman...

"I'm sorry, JP. There's no way to prove it, but I think this locks it up, don't you? I'll bring the letters to New York with me tomorrow, and let you have them. What you want to do about them is entirely your call. That was the agreement, right? I promised not to take any action. Right now, I know what I think, but there's no way to prove it and I wouldn't try anyway. I do try to keep my promises." There was something there; I wondered if it was regret I was hearing. "By the way, there's a few places where Lainey gets chatty, just making conversation. Apparently, she was a harpist for the local Baptist group, and sang in the choir. In one letter, she talks about the tent show where she and Dixon first met. Very sad, really."

"Thanks. I'll be glad to have a butcher's at those letters." I was stiff, and sore. I stood up, feeling my legs tremble. "Look, Patrick, I need to get my night meds and my shot. Let me know what you need in the way of money, and we can settle up after the show, all right?"

"Sure. Looking forward to it." He hesitated. "JP? I'm really sorry I couldn't get the second part of this locked down, but there just isn't any way I can see."

"Second part?" I was stretching. "What second part?"

"Ches Kobel." He was very quiet. "This wasn't just about your speech, remember? You came to me because there was a question of murder."

Chapter Fifteen

"...*Ladies and gentlemen...*"

"Ready?"

I turned to look at Bree. The houselights were flickering, and the music industry honcho who'd been handed the emcee duties tonight had just got up from his own table, and was waddling toward the stairs, stage left. A voice came out of the walls, introducing the man who'd be introducing me so that I could introduce Bulldog.

"...*in keeping with our recognition this year of a purely American musical form, it's a nice piece of synchronicity that this year's inductee in the category of Early Influences is one of the great unsung sidemen of that form, from the Delta to Chicago to New York to Kansas City...*"

"Yeah, notes and everything. You look gorgeous, Bree—did I tell you that upstairs?"

She did, too. I hadn't seen the dress until she'd asked me to do up her buttons, but it was sapphire blue, and had no back to speak of. She'd done something with her hair, bundled it into a soft little lace thing at the nape of her neck. We'd been edgy with each other, tense, but right now, things were fine. Good job, too. I had other stuff to cope with tonight.

"Yes, you did. Thank you, John." She leaned over and kissed me, ignoring the rest of the group. Those tables seat twelve people, and there were eleven of us, with one empty seat: Patrick Ormand's. No sign of him and no way to get hold of him. Cell phones are frowned upon at this kind of party. "You look pretty spiffy yourself."

"*...a legendary session man and leading light among English bluesmen himself, second guitarist for Blacklight...*"

Right. Showtime.

"*...ladies and gentlemen, please welcome JP Kinkaid!*"

I got to my feet. Just before the spot from the second level of private boxes found me and the applause broke out, I gave the rest of the table a fast look. Bulldog, in a shiny threadbare suit that looked to be thirty years old at least, was front and centre, with Sallie beside him. The women, including Domitra, had dressed for maximum flash; Katia and Carla were tarted up to the nines. I'd been dragged off into the kitchen and had my face dabbed by the production team's makeup person, apparently so that I wouldn't be too shiny on camera. The band and the crowd were ready, and so was I.

I took the stage, knowing where the cameras were, mindful of the trough the production company had built into the stage extension to house all the monitors. The stage backdrop was gorgeous, a representation of the Mississippi cotton fields, in that old-fashioned brownish tint from period newspapers, looking as if it stretched out for miles. The lighting crew had done something subtle; whatever they'd worked up, it made the backdrop sparkle, as if there was sunlight on it.

We'd had a dry run rehearsal with the production company this morning, dealing with the staging of it, making sure we didn't do anything that couldn't be fixed in the mix. As soon as I was done up here, everyone coming in on "Moody's Blues" would slip away from the table. They'd be waiting just offstage, waiting for that moment in the song when Bulldog and I had finished the lead-in, waiting for the downbeat, waiting for their time to play. All the amps were behind that gorgeous backdrop, the Mississippi Delta, brown in the sun.

I had the pages of my speech ready to go. I'd done a read-through about an hour before we'd come downstairs, with Carla and Ian playing my audience, and Luke holding a stopwatch. We timed it at five minutes forty, just about perfect.

When I look back at giving that speech, I mostly remember wondering where in hell Patrick was. We'd set our system at home to record the show, so I was able to watch it later. When we got home and had a look at it, Bree said she thought I was just my normal self, but I think I looked distracted. And I was, which was silly. There was no point in worrying about Patrick not getting there in time; there was nothing he could tell me, nothing he could say. There was also nothing he could prove, not about Ches Kobel's death. But something about him not being there yet was something worrying me.

Also, there was that tension between Bree and me. You'd think that fight with Bree last night would have been enough for one night, especially an interferon night, yeah? But we'd gone through another bad patch, after that conversation with Patrick.

Basically, I had a speech I'd been buried in, obsessing over. I'd been trying to get it together, make it as real and genuine and spot-on as possible. In my own head, with the discovery of those letters from Lainey Chenery to Lucius Dixon, most of it had become worthless. And I didn't know how to deal, or what to do. I'd run out of time to sort it out.

As usual, poor Bree, bless her, took the brunt of it. I'd gone silent after Patrick rang off, my head not wanting to go down the path Patrick had pointed to. Because of course, he was right; the question of whether Bulldog was the blood descendent of a family of Santeria priests and brilliant drummers or not was only part of the issue. I'd got so caught up worrying about the truth behind what I was writing, I'd forgot there was something else at stake here, the reason I'd made Patrick give me his promise not to do anything about what he might find, in the first place: Ches Kobel had died.

I was sure, now, that he'd been killed. I didn't know how, but I was sure. It was a certainty, all the way down in my bones. And not knowing how, I didn't want to look at who or why.

Bree wasn't having any of that—she just wasn't buying it. She'd made me talk, got me to tell her what I was thinking; she'd listened, without any interruptions. And when I was done, she spoke up, nice, clear, simple.

"Do you really want to know why you're freaking, John?"

I'd been reaching for my gear, the paraphernalia I use to give myself the weekly shot: the preloaded syringe, the ice pack to keep the bruising at the injection site down, the gauze pads, the bandage. But that stopped me. I just blinked at her—the girl's not usually quite so to the point.

"You think you know, do you?" Both eyebrows were up around my hairline. "Then tell me, because I'm damned if I do."

"You do know, John. You just don't want to believe it." She sounded obscenely calm. "You've been dancing around it, saying everything else, but you do know. I can tell."

I opened my mouth, and closed it again. We stayed that way, neither of us saying a word, deadlocked, looking at each other.

It hit me, suddenly, that this is was a dead turnabout from what had left her so shy, after she'd asked to play submissive the other night. She knew what was messing with my head, she knew I didn't want to look at it, and she wasn't going to let me get away with not looking at it. She was completely in control; this time, it was me who couldn't wriggle about, not without hitting some sore spots. It was a twisted mirror image of where we'd been the other night, even though the places that hurt were inside, and couldn't be rubbed to restore circulation, or eased up with an ice-down.

Bree had the whip-hand this time, and she was going to use it. She was going to tell me, whether I wanted to hear it or not. So I did the only thing I could: I caved.

"Right." I put the syringe down. "What is it you think I don't want to believe?"

"You think Bulldog killed Ches."

There it was, and of course she'd nailed it, and nailed me. Right that moment, I wanted to strangle her. *Shut up, just shut up, stop talking...*

"You think he found out Ches was going to write the story, the whole thing about Lucius Dixon and Lainey Chenery being his real parents. You think Bulldog couldn't take it, and murdered Ches somehow, to make sure that book never got written." No mercy, none at all. "Don't you?"

"Determined to make me cop to it, are you? Make me say it out loud?" I sounded as pissy as hell. "Christ, Bree, you sound like fucking Patrick Ormand. Yeah, that's what I think. I don't know how it was done, but it's what I think. Happy now?"

So there was another bad patch. She didn't walk out, not that time, but that put an end to the conversation. Because of course, she was right. I knew, down where that kind of thing lives, that Ches Kobel had been murdered. Sounds altogether too dramatic, I know. Over the top. But I *knew*.

I'd apologised in the morning. Not for the crack about her sounding like Patrick—that was true, I'd meant it and I wanted her to know that—but about being avoidant. Because the girl was right about that. It was an old story, me going on inertia, not liking to deal with unpleasantness. It had cost her quite a lot over the years. I was getting better about it, but it wasn't easy, changing those particular patterns. Who wants to have to deal with grief or extra bullshit, if they don't have to? So I'd apologised.

"Accepted." She'd leaned her cheek against mine for a moment. "I know this sucks, John. And I know how much you love Bulldog. So do I. But Ches is dead, and he shouldn't be. And if you're right about it, if he died because someone made that happen, there's no happy ending."

Now, standing onstage at the Waldorf with a spot focused on me, adjusting the mic to my height, I understood something. It was what she hadn't said that was bothering me; I remembered how shocked she'd looked, when she'd come into the ballroom behind Bulldog, and seen the change in him. It was more than age. He'd looked as if something was eating him alive, and I didn't want whatever it was to be guilt.

"...*Back in 1960, when I was nine, I went to school at Clapham Junior School, in South London. My best mate was a kid called Davey Hensley. Having Davey around, it was like having a brother—Davey was the reason I first picked up a guitar...*"

I gave them the speech, just the way I'd written it. Bree had been right about what was freaking me, but I'd been right about something else: at this moment, in the Waldorf's ballroom under the lights, what mattered most was me inducting Bulldog, that and the music itself. And that made the speech possible, exactly the way I'd written it, before Ches had died, before I'd shared the information on that thumb drive with Patrick Ormand.

It came down to one thing: Bulldog and I were still cut from the same cloth, connected by sound, by note and chord and scale and rhythm. That hadn't changed, and it wouldn't change, no matter what else did. I didn't give a damn whose genetic child Bulldog Moody was. What I cared about was that I was his child, in the only way that was allowed to matter tonight.

"...*Forty years later, when I was nine myself, I heard a song in a South London record shop, called 'Daisy Chain Blues,' and what had happened to the man who made me want to play guitar, happened to me. And that's a definition of family. It's not always about blood and DNA. Sometimes, it's about more than that, and less than that..."*

I went through that speech from a place that was a kind of weigh-station between Zen and fierceness. That turned out to be just what the speech needed, because when I came to the last bit, the crowd was silent, not a peep out of them, but they were leaning forward at their big twelve-seater tables, every last celebrity and mogul in the bunch.

"...There's a huge difference in temperament between a frontman and a sideman. As a sideman myself, it's my pleasure, and my honour, to induct Farris "Bulldog" Moody into the Rock and Roll Hall of Fame. Bulldog, come up here!"

He came onstage slowly, on his own, leaving Sallie at the table right down front, while the place erupted into applause like thunder on a summer afternoon. I felt my heart clutch up, watching him, and when he got to the mic, I did something that wasn't part of the usual set list, and wasn't part of what the prep team had run us through during the final rehearsals: I waited, and hugged him. Usually, the inductor steps back, straight off. Sod that. This was Bulldog, and it was me.

The crowd was on its feet, standing and cheering, a salute to the man's quality. Sometimes, a sideman gets a thirst to get noticed for himself; I know all about that. But when it happens spontaneously, not because he's tried for it but just because he's so damned good he deserves it and the world acknowledges him, well, it doesn't get much better than that.

He spoke to the crowd, standing there in the shiny old suit, me mostly hidden just behind his left shoulder. He didn't say much, just a thanks to them, and a separate thanks to Sara Kildare; she was at a table with the Traitors Gate blokes, since they were the big name inductees, but I saw her look startled, and then give him a beautiful smile.

237

He stopped speaking for a few moments. I got nervous; when it comes to live telly, silence is dead air, and even though they'd have plenty of time to edit, it might have been tricky. But it turned out he'd just been thinking.

"John, son, you come on up front a minute, okay? I got something to say."

His voice, the big bell, was cracked and rusty. The audience was dead quiet. I stepped out from behind him. He put one arm round my shoulders.

"I have two sons here tonight." I could barely see into the crowd—that's what happens when the stage lights are up and the house lights are down—but I could just about see Bree directly down in front. Her shoulders were shaking. "My boy Sallie down here, at the big table, he takes care of me, keeps me alive. And my boy John, he makes the music I'll be riding on down that river, when time comes for me to go. He keeps it alive. And that's gonna keep me alive. I get to be alive as long as someone out there is making the music."

I had tears in my own eyes now. Crying on telly, I hadn't rehearsed that. But I couldn't help it.

"Two boys. I love them both." The arm around my shoulder was heavy, and strong. "But I had a third son, a boy a lot of you knew. His name was Ches Kobel, and he died last week. It wasn't his time. There's no fairness there, no justice. It's a hard row to hoe, that one, and hard to bear. A man ain't supposed to live longer than his children."

He stopped.

For a moment, just one sick dizzy moment, I thought he was going to confess to killing Ches on national television. The room was moving, all the glitz and the glitter becoming blurry. Sweat ran into my eyes.

"John, here, wrote me a fine piece of music, called 'Moody's Blues.' We gonna play that for you. And we mean to play it so

238

well, Ches will be able to hear it, no matter where he is right now." He glanced at me, brown to brown, the eyes that were so much like mine, and something moved between us. "Give us a couple minutes, we get this set up for the boys in the band."

After that, there was no way the music would be anything but amazing. The sound crew and production company techs got it set up, fast and clean; they're really good at what they do and anyway, they'd rehearsed their part of the deal as much as we'd rehearsed ours. So they set up, while Bulldog and I got offstage and waited, with the rest of the band queued up right behind us. Everything was worked out, all the nuts and bolts.

I started out nervous, I'll admit that. That's unusual for me, because what the emcee said when he was introducing me was the simple truth: I was a session player for a long time before I became a permanent member of Blacklight. And session players just don't get nervous. When you don't know from day to day who you're going to have to satisfy in the studio the day after tomorrow, you develop a thicker skin.

But that night, waiting for the cue, I felt like the new kid on the block, as if this was my first public gig ever. My stomach was jumping all over the place, pure nerves, needing to get it right, play it perfectly, do it for Bulldog, do it for Ches. And when we settled in, and the house lights went back down, I picked up the 335 and I remember thinking, *right, Johnny, here we go, this is the only thing that matters right now, don't fuck it up.*

Just before the two spots hit us, my guitar tech slipped out from behind the amps, and caught my eye. I nodded at him, an old signal between me and Jas, letting him know my gear was fine. He waited for Bulldog to settle on his stool, and had the Byrdland ready for him.

Bulldog nodded his thanks, plugged in, powered up. The spots hit us, pooling around us, nice soft light, long shadows dancing on the Mississippi delta behind us.

Eight bars in, I was in heaven.

There's a zone a musician gets into, where it's dead on, perfect, sex and chocolate and every drug you ever imagined, and you're in a place where you can do all that without any of the consequences, just perfection and magic. We hit that point, both of us. By the time we'd finished the lead-in, he and I were grinning at each other, oblivious to the entire world, just us playing, making the guitars sing. We were so locked up, I barely even noticed the rest of the band coming in, but when they did, they rode the music like paying passengers on a luxury liner; Luke followed everything we did and laced his own guitar's voice around it, Mac's harp managed to be bitchy and mournful at the same time, and what Tony was doing on the piano, it might have been Dance Maxwell back there.

The crowd was with us as well, all those invitees. And no, it wasn't just me painting a pretty memory to take out and romanticise on bad days. I've got the show TiVo'd, and it's all there, right there, for the watching world to see.

We left the crowd standing and cheering and came offstage, back to our table. The original plan had been to shepherd us out into the Crystal Corridor, to give a couple of sound bytes to the media, while we waited to sit back down to watch the Traitors Gate induction. They'd taken a good look at how frail Bulldog looked, and changed their minds. So we were allowed to get back to our table and sit down.

"Oh, wow. Just—wow." Bree reached for my hand, and spoke straight into my ear. "You made me cry, damn it. That was so gorgeous, John. I had to sneak off to the bathroom and redo my damned mascara. How dare you break my heart like that?"

"It was good, wasn't it?" I turned and kissed her. Twelve seats, eleven people. Over her shoulder, my eye went to the one empty chair, and saw it was still empty. No Patrick. "Sorry, love, I've messed your lipstick. Worth it, though—here, give us another kiss, then. What's up next? Right, Traitors Gate. Winston's going to love this bit."

"...*Ladies and gentlemen, may I introduce...*"

Traitors Gate had a very nice induction ceremony, Gregory Carver doing the bulk of the serious acceptance speaking, Winston bouncing like a tennis ball and cracking everyone up as a follow-on. They played their set, two songs. We were nearly three hours into the evening; it was time to assemble out in the West Foyer, lining up, all of us who were heading on stage for the Back to the Blues finale ready to close the show.

I was ready to slide an arm under Bulldog's elbow in case he needed it. After all, it had been a long couple of days, all this work and rehearsal and whatnot on top of the plane trip in from Cincinnati. Actually, though, he was looking livelier than he had since Ofagoula—whatever was gnawing away at him seemed to have backed off a bit. Or maybe he'd just come to grips with it and made it give him a little peace.

I touched his shoulder. "You all right, Bulldog?"

"About as good as I'm like to be." He was standing slightly in front of me, behind Luke and the Traitors Gate blokes. He twisted his head round towards me, nodding. "Your doing, John. I got to thank you for this, one more time. Been a great night for me, getting to play here, with you boys. Never thought I'd get a chance to do this again."

I nodded. Couldn't trust myself to say anything, but I didn't have to. He wasn't done.

"I wish Ches was here, is all." His voice was sombre, sunken, sounding like it was coming out of deep water. Something moved along my nerves, something that had nothing to do with the MS. "I surely do wish for that. He shouldn't be dead. He didn't have to die. I just wish he was here, sitting at that table down there. Truth is, couple-three times tonight? I thought I saw him, sitting in that empty chair. I wanted to see that, John. No words in my

241

mouth or anyone else's to say how much I wanted that to be the truth, how sorry I am he aint here."

He gave a long sigh. I opened my mouth—I've got no idea what I was going to say, but there was no time to say anything anyway. The blokes in front of us were moving, the stage was flooded with light, the crowd was cheering, and we were onstage.

Electricity is a weird, weird thing, you know? I barely had Little Queenie up to full volume before we slammed into "Little Red Rooster," taking it all the way to the limit, jamming on it, listening to Greg Carver and Mac trade off some of the hottest, smokiest vocals I'd heard in years. Those vocals, they were like hips grinding. My guitar was wailing, and Luke and Winston were facing off and doing twisted little runs that echoed all over the place. It was brilliant.

When we segued into "Daisy Chain Blues," things went through the ceiling. I suspect most of the crowd were totally unfamiliar with the song, but after that night, I'd have been willing to bet that the out-of-print rare vinyl shops would have a run on "Laughing" Loudon's record.

We hit the middle of the song, thundering like a runaway freight, and here came Bulldog, hitting the chucks on the Byrd the way he'd done it fifty years before. He met my eye, and I felt myself grinning, just loving the man. Right that moment, I cared fuck-all about where he'd got the talent to play those drumbeat notes, whether he'd got them from just listening to the men who'd raised him as their own, or whether they came from Lucius Dixon and his battered old guitar. We were one person, back and forth, playing it, making it sing, and the rest of the band was right there, letting us take it alone for a few bars, revelling in the energy, feeding off it, before they came back in, running it out behind the closing credits the producers would add on for the eventual telecast.

And then there was that voice again, coming out of the walls, bleeding out into televisions and computers around the world:

242

"Thank you and goodnight!"

They brought the house lights up bright. We were still going, synched up, all of us. With the lights equalised, I could see the room properly for the first time since we'd taken the stage.

They were dancing down there, industry wonks and media types in tuxes getting down with women in designer gear and high heels. I looked down, over the edge of the stage, looking for a sapphire blue dress and auburn hair. She was dancing, of course she was, loving it, moving and shaking. All the women were dancing; even Domitra was shaking her hips, down there on the floor. Katia was hip to hip with a balding, stubby little bloke; I wondered if she knew she was dancing with the vice president of the network that was showing the ceremony. Carla and Ian were doing what looked like their own version of the bump.

Everyone was dancing, and most of the chairs on the ballroom floor were empty. At our table, though, two of them were occupied.

Sallie was watching the dancers, looking bemused, slightly vacant. Sitting in the other, ignoring the dancers and watching me instead, was Patrick Ormand.

I know I've pissed and moaned before, about things being difficult: dealing with this damned disease, the annual MRI, getting scared Bree is going to finally get tired of having to cope with my shit, and leave me for a younger bloke. But walking off that stage and introducing Patrick Ormand to Bulldog Moody took my definition of 'difficult' to a new level. It was one of the hardest things I'd ever had to do.

I stayed onstage longer that night than I would have under any other circs. The decision to do that wasn't organic, either; the show was over, the house lights were up, we could have stopped any time. But I dragged the boys out for at least an extra seven or so minutes.

243

The post-show party—it was being sponsored by FUBU that year, and they'd done a killer spread—had already started up, out in the Waldorf's West Foyer. Quite a lot of the crowd had already slipped out and headed that way by the time the rest of the band finally hit the twelve-bar run to end the jam. Patrick was still in his chair, and still watching me.

"Are we through?" Tony ran a wicked little ripple, the length of the keyboard, and got up. "Because I don't know whether I'm more tired than hungry, or vice versa."

"You forgot to mention randy as an option. My own personal countdown would be randy, hungry and tired, in that order of precedence, but that's just me." Mac took his wireless belt-pack off, and headed for the edge of the stage. "Patrick! Cheers, mate—Johnny said you were coming along tonight. How've you been? Did you just get here? Because if you did, you missed a decent dinner and a monster jam."

"No, I've been here a couple of hours. I've been on planes a lot the last few days, so I thought I'd stay near the back of the house for a while. Didn't really feel like sitting. Oh, how've I been? Busy."

Patrick was shaking Mac's hand, nodding hello to Dom and Bree, but he wasn't looking at any of them. He wasn't looking at me anymore, either; he gave Sallie a long look and then his stare moved to just beyond me. "Nice jam. And that was a great induction speech JP wrote. Very moving."

I was keeping myself busy as I could, anything at all to avoid making eye contact, doing nothing my guitar tech couldn't do just as well: coiling up cable, moving things from one place to another, putting guitars away. It couldn't last, I couldn't stay up here avoiding him forever...

"John? Is that a friend of yours, son?" Bulldog had caught Patrick's stare. "You introduce us, maybe? He seems to want to talk to me, or maybe I'm imagining things."

"Yeah, okay." On my knees, I snapped Queenie's case shut. My palms had gone damp. "Hang on, Bulldog, will you? I'm a bit dizzy."

Bree'd already caught it, and come up onstage. She was kneeling beside me. "John? Do you need something?"

I shook my head at her, and got up, trying to shake off the vertigo. It was time to deal.

"Patrick, glad you made it." I came down the steps, the room still moving around me. Bulldog was right behind me, leaning on Bree's arm; Sallie had got up, but his father waved him back into his chair. "I need to introduce you to a very important person in my world. Bulldog, this is Patrick Ormand—he's a friend of ours, from San Francisco. Patrick, this is Bulldog Moody."

"It's a pleasure." Bulldog was looking down at Patrick, and he meant what he said. If Patrick was a friend of mine, then meeting him was a pleasure. I felt sick suddenly, bile rising at the back of my throat. "Glad you could make it."

He reached past me, and held out his hand.

For a really bad moment, I thought I was having a heart attack. I don't know why I was so sure Patrick wouldn't want to shake Bulldog's hand; something, somewhere in my head, was remembering all those mystery story clichés, where the policeman can't make himself shake hands with the murderer. Behind my other shoulder, I heard Bree suck in her breath.

It was one of those moments, just hanging there, not moving, no way of knowing how long it would last. I had no way of knowing what else Patrick had sniffed out since we'd last spoken. In my head, it had come down to this reality, right here, right now: if Patrick thought Bulldog had murdered Ches Kobel, he'd refuse to shake his hand, because cops don't shake hands with murderers. *Come on, mate, put your hand out and shake, come on Patrick, just bloody shake hands...*

Patrick smiled. It was a real smile, without the teeth. He reached out his right hand, and took Bulldog's, and shook it.

245

"I'm glad I made it too." I heard a soft exhale of breath, but I couldn't tell you whether it was Bree or me, exhaling. "It's a treat, getting to be here for this kind of thing. My father had some of your studio stuff—did I tell you that, JP?"

"Yeah, you did." I sat down in the nearest chair; my legs had gone limp. "The old Sundial stuff is brilliant."

Patrick Ormand had taken that offered hand. He'd taken it, and he'd shaken it. And I couldn't see any way in hell he'd have done that, not if he thought Bulldog had committed murder.

"John?" Bree was beside me, speaking softly into my ear. "I think they want us all out of the ballroom. It looks like they're starting to load out. Are you up for this party, or do you want to head upstairs? I'm fine either way—we can get room service, or something."

"No, let's hit the party." I was suddenly feeling better than I had since that early morning phone call from Sara Kildare, Christ, was it really less than two weeks ago?

Patrick had shaken Bulldog's hand. He didn't think Bulldog had killed Ches. It was all right. It was okay. "Oi! Everyone ready for some food, then? I hear there's a decent spread out in the West Foyer."

The party went on into the small hours. Half the attendees seemed to be media, and we all ended up giving off-the-cuff interviews, and answering a shitload of questions. I drank ice water, and orange juice; Bree, who I would have expected to at least try some of the pricey bubbly, stuck with water as well. She also stuck with me, staying with me even when me and Bulldog found ourselves up to our armpits in reporters. That left me with a nice warm glow on; even three years ago, she would have been hiding, and hating every minute of this.

But here she was, being introduced as my wife, letting me show her off, willing to admit that yeah, now and forever, we were a couple. I suppose we'd actually been a couple since the moment we'd met all those years ago, however bizarre the road had got; it had been a long, very strange trip. But that didn't make this any less cool.

About an hour into the party, I'd gone off into a corner with Bulldog and Winston Dupres, three session blokes swapping stories about the good old days, which of course were often bad old days. I'd just finished a pungent story about working with a superstar bass player, back in 1973—he hadn't paid me for two years after the album had come out, and I found out later that he not only made a habit of doing that, he was perversely proud of it—when Bulldog suddenly lifted a hand to his heart.

"What is it?" I'd stopped mid-sentence. "Bulldog?"

"Forgot my medicine." He winced. "We were onstage—Sallie's got it—upstairs. No, don't worry—I just need–"

"I'll get him. You sit."

I looked at Winston, and he nodded at me. It was a clear signal between us, without a word spoken; he wasn't going anywhere, and he wasn't leaving Bulldog alone. I touched Bulldog's arm. "I'll just head upstairs, to your room. Back in a minute, all right? You stay with Winston."

I was actually at the lift to the Tower when Patrick's voice came from behind me.

"Had enough of the party?"

"Jesus! Would you not do that, please? You trying to give me a heart attack?"

"Hell, no." He wasn't smiling. "That's the last thing I want to do. For one thing, Bree would carve me into small stew-sized chunks."

"Yeah, she would. And then she'd sprinkle whatever was left with paprika, and feed you to the cats." The corridor was empty; everyone seemed to be back in the West Foyer, boozing it up on rock and roll's dime. "Patrick, look. I need to thank you."

"For what?" He yawned suddenly, a huge jaw-cracking gulp of

air. "Sorry. For some reason, I'm just wiped out."

"For not thinking Bulldog is a murderer." It was out. I'd said it. "For shaking his hand. Because I love the bloke, and I didn't want him to be guilty of murdering Ches. And you shaking his hand, I just couldn't see you fancying doing that, not if you thought he'd–"

"I do think he's a murderer."

I stood there, staring at him, not believing what he'd said, not believing the calm, crisp, matter-of-fact tone of voice, either. There was nothing believable about any of it. Patrick just watched me, waiting, saying nothing at all. The silence stretched out.

The lift came down from the tower, opened, let two women out. They glanced at us, and I saw them recognise me. But right then, I was locked up in this little bubble, stuck in there, just me and Patrick Ormand. The women edged away, moving much too slow, stopping to look back at us, whispering.

I finally got my voice back. I must have looked like death.

"What did you say?" Those light eyes, just like a hyena's. You couldn't trust him, trust his reactions, trust anything he did. He was a fucking predator, now and forever, him and his taste for other peoples' blood. "You think..."

"I think he killed Ches Kobel." His face was smooth, blank, as calm as his tone. "Don't get me wrong, I don't think he's a mean killer, or a vicious killer, or even a deliberate one. He certainly isn't a repeat killer. This wouldn't be first degree, if it were being prosecuted. I think this was a panic killing. He has a very high respect for family, for roots, and here was Ches Kobel, threatening to kick the foundation of his entire life out from under him. I don't know how he did it, but there's no doubt in my mind that he did do it. It's all right there, in his face. I'm a cop, JP. This is my meat and drink—not just the nuts and bolts of murder, but the way it smells. And this one, I can smell a mile away. It reeks

248

to high heaven. He murdered Ches Kobel."

I stepped away from the lift, listening to the doors slide shut quietly behind me. My head was thumping, beating away like bata drums, like an Afro-Cuban rhythm on a summer day in Mississippi, like *clave*, like Bo Diddley... *Bulldog needs his medicine. I can't stand here. I need to get his medicine. Say something, damn it!*

"You promised me you wouldn't take any action." I sounded dry, scratchy. "And you shook his hand."

"Yes, I shook his hand. I like him; I respect him. And yes, I promised you." Still nothing to read in that face. "But you know what? Even if I hadn't promised you, I wouldn't pursue it."

"Why not?" My voice was all over the place now, cracking along the edges. "That's what you do, isn't it? Pursue things, pursue people? If you hadn't promised—"

"He's an old man, JP. He hasn't got much time left, does he? Heart condition, coming up on ninety. What possible purpose would be served, trying to track down evidence, trying to convince the Cleveland police? None that I can see." Something flickered in that cool unreadable face. "Besides, I met Ches Kobel. You knew him. Do you think that's what he would have wanted? Bulldog spending his last months in prison?"

I shook my head. That was the best I could do, just then; I couldn't have got any words out. Luckily, Patrick didn't seem to care. He was busy choosing his own words, and choosing them carefully.

"One of the things I've learned over the past couple of years is that, sometimes, there's a difference between what's legal and what's ethical." He was watching me now. "And sometimes, there's a difference between what's ethical and what's right. I never thought about that, before I met you and Bree. But with you two, it's kind of hard to miss. Hell, you guys ought to have matching tee-shirts made, with that on it. You know what I mean? Arrow pointing at the other person, *I'm With Ethical.*"

I blinked at him. I must have looked a complete nit, just standing and gaping. I hadn't got a clue what he meant, not by that last bit, anyway.

"I'm a cop, and you're right, pursuing things is part of my job. Mostly, I don't get a choice in what to do. This time, I did: Legal, ethical, or right. I'm going with Curtain Number Three on this one."

He stretched suddenly, and reached out to hit the lift button. "You'd better go get Bulldog his heart meds. Thanks for a great evening, JP. I'll let you know how much I spent, once I'm back in San Francisco and I total up all the receipts. Would you say goodnight to everyone for me?"

He turned and went.

I took the lift upstairs, and woke Sallie up; he'd been dozing on the sofa. Sometime during that nasty little head-on with Patrick, the MS had decided to back off. Sometimes, you have to be thankful for small favours.

Sallie came downstairs with me. Between the three of us, me and Winston and Sallie, we got Bulldog up and through the mob. It took longer than I liked, but of course, he'd been one of the main events, and everyone wanted to make some kind of connection with him. Bree finally attached herself to us and got businesslike; she had us through and out in about three minutes. I don't how she did it. Dom, yeah, that I get, but Bree's not particularly scary, unless she thinks she's protecting me from something or someone.

We lost Winston right at the lift—for some reason, he suddenly went all diffident. First he shook Bulldog's hand and said something slightly incoherent about this being about as cool as cool could hope to get. Then he kissed Bree's hand, slapped me on the shoulder, and disappeared back off toward the party.

"Good idea that boy has." Bulldog gave Bree a smile, but it was an effort; he was fading out. Luckily, we'd reached the Moody suite, and Sallie had got the door unlocked. "You should take that dress and those shoes back down where they'll get better use than watching an old man take his pills. Those shoes, they're dancing shoes. John, take this girl back down, and let her see about that."

"I will, in a minute. I want to see you settled in first." I turned to Bree, trying to hide some of the things that were spiralling round in my brain, over and over: Patrick Ormand was nuts. He was off his damned head. There was no fucking way this man had murdered a boy he loved; that was bollocks, pants, total shite. I was going to have to tell Bree what he'd said. Oh, Christ. "Do you mind, love? I'll just be a few minutes, so if you want to head back down–"

"Not a chance."

She knelt down next to Bulldog's high-backed satin chair, the same way she'd knelt next to me, when Patrick had rung two nights ago. She got hold of Bulldog's hand, and held it against her cheek, closing her eyes. I thought she was being tender, and got a lump at the back of my throat for a moment, but it turned out she was just being Dr. Miranda Godwin's daughter. "Oh, good, your circulation's good and your pulse is normal. Chest pain? Is the angina backing off?"

"I'm right as rain, child." He was already drowsing. "Sallie, you get me off to bed. John, your girl Carla—she's something, that girl is—told me there's a car coming for me in the morning, along about half past ten. I have a plane to catch after breakfast. Will I see you before I go?"

"Hell, yes. Count on it."

I knelt at his other side. We stayed that way for a few moments, bracketing him, me and Bree. None of us said anything; we were silent, listening to Sallie moving around in the big bedroom, turning down his father's bed, getting ready for sleep.

Bulldog was snoring gently when we said goodnight to Sallie and left. Out in the hall, I looked at my watch.

251

"It's just gone midnight." I nodded toward the lift, and kept my voice down low. That was pure habit, since we had two floors to ourselves, and everyone else booked in up here was probably still partying downstairs. "Did you want to go back down? We can. I don't mind giving you a shot at dancing the night away. Bulldog has a point, about that outfit you're wearing. Shame to let it go to—"

"No." She pulled her hair free. She was looking at me, straight and steady, not smiling. "No, I want to go to bed. I think we need to talk, John, don't you? For one thing, I want to know what Patrick told you. Also—no, that can wait, I think. But I want to know why you looked so—so—I don't know. Freaked, maybe. Because you did, after you went out to get Bulldog's medicine from Sallie. Patrick went out after you—I saw him do it. And he didn't come back."

"Right." The girl was too damned sharp for my comfort. I jerked my head, towards our own suite. "Let's call it a night, yeah? I'm damned if I want to have this talk in the hall."

We've had nearly thirty years together, me and Bree. Plenty of time to get into routines, rituals, habits. After that much time, it takes something major—getting diagnosed with multiple sclerosis, losing a cat to age or illness, a really grim three days when Bree had cancer surgery—to get us to change anything. We both like our rituals. They're comforting things.

Tonight, we went through the usual hotel routine, but instead of relaxing into it, I was tight as a drumhead. She was going to ask me about Patrick. That was bad enough, but it wasn't what was making me want to put off bed as long as I could. I couldn't even guess what that second thing on her mind was. The whole deal with Patrick had left me unwilling to deal with anything at all.

I wasn't given a choice. Bree was in bed and wide awake when I'd finished up in the loo. I'd barely got settled in next to her and pulled the duvet up, when she rolled over and looked into my face. She didn't say anything, she just looked. But the eyes were straight at me, and she wasn't going to look away without an answer. I looked straight back at her.

"Okay. You wanted to talk. You want to know what Patrick said, what he found out, what he thinks?"

She nodded. We weren't touching anywhere—my doing, that slight pulling back. I didn't know how she was going to react to what I was going to say. I also didn't have a clue if I was going to be able to just tell her, without getting the shakes or getting upset. My reactions, her reactions—I just didn't know. Hanging back seemed the way to go.

I took a breath, and told her.

She didn't say anything, not at first. She stayed where she was, curled up, looking into my face. As for me, I was silently telling her to reach out a hand, touch me, do something to make contact, because I felt like someone who'd brought bad news, and I didn't want to instigate a touch that she might reject. I wanted to hold her, but just then, if I'd reached out to her and she'd pushed me away, I'd have lost it.

"I'm sorry, John." She still hadn't touched me, but she didn't have to; her voice, when she finally did speak, was soft, and warm, and regretful. "I'm so sorry."

It was an invitation, and I took it, reaching out and gathering her in. My eyes were stinging.

I held on to her a good long while, neither of us saying anything. She agreed with Patrick—that was right out front. That "I'm sorry" had been for the bad news, not because she thought Patrick was wrong. It took me a few minutes longer to understand she was also sorry about me having to believe it, as well.

"Nothing to be sorry about—or, no, that's all wrong, isn't it? There's plenty to be sorry about. No point in being sorry, is what I should have said. Being sorry doesn't fix anything, so let's take that one as read." I sighed, and kissed her hair. "Okay. Now, lady.

What was the other thing you said we needed to talk about? If you're breaking the news that you're bored with the tired old man and you're running off to Aruba with a twenty-year-old yoga instructor or something, you should probably wait until morning for that one. I'm already on overload tonight."

"It's about the other night." She'd rolled over on her side, facing away from me. "When I—when you—"

"When you put my favourite lioness away for the evening, and put me completely in charge?" The light had gone off in my head. I rolled her back over, keeping my arms around her. "I think you ought to be talking to me about it, Bree, not the bathroom door, yeah? That's if you want to talk about it at all. Right now, you're not doing too well with it, are you? What's all this, then? Embarrassment?"

"No, not really. I'm just thinking—trying to figure out how I felt about it."

She was still having trouble getting it out. That wasn't like Bree—she's not big on talking about her feelings, but when she does, she's generally pretty clear about things. During our early days together, she'd got into the habit of thinking she'd do better to just shut up about that kind of thing. That might have been true then, but it wasn't true anymore, and she needed to know that. I got one hand up, and stroked her cheek.

"Just dish, love. I'm right here, and you've got to admit, I'm half the problem, whatever the problem is. Talk to me. Not embarrassed, you said. Ashamed? Because don't be."

"No." She smiled at me, but her brows had drawn together. "Not about dumping the Queen Bee for an hour. I was, a little, the next morning, I mean. But when I thought about it, I was the one who instigated it, not you. Besides, you said no complaining about it afterwards, and you were right. So, that wasn't it."

"Good." I kept up the stroking, light, easy. "What's on your mind, Bree? I'd have sworn that was shame, or embarrassment or something I saw on your face, when we talked about it that first night we got here. If I was wrong, then what was it?"

"It—oh, shit." Her lip was trembling. "Okay, to hell with it, I'll just say it."

I waited. And here it came, in a long fast rush.

"I liked it, John. I liked it way too much. I want to do it again. But I didn't know if I could. Because—it felt like I'd forced you into some kind of weird turnaround, like all of a sudden I'd stopped being what I'd been forever and made you be something you didn't want to be, made you cope with me not being some kind of superwoman control freak goddess thing for a change. I know you don't like having to decide about things, and I know you like me doing that for you and I thought, what the hell am I doing, he's going to hate this, and then you liked it, and I thought you might resent me for making you look at that, and then I didn't know what to do–"

"Gordon *Bennett!*" I'd sat up, the covers pooling round my waist, and dragged her up with me. She was in tears, right at the edge of total meltdown hysterics. "Stop. Bree? Stop, and just listen, all right?"

She nodded. Her breathing was all over the place.

"I don't resent a damned thing." I slid my hands down, rubbing her arms, making her look at me. "Can you get that through your head, please? Am I getting this right? You freaked because you thought I'd wanted to be the Bloke in Charge, all these years, and that I just didn't realise it until the other night, when you woke that bit of me up?"

"Yes." She was sniffing, bits of damp hair sticking to her cheek. "Sort of. I think so. You seemed to get so into it, I felt afterwards like I'd kept you from doing something you would have really dug. And I don't ever want to do that. What the hell are you smiling about? It's not funny, damn it!"

"No, not funny. But not real, either." I tilted her chin up. "Love,

255

it's a game. That's all it is. It's got nothing to do with what happens two minutes later. I'm all about you and me, and that means any way at all you want to get through life, you know? If there's a problem, I'll tell you. Yeah, I know, I don't do confrontations much. Not to worry—this is you and me. This is us. So whatever it takes, just say what you need, and I promise I'll listen. And no, not asking for you to promise back. I already know you will."

"God, I love you. You know that, don't you?"

She was looking right into my face, into me and through me. I made a mental note to myself: *next time you even think about moaning about the MS or anything else, Johnny my lad, shut your gob, and remember this.*

"I know it," I told her, and reached for the light. "And aren't we the lucky ones?"

We actually did get to wave Bulldog into his limo in the morning, just before breakfast. Our own flight wasn't until after lunch, and checkout wasn't until noon, so we weren't in any rush. We'd just said goodbye, and watched the car pull off into traffic, when I heard a woman's voice behind me.

"JP Kinkaid!" Sara Kildare was wrapped up warm against the March weather. Wise move, that was—it was chilly as hell out there. "Good morning."

I hadn't actually got to talk to Sara at all during the weekend; the rehearsal schedule had been pretty tight, and she wasn't part of the production or tech crew, just the liaison from the Foundation. It was nice to get a moment to thank her properly—if it hadn't been for her, Bulldog wouldn't have got chosen for the Hall. I held out a hand.

"Morning, Sara, how are you? You've met my wife Bree, haven't you?"

"Yes, back at the Blacklight exhibit opening in Cleveland." She smiled at Bree. "It seems like months ago, now, doesn't it? I wanted to say thank you, for suggesting Bulldog Moody. That speech you wrote was absolutely wonderful, and the music, of course—well. It left me a lot happier than I'd been in a while." The smile was gone, suddenly. "It's been a very hard couple of weeks. The last thing I did before getting on the plane for the ceremony was cleaning out poor Ches's apartment."

"Oh, lord, that's horrible." Bree was hugging herself, shivering, but I couldn't tell whether it was the cold or the picture of Sara, small and composed, having to sift through Ches's stuff. "Everything? Not the fridge too? Why did you have to do it? I thought Ches had a sister."

"The fridge, yes. Everything. The problem was that his sister was only able to stay in town for a day, and I was the one the police had been talking to about things, so the entire thing ended up in my lap. I hope I never have to do anything like that again."

"I don't blame you." The picture was disturbing, her having to sweep two-week-old rotting food out into plastic sacks and cart them off to somewhere. The image of piles of Ches's clothing was morbid enough. "That's nasty."

"Yes, genuinely grim." She'd turned toward the Waldorf's entrance, where a uniformed doorman was waiting to let us back in. "There's nothing nastier in the world than plastic storage dishes with biology projects that used to be catfish and dirty rice in them, unless it's what used to be fruit that has to be disengaged from a hanging wire mesh fruit basket. Good heavens, are you all right?"

I'd stopped in place, Bree running into me, saying something. There was a memory cycling round, something to do with Bulldog, something to do with Ches. Catfish and dirty rice, standing on the porch at Manassas Road, going indoors, Tony laughing, Bulldog talking, the smell of catfish frying...

"Sara?" I heard my own voice, from light years away. Bree was in front of me now, looking at me, her eyes going wide. A light had gone on in my head, in my memory. "Did you say there was

257

catfish and dirty rice in the fridge? Was it in one of those tubs with the blue tops?"

Ches, eating Bree's cooking in our kitchen, the night before he headed south. What had he said? *This is a research trip—there are a few leads I need to check out down there, a few facts I want to check on for the book. I'll stop in Ofagoula Friday night, see if I can talk Bulldog and Sallie into having some dinner with me...*

"Not in the fridge, no." Her eyebrows had drawn together. "In the sink. Poor Ches's last breakfast. There was a little bit left. Why?"

"Nothing. I don't know." It was a lie. I did know. Bree had caught up, a hand at her mouth, her eyes wide and horrified. I was hearing my mother-in-law's voice now, clear and concise: *I'd bet on him somehow having taken a massive overdose of his medicine, just before he went for his run.* "Yeah, we ought to get back inside. It was a great weekend, wasn't it? Oh, one more thing—what sort of fruit?"

"What do you—oh, in the basket? Citrus, mostly. Hard to tell, because it was all very rotten." Sara looked puzzled. "Oranges, I think. Maybe a couple of nectarines or something. Why on earth do you want to know that?"

"I'm curious, that's all." There it was, the way it had been done, right there in front of my nose. I heard Sallie's voice, talking about his dad's medicine, trusting me to take care of Bulldog for the day, me asking why I couldn't just break one of the capsules open.

They have to get into Dad's blood slow. You got to promise me, okay, Mr. Kinkaid? Take them down whole, and no grapefruit.

Little blue-topped storage tub, with Ches's breakfast in it, fried catfish and dirty rice. Breakfast of champions, that was, good southern cookery, with a nice strong taste to cover up the taste of a Verapamil or three... "No grapefruit?"

"No, there wasn't any grapefruit, at least not in the basket."

She tilted her head, watching me. "Just the peel of the one he had with his breakfast."

Epilogue

"*...April 3: Moody, Farris, peacefully in his sleep, at his home in Ofagoula, Ohio. Farris Moody, known as Bulldog, born in 1921 in Hattiesburg, Mississippi, was the son of a career Army engineer. The descendent of a long line of musicians, Moody began playing guitar at the age of nine. In the course of an often unsung career as a sideman for other, more famous bluesmen of his era, many of Moody's recorded contributions remained uncredited. Moody was recently inducted into the Rock and Roll Hall of Fame, in the category of Early Influences. He is survived by his son, Salas Moody II. A memorial concert, to be held at the Backroom Club in Ofagoula, is being planned...*"

I love my morning newspaper, usually. News before coffee isn't Bree's thing; she says she's got to be fortified with a shitload of caffeine before she can cope with looking at just how stupid our species can be. She'd rather get her information later in the day, off the internet. I'm a lot less computer-aware than she is, and besides, I like the crackle of paper, something I can fold when I've done reading it.

But there are days I think I've nearly lost my taste for the news. It's not just world news, either. I'm getting to the age where a lot of the musicians I've worked with in my time are showing up in the obits, and not just because of drugs or booze. It's the percentages, you know? It's just time, taking a toll.

"John?" Bree looked up, over her own cup of coffee. "What's the matter?"

"Bulldog." I folded the paper back, and pushed it across the table to her. My hands were completely steady. "He's gone."

She took the paper, reading it, not saying anything. I wasn't saying anything, either; I was too busy trying to sort out how I felt about it.

The realisation I'd had, the understanding of what must have happened, had done something to my feelings about Bulldog. I just couldn't shake this picture of him, this bloke I loved and admired and felt so connected to, hearing about the book Ches was going to write, being unwilling or unable to stand it, opening one of those Verapamil capsules, stirring it into the dirty rice and fried catfish left over from Sallie's cookery, sending it home with Ches. I couldn't shake the picture of Ches, eating the breakfast they'd sent home with him, eating the nice healthy grapefruit, jogging out toward the complex by the lake, feeling the first hit of it in his system, faltering, stopping, falling to the pavement, seeing that glass behind him, dying alone. Had he wondered about it, those last moments, wondered what this had happened? Had he suspected, even for a second, that the man he loved and admired and respected had killed him?

I'd read up on Verapamil, once I'd got home, and the more I read, the more certain I got. Ches would have done his daily hit of Digoxin just before he'd headed out for his morning run. He had his routine, just like the rest of us who take daily meds: keeping that irregular heartbeat under control, slowing it down. The routine is automatic. It has to be, to work properly.

But he didn't have angina, and he didn't take Verapamil. So

261

just one capsule would have been enough to do serious damage, once it interacted with the Digoxin already in his system. More than one would have been enough to kill him, even if it had been taken whole, doing the timed release into his blood that it was designed for.

But it hadn't. I was sure of that, as sure as I'd ever been about anything. However many of those coloured capsules had been stirred into his catfish and rice, he'd eaten it all at once. There was nothing in there that could dissolve slowly, and of course, he'd accelerated the effect by eating the grapefruit, giving himself the citrus hit as a jumpstart to the daily exercise that kept him healthy.

I kept seeing it in my head, and I hated seeing it. There was that question, never to be answered, now: what would have happened, if luck or chance or whatever had been on his side that morning? Suppose he'd eaten a nectarine, or a pear, or an orange instead? Would he have died?

I hadn't said much to Bree about it, but of course, I didn't have to. She'd followed the reasoning and got there even faster than I had. Doctor's daughter, yeah?

One thing she did ask me was whether I was going to tell Patrick Ormand about it. I'd said no, and I'd said it without thinking twice. That conversation with Patrick, back at the Waldorf, was still fresh in my head. The way I saw it, I'd got him to promise not to touch Bulldog. He'd abided by that. He'd talked about the difference between legal and ethical, about the difference between ethical and right. It couldn't have been easy for him, doing the right thing; all his instincts and all his training had to be pushing him toward doing the legal thing. So if I told him, I'd be piling it on. Not fair to him.

I hadn't spoken to Bulldog since that morning out in front of the Waldorf. And just now, I was trying to wrap my head around the fact that I'd never speak to him again, whether I wanted to or not. It was too late. He was gone.

However muddied my feelings about Bulldog had got, though, the feelings about the music hadn't changed at all. So when Carla rang me from LA the next day to say that she'd got a call from Dance Maxwell, asking if I wanted to come and play at Bulldog's memorial, I said yes with no hesitation, and Bree announced that she wasn't staying home for this one.

The idea of the memorial should have left me feeling bouncier than it did; after all, this sort of jam was right up my alley and hell, and damned near every great bluesman still alive was probably going to be there. It had been set up for the following weekend. I told Carla to book it, get me a car and a driver. Turned out Dance had asked for Tony to come along, as well, so we set that up. Tony was getting eased into how Blacklight Corporate operated, just how easy they could make it, and *Book of Days* hadn't even been released yet.

On the Friday before we were due to leave for Ofagoula, I was down in the studio, working out a tricky bridge in a new song Luke had written, when Bree walked in.

"John?" She had a really peculiar look on her face. "Can you come upstairs for a minute, please?"

I followed her up. I don't know what it was about that look and that tone of voice, but it kept me from asking her anything. At the top of the stairs, she turned and headed for the kitchen.

Sallie Moody was sitting at the table. On the floor at his feet was a battered old Gibson guitar case.

I looked at it, and looked at Sallie.

"Mr. Kinkaid." He got up, and offered me a hand. I shook it, but my eyes kept wanting to go to that case on the floor. "Pleased."

He looked just the same, that vague smile, the voice that could have been the lowest end of the old Bechstein in my basement studio, with the soft pedal on, never really changing in tone or volume. Something moved around my heart. He looked like

263

his father and yet, you know, he really didn't. But somehow, Bulldog was in the room with us for a moment. Maybe it was the guitar case.

"Sallie, it's good to see you." I had no clue what to say to him, no clue what he was doing here, no idea how he'd got our address. "I heard about Bulldog—I'm so sorry. I'm coming out to Ofagoula tomorrow, to play his memorial."

"That's good. Dad, he'd like to know that. I'm glad to know, too—I been on a train for days now."

"Are you hungry, Sallie?" Bree had to be finding the situation as bizarre as I was. But Sallie was a guest in her kitchen, and he might be hungry, and when you have hungry guests, you feed them. That's just basic Bree. "Would you like some lunch?"

"No, ma'am, thank you very kindly. I had me some food over across the Bay, where the train from Ohio left me. But I wouldn't say no to something cold to drink, if you could see your way to doing that. Riding the trains, that dries a man's throat out."

"What brings you here, Sallie?" Sallie was a simple bloke. It was best to just ask.

"My dad wanted me to come. He wrote a letter about it." He had a hand in his jacket pocket, fumbling around; he had huge hands and it looked to be a very small pocket. "He gave this to Dance Maxwell, before he passed. Dance told me, when we had the viewing out to the house, and all Dad's friends from the old days come to see him before we put him in the ground, Sunday last. Made me read it, so I could see it. Dad wrote that he wanted me to come here. So I came."

He had it free now, a folded piece of pale blue notepaper, holding it out to me. I smoothed it out, and read it aloud.

"*Dance—I need you to give this note to Sallie. Tell him to take the Byrdland out to San Francisco, and give it to Johnny Kinkaid. I got trust in you, make sure nobody else gets it—make the boy understand. The Byrd is for Johnny. He loves that guitar, and it loves him right back. Tell him to play "Moody's Blues" on it one time for me. Tell him I'll hear it."*

Bree's hand closed over mine. I hadn't realised that my voice had broken, that I'd closed my eyes, that I was swaying on my feet.

"Sit," she told me, and pushed me into a chair. "Just sit."

I sat. I couldn't have stood up right then, not if the house had been on fire. The reality of it, that black guitar case just sitting there on our kitchen floor, that letter in my hand—it was too much, too enormous.

Whatever he'd done, whatever his reasons for doing it, Bulldog was gone and I hadn't been there. I'd backed away during his last days. I'd blamed him in my heart, not only for killing Ches, but for being too weak to own his own history. *Christ.* Who was the weak one, then? Him, or me?

I couldn't go back. I couldn't fix it. I couldn't do a single thing to make it right. And he'd left me the Byrdland.

I wish I could tell you more about that afternoon, but I don't remember too much of it clearly, at least until Sallie was leaving. I was a wreck, things out of the past getting mixed up with right now, in my head.

I know I took the Byrd out of its case, hung on to it for a moment, got my hands on it, really on it, tuned it up. All the time I was doing that, I was remembering the first thing Bulldog ever said to me, when I'd walked in with butterflies in my stomach, nervous as hell about meeting him, and got distracted by the Byrdland, the first of its kind. I could hear him now, his voice clear as the voice of the guitar itself, ringing in my head, bringing him back to me: *You like that axe, son? Because you lookin' at her like you were wanting to buy her a drink.*

I remember that I played the song I'd written for Bulldog, played it for his son. Sallie wasn't a musician; he'd taken after his mum, that way. But Salas Moody, the man Sallie'd been named

265

for, wasn't even his real grandfather. So what the hell good were genetics? What in hell was history? Was any of it true, any of it any good?

I'd loved Bulldog. But I'd turned my back those last three weeks of his life. He'd died, and I hadn't been there. Yet he'd loved me enough—and loved the Byrd enough—to send the child who'd been there all along halfway across America with the guitar, to make sure it came to me.

What he'd done had stopped mattering to me. The only thing that did matter was that I'd failed him, somehow. I'd turned my back.

I remember that, fumbling around in that funky old case, I found a slide. That damned near broke me. The slide was new, bought recently, probably after we'd sat in the house on Manassas Road, and I'd showed him the slide moves for the stuff he'd wanted to learn off *Blues House*, that old out of print album I'd done as a teenager.

Bree got to feed Sallie after all, cooking him a simple, hearty meal, no fusses or frills, pork chops done just right, mashed potatoes with garlic, greens, crusty bread and butter. He cleaned his plate twice.

It was late in the day when we walked him to the front door. I'd thought to ask if he needed a bed—that was worrying me, and I could see that Bree was fretting over it, as well.

"Thank you, Mr. Kinkaid, but I got me a motel, over on Lombard Street. And I got some money for a taxi, especially since I don't need to spend any of it on dinner."

"Good." I was holding Bree's hand, and swinging it gently back and forth. "Thanks, Sallie. I'm glad I got to see you again. I just wish I'd got to see your dad one more time. It was bad enough, him losing Ches."

"That was like to break his heart." He was buttoning his jacket. "Least this way, though, Ches didn't get to tell my dad any of his lies about my granddad, like he was fixing to do."

Bree's hand, resting in mine, suddenly tightened, clamped down hard. Or maybe it was the other way around.

"Lies?" I was watching his face. Smooth, a bit vacant, hardly ever showing any feelings. Was that something flickering in there after all, anger, memory, something...? "About your grandfather? What sort of lies, Sallie?"

"Lies about my granddad being in jail, about him robbing a store. He was lying." The eyes looked darker, somehow, and there was some colour in his voice. "He said that to me, about jail and robbing a store. He told me my granddad got kicked out of the army. Said he was gonna write that in a book somewhere, but all that stuff, that was just lies. I saw paper and a pin the army gave my granddad, saying they liked him, that he was a good man. They never kicked him out, and he never robbed any store. Would have broken my dad's heart, Ches telling him lies about my granddad. Never did, though."

He smiled, a real smile, pleased, satisfied. There was no malice in there, none at all. There was no guile.

Just off my shoulder, Bree was holding her breath. Her hand in mine wasn't moving at all. Nothing seemed to be moving, not even my heartbeat or the air in my lungs.

Standing on the porch in Ofagoula, the smell of catfish frying. It was Sallie who was the cook in that house, Sallie who'd offered to wrap up some leftovers for Bree to bring back to San Francisco, just put some in one of those little tubs with the blue lids.

Bulldog didn't cook. It was Sallie who had access to the food, to the leftovers, to the meds. Why had I assumed it was Bulldog, assumed it so easily? Why had Patrick assumed it?

Here it was, loud in my ears or at least in my memory, Bulldog asking me to convince Sallie I could be trusted to give Bulldog his meds, not let him get away with not swallowing the huge capsules, make sure he didn't have any grapefruit with it: *Times I'd be*

267

aching in my bones and Ches would be here, and all I'd want was a good sleep. They'd cover me up and the two of them, they'd be all over the place, down to the market, get some fish or some chicken, maybe. They'd let me sleep and they'd come back and I'd hear them in the kitchen, cooking, laughing, just letting me rest.

Bulldog had known.

That's what Patrick had smelled out: knowledge, guilt, that unbearable load of responsibility in Bulldog's face. I wasn't a hunter, or a cop, but that was why I'd believed it, as well. I'd seen it in Bulldog's face. He'd known there'd been murder done.

There was no way to know what had twigged it for Bulldog, not now. Had he looked in his little plastic jar of Verapamil and realised he was short one capsule, three, ten? Or was it just him knowing Sallie?

Bottom line was, he'd known. And knowing had broken him.

"Well, that was a very unpleasant thing for Ches to do." Bree's voice sounded easy, interested, completely unsuspicious. If I hadn't had her hand holding on to mine hard enough to bruise, I would have thought she hadn't got to where I was. "He said your grandfather was kicked out of the army, and was in jail? That's just silly. But you didn't let him bother Bulldog with that non-sense, did you?"

"No, ma'am, I did not. Don't know what was going on in Ches Kobel's head to be saying stuff like that. And he said he was put-ting all that in a book." He finished buttoning up his coat, and gave a satisfied little nod. Just before he turned to walk off into the evening, he paused for a moment. "I was named for my granddad. A man's got to stand up for his family, don't he? Fam-ily's all we got in this world."

"Are you going to tell Patrick?"

The house was quiet, and the moon was long down. We'd come up to bed late; I'd had every intention of burying the black painful stuff in my head by burying myself in my wife instead. Either my body or my head had other ideas, though. I'd fetched up with Bree wrapping her arms around me, holding me tight against her, while I went through a crying fit.

"No. I'm not." It was very weird. I felt as if, by crying it all out against Bree, I'd somehow committed to something. It wasn't until she asked me that question that I realised that what I'd committed to, was complicity.

"Good."

"Good?" I looked into her face, barely visible in the shadows. "You think that's the right thing to do, then, Bree?"

She put a finger against my lips. "Yes, I do. I think it's the only thing to do. You can't change anything, John. You can't bring Bulldog back, or Ches. They're gone. And Patrick was right, about what Ches would probably have wanted. He loved them both, as much as Bulldog loved you."

"I know." Legal, ethical, right. Maybe just what my own parents would have called grace? Damned if I knew. "And Patrick kept quiet. He's going to keep quiet, even though he still believes it was Bulldog. That makes up for a lot of the past, in my book— easier for me to forgive Patrick for some of his own shit. I don't want to make it harder for him."

"No," she agreed, and moved up close to me. Her voice was very gentle, full of love. "But that's not really what's bothering you, is it?"

"No, it's not. I failed him, Bree. He was old and I loved him. But the minute I thought he was weak and had done something I couldn't personally forgive him for, I turned my back. Not going to be able to forgive myself for that any time soon."

"No, you won't." She was up against me, passive in my arms, soft as a baby's blanket and just as comforting. "But that's okay too, as long as you don't overdo it. Believe me, I'm intimately acquainted with the scars a person can get from an overactive

269

conscience. Just let it lie, John. They used to call this sin-eating, or something like that. We can be Sallie's sin-eaters, can't we? He's old, and tired, and not all there, and what he did, he did because he wanted to protect his father and his family memories. Let's carry it for him. Hell, it can't possibly weigh as much as the Byrdland."

"You got it." She was right, of course she was. "All in the family."

JP Kinkaid

Photo by Nic Grabien

Deborah Grabien can claim a long personal acquaintance with the fleshpots—and quiet little towns—of Europe. She has lived and worked and hung out, from London to Geneva to Paris to Florence, with a few stops in between.

But home is where the heart is. Since her first look at the Bay Area, as a teenager during the peak of the City's Haight-Ashbury years, she's always come home to San Francisco, and in 1981, after spending some years in Europe, she came back to Northern California to stay.

Deborah was involved in the Bay Area music scene from the end of the Haight-Ashbury heyday until the mid-1970s. Her friends have been trying to get her to write about those years—fictionalised, of course!—and, now that she's comfortable with it, she's doing just that. After publishing four novels between 1989 and 1993, she took a decade away from writing, to really learn how to cook. That done, she picked up where she'd left off, seeing the publication of seven novels between 2003 and 2010.

Deborah and her husband, San Francisco bassist Nicholas Grabien, share a passion for rescuing cats and finding them homes, and are both active members of local feral cat rescue organisations. Deborah has a grown daughter, Joanna, who lives in LA.

These days, in between cat rescues and cookery, Deborah can generally be found listening to music, playing music on one of eleven guitars, hanging out with her musician friends, or writing fiction that deals with music, insofar as multiple sclerosis—she was diagnosed in 2002—will allow.

Visit her website at www.deborahgrabien.com